WHEN THE DEVIL DOESN'T SHOW

ALSO BY CHRISTINE BARBER

The Bone Fire
The Replacement Child

WHEN THE DEVIL DOESN'T SHOW

Christine Barber

MINOTAUR BOOKS
A Thomas Dunne Book
New York

This is a work of fiction. All of the characters, organizations, and events portrayed in this novel are either products of the author's imagination or are used fictitiously.

A THOMAS DUNNE BOOK FOR MINOTAUR BOOKS.
An imprint of St. Martin's Publishing Group.

www.thomasdunnebooks.com
www.minotaurbooks.com

Library of Congress Cataloging-in-Publication Data

Barber, Christine.
    When the devil doesn't show : a mystery / Christine Barber.
       p. cm
    "A Thomas Dunne Book."
    ISBN 978-1-250-00472-7 (hardcover)
    ISBN 978-1-250-02385-8 (e-book)
    1. Women private investigators—Fiction.   2. Arson
investigation—Fiction.   3. Santa Fe (N.M.)—Fiction.   I. Title.
    PS3602.A7595W44 2013
    813'.6—dc23

                                      2012040103

Minotaur books may be purchased for educational, business, or promotional use. For information on bulk purchases, please contact Macmillan Corporate and Premium Sales Department at 1-800-221-7945 extension 5442 or write specialmarkets@macmillan .com.

First Edition: April 2013

10 9 8 7 6 5 4 3 2 1

To my father,
thank you for showing us the world

AUTHOR'S NOTE

The Spanish words used in this book reflect New Mexico's unique Spanish dialect, and, as such, do not share all of the characteristics of the better-known, modern-day Spanish. For instance, most Spanish speakers today would say *"mi hijo"* when referring to their son, while Spanish speakers from Northern New Mexico would say *"mi hito."*

Additionally in the book, the term "Hispanic" is used instead of "Latino" when referring to someone from Northern New Mexico who is of Spanish descent. While Latino is the term most used in the rest of the country, Hispanic is the commonly used local term.

WHEN THE DEVIL DOESN'T SHOW

CHAPTER ONE

December 20

The devil was wearing a black cowboy hat with red plastic horns when he came out onto the balcony. The crowd started booing, and he waited for a moment for the noise to stop before yelling at them in Spanish to be quiet.

Below him in the dark, a hundred or so people filled the Santa Fe plaza. The block-wide area, lined on four sides by pueblo-style buildings, was packed with snow, as it had been since the end of October. The leafless trees were draped with Christmas lights and porch posts were wrapped in evergreen branches. *Farolitos* lined the sidewalks and roofs, the candles glowing orange through the paper bags that held them, making the buildings look like triple-tiered birthday cakes.

The devil yelled at them louder, telling the crowd the inn was closed. The people, with a few last hisses and growls, moved en masse to the next balcony, a half block away. They followed behind strumming guitar players and a choir singing in Spanish, all led by a couple dressed as Mary and Joseph. The crowd carried slender white candles that dripped wax onto the snow.

"Daddy, I'm freezing," said Therese Montoya, eleven, not looking up from her cell phone as she texted. Gil Montoya unbuttoned his coat and wrapped it and his arms around his youngest daughter as she stood in front of him, careful to keep his parka sleeves clear of the candle she was holding. The candles had been handed out to the crowd by a local museum as part of their effort to keep the tradition of Las Posadas alive. The outdoor folk play, which told a revised version of the Nativity story, used to last for nine nights when Gil was a child. Now most of the mountain villages had followed Santa Fe's lead, shortening the play so it was over within forty-five minutes.

The crowd stopped in front of a trading post on the southwest side of the plaza, where another devil, this one in a red cape and mask, came out onto the balcony above. The booing got louder, but this devil hissed back and stomped his feet at the crowd. The icicles hanging under the balcony shook but didn't break. The devils were playing the conscience of the innkeepers who'd denied lodging to Mary and Joseph on Christmas Eve. They were the villains of Las Posadas, which had been brought over to New Mexico by the conquistadors in the sixteenth century and reenacted every year since.

Gil looked over at his wife, Susan, whose face had a soft glow from the candle she was holding while she chatted with her aunt. His eldest daughter, Joy, thirteen, seemed to be the only one who was paying attention to the play. "What are they singing?" she asked. Gil strained to make out some of the words. He listened for a moment before saying, "*Hermosa Senora . . . Danos tus auxilios . . . O Madre Divina.*"

"*En Ingles,*" Joy said. "*Por favor.*" The girls didn't speak Spanish. Like most local teenagers, all they could understand were a few words of the Castilian dialect spoken in Northern New Mexico.

"Loveliest of Ladies, grant us your protection on this divine night," Gil said.

"That's beautiful," Susan said, slipping her arm through his.

Gil had been home for dinner the last twenty-one days. It was a family record. There had been no murders in Santa Fe since the beginning of November, meaning he had been able to keep regular work hours. In that time, he had become less of a detective and more of an administrative assistant, clearing out paperwork and helping with reports. He was surprised how much he liked the normalcy of it. But he knew it wouldn't last. Santa Fe averaged eight homicides annually. This year there had only been three, but there were still eleven days to go before New Year's Day.

The fire was an orange pinprick across a dark plain dotted with piñon and juniper trees. The glow could have been the angry red of a campfire, except Lucy Newroe knew better. It was a burning home.

She watched the distant flames through the front windshield of the ambulance as it left the fire station. It was 5:23 P.M. Full dark. Yet she could see the shadows of mountains on the horizon and, behind them, muted stars, smudged out by a high haze of cirrus clouds.

In front of the ambulance, the fire engine turned onto the highway. The words PIÑON VOLUNTEER FIRE AND

RESCUE—SANTA FE COUNTY were a blur of gold and reflective red on the vehicle's side. The tanker truck carrying the water they would use to fight the fire followed behind the ambulance—a convoy of lights and sirens making its way down the dead quiet highway.

Gerald Trujillo, who was in the driver's seat beside her, keyed the radio, saying, "Santa Fe dispatch, Piñon Medic One responding to the structure fire on Calle del Rio." His voice was calm, as always. Lucy could hear the three firefighters who had hitched a ride with them laughing in the back of the ambulance.

"It's time to do a surround and drown, *que no*?" She couldn't make out who had said that.

"I don't want to be a hero. I just want to get there," another voice said.

"Hell, I want to be a hero." More laughing.

She was tapping her leg hard against the passenger door, making the window rattle. Gerald looked over at her but didn't comment.

As they pulled up a winding driveway, Lucy got her first look at the house, which seemed strangely intact. She didn't see any flames coming out of the front picture windows. The fire must be in the back of the house. Their headlights swept across the front of the house, which was painted the usual Santa Fe adobe beige with the usual wooden beam vigas jutting out from the roof and the usual chile *ristras* hanging near the huge carved front doors.

Lucy hopped out of the ambulance and into a drift of snow that went up to her knees. She did her best to stomp most of it off her combat boots before pulling her firefighting gear out of a side compartment. The firefighters in the back of the ambulance piled out with a loud "Let's play," and another set of laughs. But their voices were tense. More fire trucks came up the driveway, with firefighters jumping out even before their vehicles had stopped. Some pulled hoses off the truck beds while others started gearing up, snapping helmets and pulling on gloves. The scene quickly became a cacophony—sirens, yelling, motors, pumps. One truck turned on its roof-mounted stadium lights, instantly bleaching everything in brightness and creating elongated shadows that reached out to the dark trees around them. Lucy tried to ignore it all and concentrate on one thing: Gerald Trujillo's voice.

"What's the first thing you need to know before we go into that house," he was saying over the noise.

"I don't . . ." Lucy was trying to put her heavy yellow bunker pants on over her clothes. Left foot in left boot.

"We need to know if there's someone inside," Gerald yelled. Lucy nodded. Right foot in right boot.

"What if we have no way of knowing if someone is inside?" he asked. He was already pulling on his bunker coat. The reflective stripes glowed in the undulating flashes from the emergency lights.

"We proceed as if there is a victim inside by doing a left-hand search," she said as she zipped up her pants and struggled into the red suspenders—firefighter red suspenders.

"Right," Gerald said. "At this point, Command says they don't know if anyone's inside, so we go in. But what's our main problem?"

"We don't know how many people could be in there. We could be searching for seven people or just the family dog," Lucy said, zipping on her recycled bunker jacket and slapping closed the Velcro. The department couldn't afford new equipment, so the coat was one that had sat in a box of used gear until she pulled it out. The smell of the jacket always made her a little nauseated: burned plastic in a wet campfire. It was the smell of all the fires the previous owners of the jacket had fought.

"What else do we need to know?" Gerald asked as he pulled a two-inch-diameter attack hose off the bed of the engine.

She couldn't think. Her long hair kept getting in her face as she pulled on her fire retardant hood. "I guess something about what the house is made of?"

"Right. This is a new house made with stucco, so it won't burn that fast, but our main problem is the roof."

She remembered something about that from the firefighting class she had finished two weeks ago. Something about roof joists. All she could think then was, *What's a roof joist?*

Lucy pulled on her heavy fireproof gloves and yanked a SCBA out of a compartment on the side of the fire truck. She slipped the air tank on like a backpack and pulled the rubber breathing mask over her face, cutting off her peripheral vision and her ability to breathe until she was able to connect with the air hose from the tank. She felt for the tank on her back, trying to grab the hose connected to it, but the heavy gloves made her fumble. Gerald was suddenly in front of her, a hand on her shoulder. He guided her hands to the air hose, which she pulled to her face mask and snapped in place. She took a grateful deep breath, making the seal on her mask whoosh as she breathed in air from the tank. She clicked the clasp of her fire helmet closed. The other firefighters scurrying around her like worker bees wore the traditional red fire helmets, but she and Gerald both had blue helmets with EMT emblazoned across the side.

Gerald got on his handheld radio, and said, "Command, this is the interior team. We are ready to go."

A voice came back, "Interior team, you are cleared to go in. The fifteen minutes has started."

Lucy looked up and tried to focus on the other firefighters on scene, who would stay outside the house, fighting the flames from the exterior. Only she and Gerald would go in, and they were going in for one reason: to look for survivors. They had only fifteen minutes to do their job. The fifteen-minute rule was in place for two very practical reasons: because their tanks held only fifteen minutes of air and because a house on fire would become too unstable after that.

Another voice came over the radio, "Interior team, this is RIT. We are on standby. Stay safe."

"Thanks, RIT," Gerald said into the mike. "Hopefully, we won't need you guys, interior team out."

Lucy could see the four-man Rapid Intervention Team standing off to the side of the scene. They were all geared up like her and Gerald, yet they had nowhere to go unless something went wrong. The only job of RIT was to come get the interior team if they ran into trouble. Lucy hoped the RIT guys would be bored tonight.

The crowd slowly followed along behind the couple portraying the holy parents, who were actually Ted Ortiz and Sylvia Montoya—a brother and sister from the parish of La Iglesia de Santa Cruz de la Cañada. They had been playing the parts of Mary and Joseph for more than twenty years. The couple stopped again, and the crowd stopped with them, this time in front of the Ore House restaurant on the northeast side of the plaza. Another devil came out onto another balcony. This time it was a man dressed in black leather pants with red face paint. Before the crowd stopped booing and hissing, the man started to yell. He seemed unsure of the words at first but then smoothed out. The voice sounded familiar to Gil. He was trying to make out the man's face in the dark just as Susan leaned over and whispered, "Isn't that your mother's cousin?"

His mother's cousin, Robert, worked for the state museum as a historian, mostly supervising the half dozen or so archeological digs going on in the city at any given time. Robert had helped coordinate Las Posadas for the last few years, but normally he didn't get involved in the celebration. He didn't like crowds, but he seemed to be warming to his role, which was made more menacing by his rough voice, the result of a pack-a-day habit since he was seventeen.

Gil looked down, his arms still around Therese, and caught a look at what she was texting: "That is so lame. LOL. Like she really said that."

"What's so lame?" Gil asked her.

"Daddy," Therese said, pulling the cell phone to her so he couldn't see the screen. "Stop looking."

"Just show him. He'll read it later anyway," Joy said to her sister. "You know he checks our phones, right? And our e-mail. And the names of who we hang out with."

"No, he doesn't," Therese said. "You're teasing."

"He's a cop, silly," Joy said. "You don't think he investigates his own daughters?"

Therese looked up at him and asked, "Do you really read our e-mails?"

"No, honey," he said; then added, "but I'll start reading your sister's if she doesn't leave you alone." Joy rolled her eyes in mock annoyance.

Gil glanced over to his wife, Susan, who was chatting to a neighbor she had run into, when he felt the phone clipped to his belt begin to vibrate. He assumed it was work, but when he looked down, he saw that it was his mother. He let it go to voice mail.

* * *

Gerald hauled the attack hose over his shoulder then made a signal to the engineer at the control panel to flood it with water. The hose sprang to life, going from a limp line to one that tried to twist its way out of Gerald's grip. Lucy grabbed a section of the hose farther down and, like Gerald, pulled it over her shoulder, trying to steady its bucking movements. With her free hand, she grabbed an axe from the side of the truck. Then they walked slowly forward into the house, pulling the fire hose behind them. Her movements felt stilted in the heavy bunker gear and boots, like trying to swim in pudding.

They reached the front door, which someone had smashed open before rescue crews got there. It had a gray wisp of smoke coming out of it. They immediately dropped to all fours. Gerald crawled through the door to the right, keeping one hand on the wall as he pulled the hose behind him with the other. Lucy did the same behind him, her right hand holding the axe and guiding the hose, her left hand holding Gerald's right ankle, like in a weird game of Twister. As the nozzle man, Gerald's job was to find them a low path through the house and take care of any flames they might run into. Lucy's job was to search for survivors.

Within a few feet, they went from being able to make out hazy furniture to seeing only stark blackness. This was why she and Gerald had to stay in physical contact, so they wouldn't lose each other in the smoke. She could barely make out his silhouette two feet in front of her. Their game of Twister had become one of hide-and-seek. With the head of the axe in her right hand, she made arched sweeping movements across the foyer floor with the axe shaft, searching. If the handle connected with something, they would stop to investigate, but at the moment, she was reaching out into open space. She could feel hard tile under her knees as she crawled. She moved the axe as far she could reach to the right, but she didn't make contact with any furniture or walls. She might as well have been reaching into a black abyss.

The house was making noises that she could hear through her hood—loud banging and long groaning: the sounds of walls and floors warping from the heat. She heard her radio squawk and tried to listen as the outside teams confirmed that electricity to the house had been cut off. Gerald turned, and her grip on his ankle slipped. He stopped until she found it again.

They moved into a hallway. Hallways were good. If she wanted to, she could feel across to the other side of the space as they crawled, but she wouldn't. Her left hand stayed on Gerald's ankle and his left hand stayed on the wall. Period. They were doing a left-hand search, and that was protocol. Firefighters who didn't follow protocol died. If something happened, the RIT guys would know exactly where she and Gerald were—they just had to follow the left wall.

She stopped every few feet to pull the hose along. Then put her hand back on Gerald's ankle before crawling forward and reaching out with the axe handle, bumping and scraping its way along the other wall. It was awkward and slow. Her knees were getting sore and her back ached, but she knew that if she stood up to stretch, the upper gas and smoke layers would quickly kill her. She was safe only down here, on her knees, but being safe didn't mean being comfortable. She was so hot. She forgot what she was wearing and tried to wipe the sweat off her forehead, only to have her gloved hand meet with the plastic of her face mask. For a second she panicked, and then took a few deep breaths to calm herself.

She crawled forward again, her hand on Gerald's ankle—until she hit something with the axe handle. She pulled back on Gerald's ankle to make him stop. She reached across to the other side of the hallway and felt along the baseboard. There was a finger-wide vertical gap in the wall—then something metallic. It took her a second to realize it was a hinge sticking less than an inch out into the hallway. That was what her axe had hit. A hinge meant a door. She pulled back on Gerald's ankle again. His face appeared in front of her, their masks almost touching.

"A door," she yelled and pointed. Probably a closet. Maybe a door to the outside. Maybe a door to where the fire was. He nodded and put his gloved hand on the door to feel if it was hot. She could barely see him, yet they were shoulder to shoulder. She felt him shake his head "no" instead of seeing it or hearing him saying the word. She crouched down and flattened herself up against the wall as Gerald did the same against the wall on the other side of the door. If the fire was in the closet and they opened it, they could have flashover, which would instantly ignite everything in the room, including them. But they still had to check. Children often hid in closets to escape fires. Gerald cracked the door slowly. Nothing happened.

She pulled the door open enough so she could squeeze her upper body through it, then grabbed Gerald's ankle again and, with her other arm, reached into the closet as far as she could. She pushed through long hanging pieces of clothing—maybe dresses or coats—until she touched the back wall, then swept her hand along the sides. There was no one in there. She edged back out and tugged on Gerald's ankle to let him know they could keep searching.

They crawled out of the hallway and into a bigger room, where Lucy's axe once again reached out into blackness.

But here, instead of a smooth and uninterrupted wall, there were things in their way, pushed up against the wall: furniture. They had to stop and feel everything as they tried to keep the wall to their left. A chair. A couch. A table. It was like a Halloween game Lucy had played when she was six. Her friend had told her to stick her hand into a box and figure out what was inside by touching it. Cooked spaghetti noodles were supposed to feel like intestines, and peeled grapes like eyeballs. Here it was much the same, but she had to figure out what the secret something was through heavy work gloves. She groped over a chair. A bookshelf. She crawled along, feeling a table. A desk. A lamp. A sofa. She was getting better at this. Another lamp. A chair leg. And something else. A shoe.

Her hand crawled around the shoe. It was next to something—no, attached to something—a leg. The skin felt soft under her glove, like a half-deflated water balloon. Her hand tightened on Gerald's ankle. She tried yelling to him, but she sounded like she was talking through a tin can on a string. His face appeared in front of hers. He put a hand on her arm to quiet her.

She breathed and said slowly, "There's someone in the chair."

He nodded. She felt for Gerald's foot and hooked her own ankle over his. She put her hands back on the shoe and felt her way up the leg. Just below the knee, something caught on her glove. It was sticky. She felt a smooth strap that wrapped its way around the leg. She thought at first it was a belt, but it wasn't thick enough. And it was sticky: tape. It was tape. The person was taped to the chair. She felt her way to the thigh, then to the torso. She felt Gerald reach forward to feel for himself and then edge his way slightly to the right. A moment later she heard Gerald yell, "There's something else over here." She stopped and listened, trying to hear Gerald through her hood. Then his face was in front of her: "Another body—in a chair."

She could hear him, but not see him, talking on the radio to Command.

She reached out to touch the person in front of her again, and felt her way up their chest, kneeling up as much as she dared, trying to keep her head low so as to not disturb the upper gas layers in the room. The smoke here was even thicker. She couldn't make out a damn thing. She should pull off her mask so she could see better. Maybe pull off her gloves to feel for the person's pulse. She eased her panic back down and breathed slowly. No one could have lived through this smoke. No one. Whoever it was, they were dead.

Gil, Susan, and the girls stood in the courtyard of the Palace of the Governors museum, which had served as the governor's mansion for more than three hundred years. The play had ended when Mary and Joseph knocked on the museum door and, after no devil appeared to bar their way, they were allowed inside. The crowd was now gathered drinking hot cocoa and eating *bizcochito* cookies. Therese and Joy weren't on their cell phones for the moment, and were warming their hands against the sides of the paper cups full of hot chocolate they held. It was only 7:15 P.M. but already almost freezing. A group of carolers stood near an old stagecoach that was on permanent display in the museum's open inner courtyard and sang "Silent Night." A few small bonfires and even more *farolitos* circled the space. Gil looked up at the huge cottonwoods laced with snow.

"Daddy, how old do you think these trees are?" Joy asked.

"At least a hundred years," Gil said. "Maybe they were

even here when Lew Wallace was governor." Wallace had lived in the palace in the 1870s, while he was writing *Ben Hur: A Tale of the Christ,* with all the windows shuttered because he thought Billy the Kid was coming to gun him down.

Next to Gil, Susan scrunched up her face as she took another bite of a *bizcochito,* making him laugh. "They aren't that bad," Gil said, taking a bite of his own cookie.

"It tastes like they used maple flavoring and butter," she said, shaking her head. "Why can't anyone ever make it right? It's just a sugar cookie with a little anise." She took another bite before saying, "Did you remember to invite Joe over to your mom's for Christmas Day dinner?"

"He's actually going out of town," Gil said.

"Is he going back east to visit his family?" she said, making a face before taking another bite.

"No. To Las Vegas," Gil said.

"Who goes to Las Vegas for Christmas?" Therese asked.

"Someone who likes to get drunk and gamble," Joy said.

"Mom, can we go to Las Vegas for Christmas?" Therese asked.

"*A la,*" Joy said, in response to her sister. "No way."

"Watch your language, young lady," Susan said.

"*A la* is not a bad word," Joy said.

"But it's part of *a la verga,* and that's bad . . ." Therese said.

"Girls . . ." Susan said in warning.

"That just means a male body part," Joy said. "It's not worse than *hell* or *damn* . . ."

"And we do not use any of those words," Susan said.

"It's not like I said *chingadera,*" Joy said, teasing her mother.

"Okay, enough," Gil said as Joy and Therese started

laughing at their mom's frustration. "Let's talk about something else. What did you get Grandma Montoya for Christmas?"

The girls started talking about what they'd bought for his mother as he saw his mother's cousin coming through the crowd. Robert was still wearing red face paint with black around the eyes but had changed into his street clothes. As the two men shook hands, Gil said, "I didn't know you could act."

"I don't think what I did could be called acting," Robert said. "They handed me a piece of paper with some words on it and said, 'Yell this really loud in Spanish.' So I did."

"I thought you did great," Susan said, giving him a hug.

"I guess it wasn't too bad for a last-second thing," he said. "I had to fill in. Remember that guy who does it every year and always puts on the red body paint and the real ram horns? He didn't show up."

Gil felt the phone buzz again on his hip. He pulled it off his belt and looked at the caller ID. This time it was work.

The sound of the warning alarm on Lucy's air tank made her jump and swear. It sounded like a car horn on steroids. Her emergency beacon went off a second later, sending bright white flashes through the smoke. Their fifteen minutes were up. If there was anyone left alive in the house, they weren't going to get rescued.

"Time to go," she heard Gerald yell through his face mask.

She could feel him moving around, trying to get himself and the hose resituated. She waited until his hand grabbed at hers and placed it back on his ankle. She reached out to the wall with her right hand and put her axe in her left. She tugged on Gerald's ankle to let him know she was ready, and they started to crawl back out. The strobe light from her beacon made the house look like a disco party gone wrong. She closed her eyes against the flashes and tried to slow down her breathing. She concentrated on her knees and hands making contact with the floor as she moved. She had about five minutes of emergency air left in the tank. She tried to think of something soothing, like getting a warm shower or breathing fresh air. Then Gerald's alarm went off. He had probably been breathing slower than Lucy, giving him a few minutes longer. They were both on reserve air now. The sound of both alarms was almost painful, but Gerald didn't crawl faster. They couldn't afford any mistakes, which was what happened when people rushed. Instead, he kept the same pace for the next three minutes, which seemed to stretch on for hours, until they saw the lights from the fire trucks streaming through the open front door. Only then did Lucy let go of his ankle and take a full breath, pulling a last gasp out of her air tank.

CHAPTER TWO

December 20

The first thing Gil heard as he walked up to the fire scene was the loud East Coast accent of his partner, Joe Phillips.

"We are clearly in the county," Joe was saying to a Santa Fe County sheriff's deputy as both men pointed flashlights at a map held between them. They stood partway down a long driveway crowded with fire engines and emergency vehicles. They were about twenty feet off the road, but Gil couldn't see the house at the other end of the driveway. The homes in the Montaña Verde neighborhood were purposely not visible from the street, their heavily forested two- to three-acre lots offering a natural screen from anyone driving by.

"Look right here," the deputy said, poking at the map. "This is where we are, within the city limits."

"You are either insane or blind," Joe said. The jurisdictional fight was an old one. The lines that divided Santa Fe city from Santa Fe County always became an issue when both sides were called to a crime scene. It became a game of "Not It," where the loser was left doing the investigation. Gil stopped and looked to the west, south, and north to get his bearings from the mountains in each direction. He could still make out the dark outlines of the Ortiz, Sangre de Cristo, and Jemez ranges. Joe was right. They were outside the city limits.

"Will you tell this guy that we are in the county?" Joe said to Gil as he saw him walking toward them.

"Hey, Paul," Gil said, shaking the hand of Deputy Paul Gutierrez.

"Of course, you guys know each other," Joe said. "I should have guessed. You're probably cousins. Everybody's a cousin."

"What's going on?" Gil asked the deputy, ignoring Joe.

For a moment, Gutierrez was quiet, then said, "Listen, Gil. My daughter is coming home tomorrow from her third tour in Afghanistan . . ."

"We are clearly in the city," Joe said, folding up the map and switching off his flashlight. "We couldn't be more in the city if we tried. Whoever said we were in the county was a complete idiot." Joe walked off toward the fire scene without another word.

"Thanks, Gil," Deputy Gutierrez, said. "And thank your partner for me. He seems like a good guy."

"Sometimes," Gil said.

"Listen, the least I can do is help you out before I leave," Gutierrez said. "How about I go interview some neighbors. Maybe I can find someone who saw the home owners."

They both turned to look as they heard the noise of car tires crunching from the direction of the street. A gray car,

with Montaña Verde Neighborhood Security written
on the side, came to a stop near the end of the long driveway. A man dressed in a security guard's uniform got out
and adjusted his belt.

"I've got this," Gutierrez said before trotting down the
driveway and shaking hands with the guard. Gil went in
search of Joe. He found him farther up the driveway, near
the front of the house, watching the firefighters work. Much
of the scene was in shadow, but other parts were lit with bright
lights mounted on the backs of the fire trucks. One group of
firefighters was guiding a truck as it backed toward a large,
red rubber holding tank full of water. Others carried saws
and ladders toward the back of the home. From this vantage
point the house looked mostly intact. It was a single-story
with a three-car garage. In this neighborhood, the houses,
with their easy access to the ski area only seven miles down
the road and views of the valley, started at around $5 million.

Gil glanced over at Joe, whose coat collar didn't quite
hide the chain around his neck that held his dog tags, which
he still wore even though his time in Iraq was long over.

"Paul wanted me to tell you thank you," Gil said. Joe
didn't respond. "He said that you are a really good guy," he
added. Still Joe said nothing. "He said it's like your heart is
filled with happiness and butterflies and a beautiful light . . ."

"Shut the hell up, detective sergeant, sir," Joe said.

Gil smiled. They had been partners for only four months
but they seemed to be easing into something resembling a
routine, based mostly on Joe constantly harassing Gil about
his crisp haircut or precise driving, and Gil occasionally
harassing Joe back, mostly about his inability to take a com-
pliment.

"You know taking this case means you might not make
it to Las Vegas," Gil said.

"My flight doesn't leave until Christmas Eve, so we have"—Joe looked at his watch—"three days and twenty-one hours to find this guy."

"What do we know?" Gil asked.

"They found two adult males inside who didn't burn up," Joe said. "Maybe they were overtaken by the smoke or something. I don't have a report on the condition of the bodies or where they were found."

"Do we have names?" Gil asked.

"Not yet," Joe said. "Dispatch is trying to do a reverse search on the address to see who owned the house. I figure we can just run the plates on the cars when we get a look in the garage."

"Who called the fire in? A neighbor?"

"Nah. Just some trucker driving by who saw the flames from the main road," Joe said. "I don't think there are any neighbors around this time of year. Most of the houses here are second or third homes."

"I guess we should go find out when we can get inside."

Gil asked a passing firefighter the location of Incident Command and was pointed to the fire engine closest to the scene. Inside the cab was a man holding a radio microphone in each hand and saying into one of them, "Make sure and check for any exposures. We have a lot of trees on the west and east sides of the house." "Copy that," someone on the other end of the radio answered.

"Charlie, how are you?" Gil asked the man in the front seat as they shook hands. Charlie Solano was an EMS commander who had retired from the Albuquerque Fire Department only to become a full-time volunteer with Santa Fe County.

"Not too bad, Gil," Solano said. "Better than the folks inside. Hold on a second." Solano listened to the radio as someone said, "Command, this is Team A. Can we get an ETA on the next tanker at the second drop tank?" Solano answered, "Copy that. Stand by." He clicked the mike in his right hand, saying, "Shuttle Five, this is Command. We need that water ASAP. Our second drop tank is getting low. What's your location?" The answer came back, "Just passing the county dump." Solano answered, "Copy that. Command out." He clicked the mike in his left hand, saying, "Team A, this is Command. Your water is five minutes out."

"What can you tell me?" Gil asked once the radios had calmed down.

"Two bodies. In pretty good shape, according to my guys," Solano said. "It looks like they weren't touched by the fire. Don't know what killed them. We haven't had a good look at them, since we were busy putting out the fire." The bodies would stay where they were until a field investigator from the Medical Examiner arrived to take charge of them. Dead bodies were not the fire department's problem.

"I would assume that would be your priority," Joe said.

"Pretty much," Solano said. They cared only about the living.

"Are you thinking accidental fire or arson?" Gil asked.

"We have no idea," Solano said. "I guess you're wondering when you can go in. We got knockdown of the main fire about twenty minutes ago, so there is no more active flame. We have a few hot spots to still mop up. Let me make sure the structure is intact enough for you to go in. Say about another ten minutes."

"Can we start limiting personnel in the house?"

"No problem," Solano said. "We're about done. I'll release everyone except me and my engine. The water on the ground from the hoses is all turning to ice anyway. It's getting too dangerous."

"Can we talk to the firefighters who found the bodies before they go?" Gil asked.

"Sure," Solano said. "One of them is out doing a tanker shuttle . . ."

"A tanker what?" Joe asked.

"He's from back east," Gil explained to Solano, "where every corner has a fire hydrant."

"Well, out here we don't really have hydrants," Solano said to Joe. "What we do have are tanker trucks that go get water and dump it into big portable tubs at the fire scene. Then we pump the water from the tubs into the hoses."

"A tub, like the red rubber thing in the driveway, that looks like an above-ground swimming pool?" Joe asked.

"Yeah," Solano said. "That's our water supply. We have to go get more when we run out. Tonight the nearest place for the trucks to get water is five miles away."

"Sounds like a lot of work," Joe said.

"Your guy will be back in about five minutes," Solano said. "But his partner is still on scene. You can't miss her. Just look for the tiniest firefighter out there."

Lucy stood outside the house squeezing water out of the hoses and packing them back into the truck. The scene had quieted down a bit now that the fire was almost out. The outside teams had found the flames and hit them hard. The structure had been mostly saved. Only a corner of the house had been burned, but the rest was wet with water and stank of smoke. She and a half dozen other firefighters were trying to get the crisscross of hoses covering the driveway onto the trucks as fast as possible before they froze with the water still inside.

She was thinking about how much she would rather be in bed when she heard someone say, "Hey, it's little Lucy."

A moment later Joe Phillips was wrapping her in a hug, his goatee scraping her cheek. "How are you doing?" he asked.

"I'm good," she said. "What are you up to?"

"We need to ask you a few questions," she heard Gil say as he stood slightly away from them.

"And a big howdy to you too, Gil," Lucy said. She hadn't seen them in four months, since the fiesta. "Come here, you big lug." She hugged Gil lightly, her head reaching only up to his midchest. "It's like holding onto a big tree. I'm a tree hugger." She laughed, as much at her own joke as at Gil, knowing she was making him uncomfortable.

"We're just here to ask you about the bodies," Gil said, as she finally let him go.

"What do you want to know?"

"Just tell me what happened," he said.

"Okay," she said. "Um . . . we made an entrance through the front door . . ."

"Was it locked?" Gil asked.

"No."

"Did you break it down?"

"No," she said. "It was that way when we got there."

"Could another firefighter have broken it down?" Joe asked.

"No. They would have had to check with Command before doing a thing like that," she said. "Opening a door or window on a fire scene is a big deal. You're introducing a new source of oxygen into the fire. That's how you get a back-draft explosion."

"What happened next?" Gil asked.

"We made a left-hand search of the house, and about ten minutes later I felt a leg tied to a chair. Gerald found the other guy nearby."

"Did you check for a pulse?" Gil asked.

"No," she said, stopping for a moment before saying, "There was no way they could have survived the smoke. If I thought for a second that they might be alive . . ." She surprised herself by almost starting to cry. She knew she must be tired. "Anyway," she continued quickly, "my fifteen-minute alarm sounded, and we got out of there."

A sheriff's deputy came over and whispered something to Gil, who turned around to look across the driveway. Lucy looked in the same direction and could just make out a person standing near a car in the street. Lucy blinked as something flashed—and then flashed again.

"I think a co-worker of yours is here," Gil said intently. It took Lucy a second to realize he wasn't talking about a co-worker from the fire department. He meant someone from her real work—or at the least the work she got paid for—at the newspaper. There was another flash as the photographer took a picture of the fire.

"Sorry," she said, feeling the need to apologize.

"Don't be," Gil said. "They're just doing their job."

"Are you going to give me your trademark don't-tell-anyone-at-the-newspaper-about-this-crime-scene speech?" she asked.

Gil smiled. "I think you probably have it memorized by now."

"You usually say, 'Yada, yada. I'll shoot you if you say anything yada,'" she said.

"That sounds exactly like him," Joe said, surprising Lucy. She had forgotten he was even there.

She added, "Then I usually swear by all that is holy never to speak to anyone at the newspaper about what I have witnessed here."

CHAPTER THREE

December 20

The double front doors of the house had been made in the local Colonial Spanish style, with crude geometric shapes carved into heavy wood, but they hadn't been solid enough to withstand several well-aimed blows. Gil and Joe looked closer at the marks next to the deadbolt, which could have been made by a metal baseball bat or crowbar. A deadlock bolt extends only about an inch into the doorjamb. One sharp blow to the door's weakest point—just to the left of the lock—can force the metal bolt to splinter through the doorjamb, which is exactly what someone had done. He would have been inside before anyone had time to react.

Gil and Joe stepped inside the house and swept the beam of their flashlights over an open foyer with cobalt blue Mexican floor tiles and twenty-foot cathedral ceilings. Two curved archways led in opposite directions out of the entryway. Gil went left, followed by Joe. Their flashlights lit the room in patches, giving slight hints of what the walls and floor looked like. They appeared to be in a living room with carpeted floors that made wet, squishing sounds as they walked. A fifty-inch plasma flat-screen TV mounted to the wall had holes smashed through it. A leather sofa and love seat were arranged nearby. Gil kept his eyes on the carpet as he moved his flashlight carefully, making sweeping motions across the floor. He didn't want to disturb the scene any more than it already was. He looked up just as the beam from Joe's flashlight bounced off something across the room. It took a moment in the darkness to realize the light was reflecting off the open eyes of one of the dead men.

Gil and Joe stopped where they were, about ten feet away from the bodies, and surveyed the scene. They would do a visual examination only, leaving the field medical investigator to give a full review once she got on scene.

The dead men were each tied to wooden chairs that had been taken from the dining set in the room just off to the left. The men were bound at two points—at the chest and legs—by a wrapping of duct tape. Gil and Joe moved closer. From this angle, they could see that the men's arms were pulled behind them, their hands pinned by duct tape.

The men both looked to be in their fifties and were wearing dress shirts and pants. Only one had his mouth covered with duct tape. The other one, who had a dark beard, seemed to have a broken nose, and a few cuts on his chest were visible through his partially unbuttoned shirt. Gil shone his flashlight on the head of the man nearest to him, while Joe did the same on the other body. Unlike the bearded man's body, the one Gil was inspecting seemed to have been relatively unscathed. There was a combination of soot and water in the man's hair, and in his head, something else: a bullet hole.

"It looks like a .22," Gil said. "The entrance wound is pretty small."

"My guy is the same," Joe said. "And I can see an abrasion ring from where the gun was pushed against the skull."

"I have a good-sized exit wound," Gil said, looking at his dead man's left temple.

"Me, too," Joe said. "They were shot at close range. You see any shell casings around?"

Gil crouched down and shined his light parallel to the floor. "No, I don't see anything," he said. "But they could have been washed away by the hoses."

"You know what else I don't see," Joe said. "Burned skin. The fire never reached them."

Gil went back to inspecting the clean-shaven man's head, then swung his light back and forth as he made his way down the man's upper chest, where he was duct-taped to the chair. The tape holding him in place was unremarkable: the gray kind found at any hardware store. The man was dressed in a white button-down business shirt, making a visual inspection of his torso and upper arms impossible. But his lower arms were covered in cuts varying in length from two to six inches. The cuts were mostly shallow except for a few that seemed to be closer to puncture wounds. Gil moved back to inspect the lower torso, where the man's shirt was tucked neatly into his pants. He glanced over to Joe's body and noticed something different.

"Hey, Joe, shine your light on your guy's crotch," Gil said.

"Why, you dirty man," Joe said as he moved the beam of

his flashlight. The man's shirt was not tucked in, and his belt and zipper were undone. There was also dark staining between his legs.

"That looks really gross," Joe said. "I don't want to know what that is, and I want to stop looking at it. I'm moving my light now. You can check his crotch by yourself later."

Gil went back to inspecting his dead man's body, moving his light down the legs, which were also duct-taped to the chair. Nothing else stood out.

Solano came up behind them, carefully following the beam of his flashlight.

"Hey, Gil," he said. "We found something in one of the back rooms."

Joe and Gil followed Solano through the house, which got more charred as they moved toward the back. Joe swore as water dripped down on their heads in the freezing cold. They stepped into a bedroom that was now half open to the night air, its floor covered in charred debris. The fire had done the most damage here, as had the firefighters, who had cut through the ceiling to ventilate the room and torn down the walls to root out any remaining flames. In the middle of the room was what had once been a bed, and against the far wall was a dresser that had been turned over in the firefighting. Near the closet, something was hanging from a wooden ceiling beam. Gil couldn't make out what it was in the dark. He directed his flashlight toward the hanging object, telling Joe to do the same.

Gil thought at first it was dark clothes dangling from a wire hanger, then realized what it was.

"Now we have three bodies." he said.

The dead man was wearing blue jeans and nothing else. He had been suspended from the ceiling by his hands, which were wrapped in wire and tied above his head. The wire was hanging from one of the decorative viga beams by a screwed-in eyehook, which had probably once held up a large hanging plant. This body had burned.

"It looks like this is where the fire started," Solano said, pointing up to the blackened ceiling. "There are burn patterns here that could be from an accelerant . . ."

"You mean the fire started on the body?" Joe asked.

"It looks that way," Solano said. "My guess is gasoline was dumped on him and lit on fire."

"Any way to tell if the guy was alive when it happened?" Joe asked.

"Not just by looking at him," Solano said. "Maybe they can find out when they do the autopsy."

"If the fire started here, why didn't this part of the room burn more?" Gil asked.

"The fire probably wasn't hot enough," Solano said. "The ceiling and wooden vigas would burn at a higher temperature than, say, curtains or bedding. The thermal gasses from the accelerant probably ignited the carpet or some fabric. And then the fire would have moved toward the closest source of oxygen, which would have been a window or vent, probably toward the eastern corner of the room."

"Or what used to be the eastern corner," Joe said. He went over to where a wall had once stood and was now a hole about five feet wide. If there still had been a window there, it would have looked out over the snowy piñon forest and the view of the city in the valley below. Joe shifted his footing and slipped on a small patch of ice. He had to brace himself against a pile of debris so as not to fall. He paused for a second before looking at Gil. "I don't mean to alarm you, but our crime scene seems to be freezing."

"We should call Liz," Gil said. Liz Hahn was a field investigator for the state Medical Examiner. It was her job to collect bodies, take photos, and measure the dimensions for the Coroner's Office. Gil had already called her once tonight, on his way to the scene. She had told him she would be there as soon as she could, but was waiting for her partner, Shelley, to come home to watch the kids. Liz was as close as Santa Fe got to having a full-time medical investigator. That was because, population wise, New Mexico was a small state. More than half of its 1.6 million people lived in Albuquerque, and the other half was spread out over 122,000 square miles of desert. Only Albuquerque had crime investigators on duty at all times, and it was also home to the state's only medical examiner. When someone was murdered, the body always went to Albuquerque for an autopsy. In most towns, there was one field deputy, who, like Liz, worked only when there was a corpse and usually had another job to pay the bills. The investigator in Tucumcari was a taxidermist, while the one in Roswell was a housewife. Liz worked as a technical writer for a medical journal.

Liz answered on the third ring, and Gil explained the situation. "What do you want to do?" he asked. "We could wait until morning."

"We've gotta do it right now," she said. "I'll be there in ten minutes, and I'll call Adam to see if he can help." Adam Granger lived in Santa Fe but was technically the investigator for Española, about thirty miles down the valley. He and Liz had an unspoken agreement to cover for each other during vacations or when a scene was rough. And this scene was particularly rough.

Gil and Joe walked back out to the driveway, which was almost empty of fire trucks now. Since Solano had ordered most of the crews to go home, only a few were left to finish cleanup. The driveway was clear enough for Deputy Paul Gutierrez to pull his cruiser closer. He got out and came over to Gil and Joe.

"Do we have any names yet?" Joe asked.

"I'm still tracking those down," Gutierrez said. "According to the security guard, there are no neighbors around. The only permanent residents were these two guys." In Santa Fe, 30 percent of all homes were vacation properties. The homeowners would come into town only a few times a year, usually for the opera season in June or the Indian market in August. "The guard didn't know them except to wave," Gutierrez said. "He went to the office to get the names."

Adam Granger pulled his van up next to Gutierrez's car. Adam got out and adjusted his white turban, which must have been jostled in the process.

"Adam," Joe called across the cars. "Wass up, dude?"

"Nothing much," he said as the two men fist-bumped. "What's up with you?"

"At the moment, I am fricking jealous of your turban, man. That thing must be warm. I am freezing off some very delicate parts out here."

"It's functional and fashionable," Adam said, patting his head. Adam's family was Sikh, followers of Yogi Bhajan, who led an ashram with thousands of faithful outside the city.

"How is it inside?" Adam asked.

"Getting worse by the moment," Joe said. "I hope you brought your crampons and ice pick."

Lucy looked down at her hands, which were red and raw from handling the icy fire hose bare-handed. Her heavy gloves had quickly become frozen stiff, and she'd had to take them off in order to pack the hose. She had blisters on her palms and between her fingers.

The car ahead of her moved, and she inched forward to the drive-through window. A minute later she was taking quick bites out of a burger while trying to keep her eyes on the road. When they had gotten back to the station after being released from the scene, Lucy was more than ready to head home. Her bones ached, and her throat was raw from the smoke. But they spent another hour restacking the hose, trying to get as much water out as they could so it would be ready to use for the next call—which came just as Lucy was pulling onto her street. She listened to her handheld radio as the dispatcher called out the emergency code. A 29-Alpha 4: a motor vehicle accident without injury. They wouldn't need an EMT, and especially not one who might fall asleep on a patient. She turned her pager off so she wouldn't be tempted to join in the fun. As a volunteer, Lucy was the one who decided if she would go to a call, and she decided to go a lot, so much so that it had been interfering with her real work. She needed to get to bed. Tomorrow was her first day in a new position at the paper.

She drove down Alto Street slowly and purposefully. She'd almost run over the Martinezes' fourteen-year-old calico cat the day before, and she did not want to almost do it again. Her headlights played over adobe fences built within inches of the street curb. It might seem like that tightness would make the road claustrophobic, but Lucy found it charming and old-timey, especially at this time of year, with the electric *farolitos* lining the flat-topped roofs— real *farolitos,* with their candle-in-a-paper-bag fire danger, only for special days, such as Christmas Eve. For everyday Christmas lights, most everyone, from fast-food restaurants to government offices, used electric *farolitos.* They were just blocks of brown plastic shaped to look like paper bags that covered each white light bulb in a string; but the effect was magical.

She parked in front of her house and touched the Our Lady of Guadalupe mosaic by the front door as she went inside. She was starting to have an indecent fantasy about taking a hot bath in her claw-foot tub with a roaring fire in her kiva fireplace when she frowned. The living room light was on. She hadn't remembered turning it on. She dropped her keys in the bowl by the door and kicked off her shoes on her way to the bedroom. She stopped short in the doorway, looking at the person in her bed. She also hadn't remembered having company.

"How did you get in?" she asked Nathan, who was lying on her bed reading *Catcher in the Rye*.

"The door was open," he said turning to look at her. He was naked except for his boxer shorts and the endless tattoos that ran up his body. She must have forgotten to lock it in her hurry to get out the door and to the fire.

"Why are you here?"

"I thought we could hang out since you're leaving on your trip in a few days."

Lucy sighed. "I feel like I need to explain to you the fundamental nature of a booty call," she said. "First, I have to call you . . .

"I get it . . ."

"And, second there is no hanging out."

"Why not? Is that the law of the booty call?" He was trying to make her laugh. She smiled instead. He continued, "With as much as you are calling my booty, maybe we should . . . I dunno . . . talk about it or something. I'm here almost every night."

"Can we talk about it later? I need sleep."

"Sure," he said, standing up to give her a hug. "But why do you smell like a campfire?"

The light path made by Gil's flashlight reflected off the water in the hallway as he followed the sound of voices to the back bedroom. He stopped in the doorway but went unnoticed by the trio inside. Liz had arrived while Gil had been outside getting the names of the homeowners from Dispatch. The operator had sent two driver's license photos to his cell phone. The photos matched the men in the living room, but the person hanging in the bedroom was still unidentified. Now Gil watched as Adam and Liz moved carefully about the room, hampered by the ice and their heavy winter coats, while Joe stood in the corner, out of the way. Liz and Adam had cleared away some burned debris and set up lights on tripods aimed at the hanging body. The white light hit the man's blackened skin, which was cracked in places, showing pink tissue underneath and gleaming patches where ice had started to crystallize. The burns had been concentrated on the man's upper body and face, which had sustained the most damage. His hands were black ash, and his facial features were burned down to bone and teeth.

Gil heard a laugh. As usual, Joe was harassing someone. This time it was Liz.

"I think having kids is the ultimate form of feminism," Joe was saying.

"What do you know about feminism?" Adam asked. "Or having kids?"

"I think being a lesbian is the ultimate form of feminism," Liz said as she crouched down under the charred body.

"That would mean a man can't be a feminist," Joe said. "Can I at least be a lesbian? I have my own power tools."

Liz glared up at Joe while Adam said, "Why do you bug her like this?"

"I can't help it," Joe said. "She reminds me of my sister."

"Your sister must hate you," Gil said from the doorway.

"Hey, Gil, can you help us settle an argument?" Joe asked. "What's the definition of a feminist?"

"It sounds like you're about to tell a joke," Adam said.

"I'm being serious," Joe said before Gil interrupted, saying, "How's it coming?"

Liz answered. "Adam and I are almost done in here. Then we'll get started on the other two."

"We have an ID on the men in the living room," Gil said.

"What are the names?" Liz asked, as she found her clipboard and a pen to take the names down for her report.

"James Price and Alexander Jacobson."

"Really?" she said, looking up. "I know them. I don't know them well. I just met them through friends."

"I'm sorry, Liz," Adam said. "I can handle processing their bodies, if you want . . ."

But Liz said quickly, "No. Thanks. It's okay, really. I barely knew them."

"Do you know what they did for a living?" Gil asked.

"I know Alexander was in the theater; I think he was a makeup artist for the opera during the summer," she said. "Jim works up on the Hill."

"What's the Hill?" Joe asked.

"God, I always forget that you're not from here," Liz said. "The Hill is Los Alamos National Laboratory."

"Is that because it's up on a hill?" Joe asked.

"It's what locals called it during World War II," Gil said. "Everyone knew the government was building a laboratory, but they had to pretend it didn't exist, so they just called it the Hill."

"Why the big secret?" Joe asked.

"Los Alamos National Laboratory," Liz said, annoyed. "That doesn't ring any bells for you? Do you know anything about history? It's where the first nuclear bomb was built. The one they dropped on Hiroshima."

Gil could tell Liz was getting close to kicking them off the scene, something she did with regularity, so he jumped in, saying, "Why don't we go out into the other room and make sure it's Price and Jacobson before we get too off track."

"Fine," Liz said. "Adam can you finish up in here? We'll go take a look."

As they walked to the living room, the carpet no longer squished with water; it crunched with ice. Liz stopped momentarily before the bodies, shining her pen light at their faces. She said, "It's them," then got down to work. While she took some pictures of the overall scene, Joe and Gil set up construction floor lights. She made notes on her clipboard and then took out a measuring tape. Not knowing how else to help, Gil and Joe stood back and let her do her job.

After a few more notes, Liz approached the bodies. She looked them over, taking more pictures.

"They each have a bullet wound to the head," she said, more matter-of-fact than usual. "They have multiple cuts to their arms."

She knelt down in front of the man with the beard and the dark stain on his trousers, who matched the picture of Alexander Jacobson, and pulled back the front of his unbuttoned dark blue dress shirt. The color of his shirt had been hiding bloodstains. What looked to be the letter *T* was carved into his chest. Gil had half expected Joe to make a comment, but he was silent, his face tight. Liz took another half dozen pictures then carefully used the tip of her pen to pull out the front of Jacobson's pants so she could aim her flashlight down the length of his abdomen to his groin.

"His genitals are cut," she said, making a note on her clipboard. Her effect was flat. "The penis is sliced completely off." Without a word, Joe turned away, heading off into the dark dining room, where he could hear what was being said without having to look at the bodies.

Liz moved to the next body: James Price. She noted a similar gunshot wound to the head, then moved her flashlight down to inspect the face. She used her pen to pull the duct tape off Price's mouth. It was wet, so it gave way easily. Liz started to say something else, then stopped. Instead, she stuck her gloved hand in between Price's teeth and forced his jaw open. Using her fingers, she pulled out something. It was Jacobson's severed penis. She sat back on her heels and looked at the mass of tissue in her hand. A minute passed. Then another. Gil wondered if seeing firsthand this level of violence against people she knew was starting to take its toll. It certainly had for Joe, who was now pacing nearby. Liz stood up silently and placed the penis into an evidence bag. Only after she had written all the proper information on the bag, did she finally speak, "I've only ever seen this level of torture once before," she said. "And that ended up being a hate crime."

CHAPTER FOUR

December 21

Mateo Garcia stood watching his quarter horse, Baby, play in the new snow, her cold breath forming wisps around her muzzle. As she galloped down the field, the horse's gray coat flashed past dark tree trunks, barren of leaves. The white snow that Baby kicked up as she played flashed out like glitter being sprinkled over the ground. Mateo was watching to see if Baby was still favoring her front right leg. Yesterday, he thought he had seen her wince after they got home from their evening ride, but today she seemed fine.

Phantom, as usual, stood near the fence closest to Mateo. Her Appaloosa coat—a solid bay color in the front with white leopard spots in the back—made it look like someone had thrown snow over her hindquarters. He patted Phantom on her side while the cold snapped at his ears, making him pull his cowboy hat tighter on his head. He went into the barn to flake a bale and a half of hay into the trough, then cracked the ice that had formed overnight on the watering station. He had brought hot water down in a bucket and stirred in the wheat bran to make warm mash as a treat for the horses. His two goats had stayed in the barn, not liking the new fallen snow quite as much as Baby.

But then she always seemed happy, even when he'd first found her. Back then, she'd weighed only six hundred pounds yet was more than fifteen hands high. Mateo had been on a training maneuver with the Santa Fe County Sheriff's posse. He was riding Phantom, whom his two daughters had trained to be a barrel racer. But when the girls went off to college, Mateo trained her to be a search-and-rescue horse. Mateo had been in the posse since he was sixteen, joining his father and other members on rides deep into the rough desert or up into the heavily wooded mountains, looking for lost hikers or hunters. The posse no longer did searches for runaway inmates or dangerous criminals. That had stopped twenty years ago, but the members each still wore a gold star badge with SANTA FE COUNTY SHERRIFF'S POSSE written across it.

The day Mateo found Baby, he was following a steep path between yucca plants and *cholla* cactus when Phantom hesitated and then veered off the path. Mateo's first instinct had been to rein her in and pull her back to the trail, but he didn't. Phantom was a dependable horse who did what she was told and was eager to please. She wouldn't go off trail unless she had a reason. After a few minutes of riding through the brush, Mateo saw something move beyond the piñon trees. He sat perfectly still as Phantom made her way over to a white-and-gray quarter horse. Her ribs were sticking out of her matted coat and she was almost too weak to support her own weight. Mateo had decided then and there to take the horse home and lie about having looked for her owners. He sat with Baby through much of the first night, with an anxious Phantom in the next stall stomping her feet, whinnying, and swishing her tail. That first week, Mateo fed Baby six times a day, only tiny portions at first. By the seventh day, Phantom was nuzzling Baby, pushing her to move her legs. It was another three months before Mateo attempted to saddle Baby.

He finished with the hay and scratched the two goats behind the ears, then went out into the cold, taking the dirt path up toward the house. He needed to get to work. The store wouldn't open itself.

Gil drove his unmarked Crown Victoria down a slight hill, leaving the white-coated desert south of Santa Fe and dropping into the river bosque, where huge cottonwood trees edged in snow stood over salt cedar and chamisa bushes. He slowed as he came into the village of Galisteo and crossed himself as he passed the church. He followed the road past the old Montoya general store, owned by a relative back in the 1930s, and down Avenida de Montoya, a dirt road of frozen mud. He passed his cousin's house and then his uncle's before arriving at his parents' circular driveway. The Pueblo Revival–style house had been built in the 1920s by his grandparents. Even though it was ninety years old, his family considered it the "new" house. He got out of the car, but instead of going inside, he crossed a small field through the knee-deep snow and went to stand near what looked to be an adobe fence but was actually the south edge of the old Montoya hacienda. The house, built in the 1700s with a grant from the king of Spain, had once been home to probably close to thirty people—family members, servants, and Indian slaves. The last person to call it home was Gil's grandfather and namesake: First District Court Judge Gilbert Nazario Estevan Montoya. Gil's father had grown up in the new house, which had been built as a wedding present to Gil's grandmother. It was where his mom still lived.

The walls of the hacienda had been made of adobe almost two feet thick, but even thick adobe must be replastered every year, or it will crumble. During World War II, when his grandfather was in a Japanese prisoner of war camp, there wasn't the manpower to do the replastering. That left erosion free to whittle the house down to ruin. The rooms were mostly left to the prairie dogs and mice, except a few where the roof remained; those were still used for storage. But this winter might be the last even for that. The snow that had been piling up for the past two months had taken its toll on what was left of the roof. Gil would have to check everything over in the spring to see if any part of the building might be salvaged.

He looked across the field toward the north edge of the property, trying to catch sight of one of the flame orange survey flags that marked the spot where Gil and Susan were going to build their house. Before the weather got bad in October, a driveway had been cut through the scrub, up to a hundred-year-old cottonwood that would be in their front yard. Now everything except the tree lay under a foot of snow.

He walked back over to his mom's house and stomped the snow off his feet before going inside. He could hear his mom on the phone somewhere. Going into the kitchen, he took the cover off a pot simmering on the stove. He knew it was green chile stew before he was hit with the smell of garlic, pork, and potatoes. According to the timer, it would be done in seven minutes. He could easily distract himself for that long. He got his mother's blood glucose machine out of the kitchen drawer and sat down. He scrolled through the digital display, making sure her levels were normal so as to keep her diabetes in check.

"Hi, *hito*," his mom said as she came into the kitchen. "Do you want something hot to eat? The stew is almost done."

"That sounds great, Mom," he said. "I can just stay a minute, though." He waited a moment before asking, "Did you check your blood sugar today? I don't see the results on the machine."

"I'll do it later," she said, sounding dismissive, but she was notorious for forgetting to take the blood test every day. "My sugar has been fine."

The buzzer went off, and Gil watched his mom spoon some of the stew into a bowl before setting it in front of him. "Do you want to take a bowl to your partner?" she asked.

"I'm sure he'd like that. Thanks, Mom." The first bite of stew set off a slow burn on his tongue. Since he was a kid, his mom had spent her winters making green chile stew, making sure it was ready as soon as he and his sister, Elena, came home from school. Joe always talked about how mac and cheese was his comfort food. If Gil had one, it would be green chile stew. He finished the rest in four mouthfuls before getting up and putting his dishes in the sink. "I'm going to go shovel."

"Make sure and invite your partner over for Christmas," his mother said.

"All right, thanks," he said, not wanting to have to explain about Joe and Las Vegas. Putting his hat and coat back on, he took the shovel that was propped up near the backdoor and went outside into the cold.

* * *

Kristen Valdez looked out the kitchen window of the mobile home she shared with her mother as she kneaded dough. She punched it and turned it, sprinkling flour on the countertop when the dough stuck to it in places. She stopped long enough to stir the red chile and elk stew simmering on the stove next to her, then got back to pounding the dough and looking out the window again. Across the stream on the icy dirt road leading to Nambé Pueblo, her mother had stopped to talk with Josephine Gonzales. Growing up, Kristen and her brother had been warned to stay away from the Gonzales's house after Kristen's mother saw Josephine peeping in a neighbor's window. Kristen's mother told them, "There is only one reason to look through someone's window in the dark." She didn't say it aloud, but Kristen and her brother knew what their mother meant. Nighttime peeping was a sure sign someone was a witch. That was why you didn't leave your curtains open; otherwise the witches who prowled the night could see inside and cause harm. It was also why you didn't take food from a stranger, or you might feel an animal clawing inside your stomach. But Kristen wondered if her mother's warning about the Gonzaleses had less to do with witchcraft and more to do with the family being multigenerational heroin users. That wasn't unusual in this part of the state. Josephine's two sons, George and Luke, hadn't escaped the family's addiction of choice. The boys had been hooked on it since they were teenagers, just like their mother, father, aunt, and grandmother. Tribal police visited the Gonzaleses house often, usually after lots of yelling or gunfire.

Kristen watched her mother hug Josephine Gonzales good-bye, then start back to the mobile home. Kristen wasn't surprised to see her mother acting so friendly with a supposed witch. You had to be especially nice to witches so they wouldn't curse you. Kristen punched the dough again, trying to knead out all the lumps. She wasn't sure witches existed, but she respected how her mother felt about them.

Plus, Kristen had seen things that made her wonder. One time, she was playing up in the hills when she saw a bundle of shredded rattlesnakes and coyote hair hanging in a tree. Another time, just after her twentieth birthday three years ago, she'd seen witch lights dancing in the forest, the balls of fire seeming to float above the tree line. But then, Nambé Pueblo had a long history with witches. Among the nineteen pueblos, Nambé believed in them the most, and that belief tended to lead to executions. In the 1800s, Nambé Pueblo had more than five hundred members, but by the turn of the twentieth century, the high number of witch executions had made that number dip to eighty-eight. A local priest predicted at the time that Nambé Pueblo would be extinct in fifty years because of the killings. The pueblo arrested their last witch in 1940. Kristen wasn't sure what had happened to that final witch. He or she might have been executed. The pueblo now had about two thousand members. But as Kristen's mother would say, just because witches were no longer arrested, it didn't mean they weren't still around.

The trailer door opened and a blast of cold air came in along with a swirl of snow. Her mother stomped her feet, saying, "*Hita,* are you done yet?"

"Mom, were you talking to Josephine Gonzales?" Kristen asked instead of answering.

"Yes," her mother said as she unwrapped her scarf and took off her boots. "Her son George is missing." Kristen didn't respond. George probably had just been arrested—or had overdosed.

Kristen gave the dough one last punch before letting it rest under a towel so it could rise. She would finish the dough today, but she wouldn't bake the bread until tomorrow. Proper bread baking took two days. It would be done in plenty of time for the Christmas dances, when a crowd of people would come to their house for food. Christmas was one of the few times during the year when the pueblo tribes allowed the public to watch their dances. Picuris and San Juan put on the Los Matachine dances, while San Ildefonso, Santa Clara, and Taos performed their versions of the buffalo, basket, or turtle dances. Nambé Pueblo did the deer dance, which was given as an apology for taking the life of a deer and in thanksgiving. Intermeshed with the dances were the traditional Christmas events—waiting for Santa, going to Mass, opening presents. For as much as they were pueblo people, they were also Catholic. It was the way it had been for four hundred years.

Gil hadn't even put the foil-covered bowl of green chile stew down on his desk before Joe started talking to him.

"I have made my way through that list of friends that Liz gave us, and all I have to report is that I have now woken up every gay man in Santa Fe," Joe said, flipping through his notebook. "And that's a lot of gay men." Santa Fe was second only to San Francisco in the number of gay households per capita. The list Liz had given them last night was two pages long.

"Thanks for doing that, Joe," Gil said.

"Unfortunately, none of them had much helpful to say," Joe said. He started to read aloud from his notes: "Our guys went to a dinner party four days ago and, I quote, 'seemed fine.' They didn't mention any problems to anyone. When I asked about the chance of an affair, everyone told me the same thing: 'hell, no.' I wish I'd been that certain of my ex-wife," he said, glancing up at Gil before looking back at his notes and adding, "They had plans to meet Christmas Day with friends to open presents. That's it."

"What about threats or problems with anyone who is homophobic?" Gil asked. The idea the murders were a hate crime was not far-fetched. It wouldn't have been the first time in Santa Fe. There had been beating incidents in 2005, 2006, and 2007. In one case, the suspects included a teenage girl who, with a group of others, kidnapped a man and tried to "beat him straight." Liz had been the lead medical investigator for that case, but hate crimes against gays had become much rarer in recent years.

"Nothing," Joe said. "They didn't go to gay bars or really go out much at all, except to friends' houses. They were an old, boring married couple."

"Okay," Gil said. "What about the third victim?"

"No one has any idea who Mr. Burns could be—"

Gil interrupted, saying, "That's what we're calling him? Not 'John Doe'?"

"But," Joe continued, "the most popular guess is that Mr. Burns is an unexpected Christmas houseguest, but neither of our victims had kids or close relatives who might show up out of the blue like that."

"All of that doesn't tell us much," Gil said. "Has Liz gotten back to us on time of death?"

"Hang on," Joe said. "I'll text her." A moment later his phone buzzed; he looked at the screen and said, "She writes, and I quote, 'TOD was 4:00 P.M. yesterday. Same for all victims. Don't text me again.' It's amazing how much she loves me."

"Okay," Gil said. "They were killed about an hour before the fire department got on scene."

"Now we need to know the last time someone talked to them or saw them in public, so we can get the timeline straight," Joe said, popping a Cheeto into his mouth from a bag that had been open on his desk for three days. "I think our best bet would be to call Price's office and see when he was at work."

A half hour and several phone calls later, all they had to show for their efforts was an appointment at Los Alamos Laboratory with an assistant security director.

Joe leaned back in his chair and asked with a sigh, "What do you want to do now?"

"Go back to the house," Gil said, pulling on his coat. Joe was doing the same when he noticed the bowl covered in foil on Gil's desk. "Why do I smell garlic?"

CHAPTER FIVE

December 21

Lucy got to work at 9:15 A.M.—late on her first day. She'd had to dress like a professional since she'd now be interacting with the public. Usually, she looked more like a pizza delivery person in jeans and a T-shirt. Today, she was wearing a button-down blouse that had taken way too long to iron and gray pinstriped pants that needed to be hemmed.

She walked through the backdoor of the *Capital Tribune*. The building was a mishmash of old and new, with parts from the 1800s and the 1970s. Some of the exterior walls had seams where the old and new didn't quite line up. She went into the windowless newsroom, empty of people, where the cubicle dividers made playhouse-sized streets and alleys. The quiet made her nervous. She was used to a humming office where editors yelled headline

ideas over to the copy desk, and where the Photo Department held meetings while standing in front of the bathroom. They would all come in later. For now, all that was
making noise was the police scanner jumping from station
to station. The relative silence allowed Lucy to take in the
newsroom sans employees. It wasn't a pretty sight. The sea-
foam green walls and low-hanging fluorescent lights made
it look like an empty aquarium.

But her new desk wasn't in the newsroom. She walked
past the cubicles and out the opposite door, leaving the
squealing scanner behind her. She went up a sloping step,
then down three more. The linoleum changed from black
speckled to pink, and she made her way to the left, to the
Features Department.

She got to her desk and sat down, stowing her purse in
the bottom drawer. The top of the desk was mostly empty,
except for the computer, a few pens, and an old pad of Post-
it notes. The previous owner of the desk had been Shelley
Lovato—mother of three, native Santa Fean, lover of the
Dallas Cowboys, and employee at the paper for twelve years.
She'd been one of fifteen employees laid off without notice
two weeks ago. Just eighteen days before Christmas. Shelley, who had been in advertising, had cried when she'd
walked out of the building for the last time.

Other newspapers that had made similar staff cuts never
recovered. More than a hundred newspapers across the country had closed since the recession in 2009. That's what had
happened to the *Santa Fe Times,* the other newspaper that
served the area. After 150 years in business, it stopped its
printing presses and went completely online, with only four
staff members doing a job that used to take fifty. Lucy's ex-
boyfriend Del Matteucci had lost his photography job at the
Times in the process. Lucy had followed Del to New Mexico

from Florida when he first got the job. Their breakup, which began six months after they moved, had gone on for months. They had been the ultimate recyclers—using and reusing each other whenever one of them got lonely or wanted sex—until four months ago, when Lucy finally ended the cycle. She had thought their "breakup" would live up to its name, leaving her more than slightly broken, but she had been strangely content. Since then, they had talked only infrequently. The last time was two months ago, when he got laid off and told her he was moving back to Florida.

Though Lucy didn't lose her job, she did lose her slot in the newsroom. They had offered her the cops' reporter position, but she turned it down, not wanting to kick Tommy Martinez out of the job. Instead, she switched to Managing Features Editor, which was a title they made up just for her. While her overall job description was vague—she was to "help as needed" with feature assignments—the actual day-to-day work was clear: to write the funeral notices and birth announcements. Her boss, managing editor John Lopez, had tried to sell the new position as "restructuring," saying they would be handing her more responsibilities as time went on, but the new title and the power that might someday go along with it were just sugarcoating. And she knew it. After her meeting with Lopez, she locked herself in one of the pink bathroom stalls at the newspaper and cried. The toilet paper she spooled out from the dispenser to mop up her face ran out before her tears did. Many journalists given her fate would have quit, but there was one thing that kept Lucy from turning in her letter of resignation: Lopez had promised she'd get her own column. That was something every journalist wanted. Columnists have their own audience. They were allowed use their own voice to express opinion, something that was strictly verboten in normal journalism. Having her own column would be a step up—or, at the very least, a step sideways—from City Editor, while being transferred to Features was not. In essence, she was demoted and promoted at the same moment.

She noticed a box next to her chair and realized that the night janitor had moved her things from her old desk. On top of the pile was a stack of business cards that had been ordered for her over the summer. She took one out. It had "City Editor" embossed in gold under her name. Lucy took the entire stack and threw it into the trash can next to her desk.

It had started to snow lightly by the time they pulled up to the house. Gil parked on the street, but waited to get out until Joe finished his bowl of stew. Then they walked up the long driveway as two squirrels played in the piñon and juniper trees nearby. Joe stopped and looked down at the fresh snow in the driveway, a frown on his face.

"What are you thinking?" Gil asked.

"I grew up in Pittsburgh so I know about two things: the Steelers and snow. This driveway was plowed recently, like, by a truck," Joe said, stopping and looking at the edges where the asphalt met the forest floor. The snow off to the side was deep and piled up a foot high. "See, there are the marks from the front of the plow," Joe said, pointing at a straight diagonal mark in the snow. "It's been plowed in the last few hours." He looked back down the driveway and said, "I'll be right back," then he jogged back down to the street. In a moment he was back, saying, "The neighbor's driveway has been plowed, too. They must hire someone to do it."

"That would make sense," Gil said. "A driveway full of snow is a sure sign someone isn't home."

"We should check on the snowplow guy," Joe said as they reached the front door. "It snowed yesterday morning, then again last night. Maybe he saw something when he was plowing. He could have been the last person to see our victims. He might even know who Mr. Burns is."

Gil nodded, saying, "We can ask the security guard who does the plowing."

They reached the house, which from the front showed little evidence of the fire. The plow had taken away the tracks of the fire engines. The house itself was covered in a dust of white with red chile *ristras* hanging out front, green bows tied on each.

Inside was a different story. The sun streaming through skylights showed glistening ice on most surfaces. Tiny icicles hung from the ceiling where water from the fire hoses had found its way off the roof and into the house. In the corners, snow—blown in through broken windows and damaged walls—had accumulated in slight drifts.

Gil went through the right archway, into the kitchen, while Joe went left, into the living room. Gil called after him, "Go to channel six." He flipped his handheld radio to the right frequency and turned up the volume. He had purposely picked a channel that wouldn't bounce off a radio tower, so any conversation would be just between him and Joe.

Gil went into the kitchen, which had a large butcher block counter in the center, the kind Susan wanted in their new house. The firefighters hadn't come in here, so everything had stayed as it was: neat and tidy. Dishes put away and mint ice cream still in the freezer. It was a slice of Jim Price and Alexander Jacobson's lives frozen in time.

Gil clicked a button on his radio and asked, "Are you noticing anything missing?"

"Part of the gaming system that was set up in the living

room is gone," Joe said. "It looks like someone took the controllers and maybe a few games." Gil could hear Joe's voice on the radio and a more muted version echoing through the house.

Gil went through the other door, leading away from the kitchen, and found himself in a sunroom with a billiard table. It overlooked a flagstone patio with a lap pool and a deck that jutted out on stilts.

Gil clicked his radio on and started saying, "What about cell phones or a computer"—when he heard a ringing that sounded like an old-fashioned telephone. The sound was muffled and bounced off the walls. Gil followed the noise down a hallway and into an office. On a desk next to some bills was a ringing cell phone. A second later, Joe walked in, holding his own phone to his ear.

"I thought I'd give Jacobson a call," he said. In his hand was another cell phone. "I found Price's phone still plugged into the charger in the master bedroom." Joe punched numbers into both phones, checking their recent calling history and comparing the numbers dialed against numbers in his notebook.

"The last call made from either phone was two days ago, when Alexander called Jim," Joe said. "There were a bunch of missed incoming calls this morning: I guess friends checking on them."

Gil said, looking around the office, "I don't see a computer on this desk. Did you see one anywhere?"

"No," Joe said. "And you know they had to have at least one."

"So we're missing a computer and a gaming system," Gil said. "If this was a robbery, they didn't take much." They made their way back out into the living room. The ice covering on the furniture was already starting to melt.

"What do we think about the hate crime idea?" Joe asked.

"I don't know," Gil said. "I'm not convinced."

"I think the whole cut-off penis thing is pretty convincing," Joe said. "You're the Wikipedia of all things criminal. What kind of suspect would we be looking at if it was a hate crime?"

"Sixty percent of the perpetrators are white males," Gil said. "And, I think, around thirty percent of hate crimes take place in a home."

"It sounds possible," Joe said.

"But hate crimes resulting in murder are very rare," Gil said. "There are only about eight a year in the entire country and that includes all hate-motivated murders, including those that are about race and religion."

"I guess this could have been regular torture and not hate-related torture," Joe said. "But this is pretty extreme stuff. Our suspect took the time to carve a *T* on his chest . . . I wonder if there's a gay-bashing word that starts with *T*?" Joe stopped to think.

"Let's just keep all the options on the table," Gil said. He glanced around the room. "Even if it was a hate crime, this scene doesn't make a whole lot of sense logistically. There are two separate areas where the victims were held. From what Liz said, all the victims were alive until the end. One person wouldn't have been able to keep control of that many people at once."

"Right. You can't be in this room with Price and Jacobson and keep an eye on Mr. Burns at the same time, or vice versa," Joe said. "If there was just one suspect, he'd be running between the rooms all night long. At some point, he'd just put everyone in the same room."

"Then we have a group of suspects," Gil said. "That

means home invasion of one kind or another." Gil looked at his watch. "We should get on the road. The drive to Los Alamos might be icy."

They were just getting back into the car when a dark SUV pulled up and a sandy-haired Anglo man in his early twenties leaned out the window. "Could you help me?" he asked in a Texas accent. "I'm trying to find the ski area."

"Yeah, you missed the turn," Joe said. "Just follow this road straight until you come to the stop sign. Take a right, and you'll be on Hyde Park Road. Just follow that up into the mountains."

"Thanks. You wouldn't happen to know anything about the skiing conditions?" the man asked, with a laugh.

"Actually, there should be some sweet powder," Joe said. "But take it easy. It's twelve thousand feet up there at the top. You can get dizzy real quick at that elevation."

"Thanks for the tip," the man said. "My buddy told me there was some great off-trail skiing."

"I wouldn't recommend it," Gil said. "Outside the ski area is National Forest land. It's hundreds of acres of forest. If you get lost, you're on your own."

"Just you and the bears," Joe added.

Natalie Martin sat on a bench in the mall, watching her twin boys play a made-up game that seemed to resemble hide-and-seek. Deacon would run around the plastic tree house as fast as his chubby two-year-old legs could manage until Devon, in the tree house above, popped out his head and growled. Then they would both start laughing until Deacon began to run again. It wasn't a complicated game, but it was keeping the boys busy. And that had become Natalie's main goal in life.

She waved as she saw her friend Julie pushing her stroller

toward them. Julie's twenty-two-month-old son, Connor, was waving his arms and legs trying to get out of the stroller before it had come to a stop.

"Okay, okay," Julie said. "Hang on." She freed her son, who went running off to join Deacon and Devon.

"Hey, you," she said to Natalie, giving her a hug. "Weren't we supposed to meet a half an hour ago? I've been wandering around looking for you."

"Oh my God," Natalie said. "I am so sorry. I have such a mom brain. I can't keep even the simplest thing in my head."

"Don't you hate that?"

"Some days I wonder how I ever managed to get a PhD in chemistry."

"I know," Julie said. "I used to go into courtrooms and argue cases in front of a judge. I have no idea how I did that. I wore dresses and high heels and everything. Like a real grown-up."

"I swear, as soon as we have kids there must be some hormone that makes us forget we were once smart, successful women," Natalie said. Both women, despite sitting right next to each other, kept their eyes only on the playground.

"That'll be something for you to figure out when you get your brain back. Maybe you'll discover the mom brain hormone and make the big bucks."

"When will that be?"

"When they go to college. I hope to God."

"With any luck, the twins are both prodigies and off to college at twelve," Natalie said. "Of course, all they are prodigies at right now is creating laundry. How do boys go through three outfits a day?"

"Are you kidding me? Connor is on his fourth today."

They heard a cry across the playground.

"Speaking of which . . ." said Julie, as she got up to go to her son.

"What department did this guy work in again?" Joe asked as they drove toward Los Alamos. They had followed U.S. Highway 285 north out of Santa Fe for fifteen miles, dropping down into the wide valley cut by the Rio Grande more than thirty-five million years ago. Now they were on State Highway 502 heading west; after crossing the river and beginning the climb out of the valley, they had another twenty miles before they reached the lab.

"Primary Structural Biosystems," Gil said.

"That could mean anything," Joe said. "I wonder if he worked on bombs. Maybe the guy made biochemical weapons and someone killed him to get information. Or he was selling information to some international bad guy . . ."

"Like who?"

"The Chinese," Joe said. "They've been the ones behind most of the recent spying cases at the lab." He had been busy researching the lab on his phone's Internet connection, telling Gil every detail about what he found. So far, he'd told Gil how the lab was built on a fault line and had frequent earthquakes. He also talked about how the water runoff that came down the mesa from the Hill had to be checked for radiation, since during the early days at the lab, they simply dumped nuclear waste in the arroyos. Now Joe was researching spying, which had a long history at the lab, going back to Ethel and Julius Rosenberg in the 1940s. But they were only two of dozens of spies caught over the years.

The Crown Victoria started to groan under the effort of getting up the hill, despite the fact that the highway itself was perfectly maintained, because trucks carrying radioactive waste also used it. Every week, the lab shipped containers of waste to an abandoned salt mine more than three hundred miles to the south for storage. In the last decade, the lab had sent more than eight thousand trucks from Los Alamos to Carlsbad, and they wouldn't be stopping the shipments anytime soon. Sitting in the middle of a parking lot, on lab property, another thirty thousand containers of radioactive waste were still waiting for a ride. The trucks were followed by satellite and were equipped with warning alarms should a driver make a wrong turn or an unplanned stop. The nuclear waste was only low-level, but even so, Santa Fe had built an entire bypass highway around the city simply for the trucks on their way to the interstate.

Joe and Gil stopped at a gas station run by the San Ildefonso Pueblo and went into the attached restaurant. The menu had the usual list of New Mexico diner food: breakfast burritos, Navajo tacos, Frito pies, hamburgers, huevos rancheros, tacos, and hot dogs. Gil and Joe both ordered a Frito pie. They had barely ordered when the waitress came by holding two plates of Fritos chips covered with beans, onions, lettuce, cheese, and red chile.

"Man, this is the best," Joe said, taking a bite. "This is like three of my favorite things together: beef, cheese, and snack food. I wonder if they could make a Cheeto pie?"

Gil watched cars come and go at the gas pumps. Some people were clearly from the pueblo, dressed in T-shirts and jeans, and some were lab workers in their suits and ties.

"Okay, here's my new theory," Joe said with his mouth full of Fritos. "What if Jim Price was selling secrets to the—"

"This is not a spy thing," Gil said.

Joe rolled his eyes and said, "Fine. It's not a spy thing. What, then? Love triangle? Radioactive experiment gone horribly wrong?"

"Maybe a home invasion," Gil said.

"You still don't think it's a hate crime?" Joe said.

"I don't know," Gil said. "At the moment I'm just think-ing about how the victims were killed."

"Mr. Burns was torched and the other two were shot," Joe said. "I wonder why the difference?"

"Maybe to cover up some evidence," Gil said. "Or out of anger."

"Tying someone up and then setting them on fire is a really messed-up thing to do," Joe said, finally swallowing. "Maybe Mr. Burns resisted or—"

"Or maybe he knew his killer. Like an ex-lover. I know that's who I get raging mad at."

"Or maybe even a co-worker . . ."

"What are you saying, Gil? That you want to tie me up and burn me alive?"

"Or shoot you. Depends on the day."

CHAPTER SIX

December 21

Lucy had spent her morning checking e-mail
and watching videos online of cats playing
musical instruments. Occasionally, she considered trying to figure out how to do a birth
or death announcement, but she ended up
thinking about her column. A columnist for a
midsize daily newspaper such as the *Capital
Tribune* would often end up with a following.
Lucy knew that having a column could give
her some power. She had some experience as
a columnist. When she was in college at the
University of Florida, she'd had a column
called "The Whine List." Within a few weeks
of the first column being printed, people
started to recognize her. She got into bars for
free and had several marriage proposals. Of
course, that might have been because she came

across in the column as a drunken slut. What she had been trying to do was show the hypocrisy of college: students furthering their education while simultaneously killing their brains with alcohol. She tried to find a humorous way to portray how most college students ended up with a Dr. Jekyll/Mr. Hyde personality battle; the good side who went to class during the day and the bad side who went out every night. But the subtlety of that message got lost in the hangover shuffle. Instead, she ended up coming across as a hero for the drinking class. It was an image she didn't fight, not after she got banned from a fraternity for crashing one of their parties and then writing about it. Not after the president of the university publically mentioned her in the dedication speech for the new library.

Now she was being given a chance to do another column. Lopez hadn't told her what kind of theme to follow—advice, horticulture, sports. All he'd said was, "Do whatever feels most natural." Lucy, naturally, was thinking about doing a humor piece.

She was watching yet another cat play the piano when Tommy Martinez came in holding his reporter's notebook.

"Hey," he said. "I just wanted to come see your new place. It must be nice having your own office. Are you ready for your trip? You're leaving tomorrow, right?"

"What's up, Tommy?" she said.

"How's Nathan doing?" Tommy had met Nathan a few weeks back, at the Cowgirl, where Nathan worked as a bartender. Lucy had been there, waiting for Nathan to get off work, when Tommy came in with a few of the copy desk people. Lucy considered trying to duck and hide, not wanting to have to introduce her co-workers to a guy who was basically a one-night stand who wouldn't go away. But they spotted her, and she was forced to make the introductions, in which she referred to Nathan as a friend. Tommy, of course, got the gist of it.

"Get to the point, Tommy."

"I was wondering, boss—did you go to that fire last night? The photographer said she saw you there."

"First of all, Tommy, I'm not your boss anymore," she said. "Second, you know I can't talk to you about any emergency calls I go on."

"So, you were there?" he said. "I heard they found some dead bodies."

"No comment," she said. "Now, can you close the door behind you so I can get a nap? I need to rest up for the *bizcochito* bake off later."

From the Rio Grande Valley floor, which had only a scattering of piñon and juniper trees, to the top of Pajarito Mesa, which was covered in ponderosa pine and Gambel oak, there was almost a two-thousand-foot change in elevation. Los Alamos, built on top of Pajarito Mesa, looked out over the entire valley. As Gil followed the state highway to the mesa top, the road hugged white cliffs of soft rock made of tuff—a hardened volcanic ash into which Anasazi Indians were able to carve entire cliffside villages such as at Bandelier National Monument, just a few miles away. Where the cliffs of Pajarito Mesa met the flat mesa top, it looked like one giant step led up to the Jemez Mountains' eastern slopes, where the highest peak reached more than 11,500 feet. On top of the mesa, where the trees became much taller and the snow a foot deeper, there was the city of Los Alamos, which surrounded the lab like a protective coat. The lab itself had been safely built miles away from the mesa edge, in the crook of the steep Jemez Mountain slopes to the west. As the town of

Los Alamos grew up around the lab, it had nowhere to go but closer and closer to the top of the steep cliffs to the east. Now it looked like half the city would go tumbling down the mesa edge with the next strong gust of wind.

When Robert Oppenheimer was looking for a place to build the lab in 1944, he picked Los Alamos for several reasons. The main one being that access to the site could be easily controlled should the Germans or Japanese invade. Its location on the mesa meant there were only two roads in, both of which had cement guard stations to keep watch. State Highway 4 came down from the Jemez Mountains and into Los Alamos from the west, while State Highway 502 came into town from the valley below to the east. Oppenheimer knew what the Pueblo and Anasazi tribes knew before him: mesas make for good defensible positions.

Unlike the rest of Northern New Mexico, the houses in Los Alamos were not built in the flat-topped Santa Fe style. Instead, they were the type you might see back east, with pitched roofs and more than one story. And almost no houses were painted any shade of beige, but were white or yellow with neat trim. Many were ranch-style from the 1970s, when the lab had started to grow. The trees here were different from Santa Fe as well. The high elevation allowed for more precipitation and thus more variety. There were elm, tulip trees, and even some weeping willows with branches straining under a heavy layer of snow. All of the houses were well maintained; no foliage overhung the sidewalks. Every now and then, through a hole between houses, Gil could see down to tribal land of San Ildefonso Pueblo in the valley a thousand feet below. When it came to household income, Los Alamos County was the fifth wealthiest in the country, whereas almost a quarter of the people in San Ildefonso Pueblo lived below the poverty line.

Gil drove through a manned gate that looked more like a bunker, past a sign welcoming them to a place WHERE DISCOVERIES ARE MADE. The gates looked like they had been built in the 1950s, but Gil knew they were outfitted with state-of-the-art radiation detectors and surveillance equipment. The town likely was under twenty-four-hour watch by a host of satellites.

"They have you go through a guard post just to get into town?" Joe asked after being waved through by an armed officer. "We're not even at the lab yet."

"Welcome to Los Alamos," Gil said. The town of Los Alamos within the county of Los Alamos was supposedly separate from Los Alamos National Laboratory, but with almost ten thousand employees, everyone within a twenty-mile radius—with the exception of Pueblo tribal members—was connected to the lab in one way or another.

They passed through another gate to get into Los Alamos lab proper, showing their ID and badges to another security guard. He directed them to the correct building and sent them off with a brisk wave.

"I think I should warn you that they do things differently up here," Gil said.

"How so?" Joe asked.

Gil hesitated, not sure how to explain. The lab was one of the largest scientific centers ever created and one of only two places in the country where nuclear weapons were designed. By necessity, that made it one of the most secure places in the world. It also made everyone who worked there justifiably paranoid. "They are a federal organization," Gil said. "They don't really have to cooperate with us. They operate according to their own set of rules."

"Are you saying these are the guys who come for you in the black helicopters?"

"No. I'm saying these are the guys who built the black helicopters and trained the pilots."

"Meaning we need to shut up, smile, and don't ask questions," Joe said. "I know exactly how to do that. I was a soldier after all."

They parked between a pair of dark SUVs, just two of more than a dozen in the lot, and went to the reception center—a steel-and-brick building that looked new and angular. A minute later, they were shaking hands with assistant security chief Chip Davis. He had close-cropped blond hair with some gray in it and was wearing a red golf shirt and khaki pants with an ironed-in crease. When he talked, Gil thought he heard the ghost of an East Texas accent.

"We've got an interview room all ready for you," he said, leading them to a set of elevators that opened with a swipe of his security card. "We have notified Dr. Price's immediate supervisor about the situation. She is being brought up to talk with you."

They got out in a hallway lined with identical doors and went in the third one on the left. Inside was a wall of sound and camera equipment with a video monitor showing an interview room decorated like a funeral home: beige carpet, pastel blue walls, and several watercolor paintings of mountains.

Gil and Joe put their guns into a locker and went into the interview room with Davis, where all three of them took a seat. What Davis didn't need to explain was his presence there. Gil and Joe would not be allowed to talk to any employee without a security member present.

Davis slid a green folder across the table to Gil, saying, "We have Dr. Price leaving his workstation at 5:34 P.M. the day before yesterday and passing through all the checkpoints within a few minutes after that." Gil flipped open the folder, which had a picture with a time stamp that showed Price getting into his car and another of him driving his car through town. "We have confirmation of him leaving the city limits at 5:47 P.M.," Davis said. "Do you have any reason to believe that this is related to his work?"

"No," Gil said. "Not at this time. You've looked over our reports?"

"They have our reports?" Joe asked before Davis could answer.

"Your office sent them," Davis said. "I read the incident report and some of the scene information. It doesn't seem to involve us. But we'll keep up-to-date on it."

"I know you keep pretty close tabs on your employees," Gil said. "There must have been some red flag when Dr. Price wasn't at work yesterday."

"According to our records, he had requested the day off," Davis said.

"Do you know why?"

"No," Davis said. "He wasn't required to give a reason on the paperwork he filled out."

Someone knocked, then opened the door a crack. Davis got up to speak in low tones with a person on the other side, then came to sit back down, saying, "Dr. Goodwin is ready. Before she comes in, just keep in mind you cannot ask in any way about her work. I'll conduct the interview, and you will be allowed to ask questions at the end." Another security officer escorted a small woman with blond hair into the interview room.

"Begin recording," Davis said. "The date is December twenty-first. Present is myself, assistant security director Chip Davis; Santa Fe police detectives Gil Montoya and Joe

Phillips, and Dr. Laura Goodwin. We are meeting to discuss any information regarding an incident involving Dr. Jim Price. Dr. Goodwin, could you state your full name and where you work?"

"I am Dr. Laura Goodwin," she said without inflection. "I am group director for the Primary Structural Biosystems department at Los Alamos National Laboratory."

"And you are Dr. Jim Price's immediate supervisor?" Davis asked.

"Yes."

"When did you last see him?'

"At a group meeting last week." Her answer surprised Gil. He saw his co-workers several times a day. To not see someone in a week usually meant that person had gone on vacation.

"And how did he seem?" Davis asked.

"Fine."

"Who in your lab would have had more contact with him over the last few days?"

"I wouldn't know. My office is on a separate floor of the building."

"Is he friendly with anyone in your department?"

"He is fairly new to our group. He transferred in a year ago from the Bio Tech department to fill an opening due to a retirement."

"Did he have any problems with anyone in your department?"

"Not that I know of."

Davis leaned back. "Detectives, do you have any more questions for Dr. Goodwin?"

"You hadn't seen Dr. Price in a week?" Gil asked. "Was that normal?"

"Yes," she said. "We each have our own labs and offices. And, as I said, I work on a different floor."

"You didn't run into him in the hallway or the break room?"

She raised her eyebrows at the last part of the sentence. "We don't have break rooms," she said.

"He wasn't required to check in with you or anyone else?"

"We're all PhDs," she said, as if that explained it.

"Doctor, did anyone have an issue with Dr. Price being gay?"

"He was gay?"

"Yes," Joe said slowly. "He lived with his partner."

"I had no knowledge of it."

Gil leaned back and thought. Normally, they would get much more information about a subject from his work environment. People spent as much time with their co-workers as they did with their family. The natural consequence of that was co-workers often had valuable information about the subject the family either didn't know or didn't want to reveal. Office mates sometimes knew when a person had problems at home or financial trouble. But the distance kept between Dr. Price and his co-workers meant there was little more Dr. Goodwin could tell them.

Gil and Joe had no other questions, so Davis told Dr. Goodwin thank you, and she was escorted out of the room.

"Well, that was a bust," Joe said as soon as the door closed behind her. "The cashier at the liquor store knows more about me than she did about Price."

"That's pretty typical," Davis said. "Most scientists are ultracompetitive. You have to remember that these are some of the smartest people in the entire country. They are used to being treated differently. And they aren't very good at teamwork." Gil nodded. He had heard rumors about lab employees poisoning co-workers or framing them for espionage, all over who got their name on a scientific research paper or credit with the Nobel Prize committee.

"Honestly," Davis continued, "usually the cleaning crews and security guards are the only people the scientists might have had a social conversation with."

"Did Dr. Price interact with any of them?" Gil asked.

"Maybe one of the security guards assigned to his unit," Davis said. "Let me find out."

Davis got on his walkie-talkie and stood off to the side of the room, while Joe tried to get Gil's attention by tapping on the table. Gil glanced at him, and Joe mouthed the words, "What the hell?" Gil ignored him. Davis came back over to them, saying, "Dr. Price was friendly with the day-shift security officer Chad Saunders. He's on his way here."

Saunders came in a few minutes later wearing what seemed to be the lab security uniform: khaki pants and a golf shirt. He had ruler-straight buzzed hair and held himself with his center of gravity shifted slightly lower than normal. Gil had seen mixed martial arts fighters develop the same stance over years of training. The men sat down, and Davis gave the same introduction as earlier, before asking Saunders, "When did you last see Dr. Price?"

"I saw him around seventeen-thirty hours the day before yesterday," Saunders said. "When I went to his office to drop off some Tupperware."

"Tupperware?" Joe asked.

"He and Alex made chicken cordon bleu from a recipe I gave them, and he brought me some leftovers. I was just returning the Tupperware he brought the chicken in."

"Alex?" Gil asked. "So you knew Dr. Price's partner?"

"I had never met him," Saunders said. "But Dr. Price talked about him a lot."

"Do you know what their plans were for Christmas?" Gil asked

"They were just going to do what they always do—go to the *Farolito* Walk, then watch a couple of Pueblo dances and hang out with friends."

"Did he mention any houseguests?" Gil asked.

"Not that I remember."

"Had he been having any problems lately?" Joe asked.

"No," he said. "His biggest concern was what to get Alex for Christmas."

"Do you know why he took that day off yesterday?" Gil asked.

"He just wanted time to wrap presents," Saunders said. "Plus, he was going to watch Alex perform. He plays the devil every year at Las Posadas. He's the one that wears the red paint with the sheep horns."

Lucy walked into the conference room where the chairs had been pushed against the walls, leaving a huge oblong table in the middle of the room. On the table were platters of cookies—fifty-two platters in all. That's how many readers had baked cookies for the Best *Bizcochito* Bake Off. In almost every household in Northern New Mexico, the Christmas season officially started with the first batch of *bizcochitos*, which was how it got named the New Mexico state cookie. Lucy had heard many arguments about what made the perfect *bizcochito*. Some said it was anise; others said vanilla. Some said it depended on the lard used—it had to be Snowflake brand—while others insisted it was the right consistency of butter. The newspaper had been advertising the contest since Thanksgiving, telling readers it would determine "once and for all, what makes the perfect *bizcochito*." The bakers were not allowed to be present while select members of the newspaper staff judged the cookies.

"Lucy, I'm so glad you're here," said Connie Dominquez, the office receptionist. She had fake holly in her hair and peppermint stripes painted on her fake nails. Connie, who was in charge of the contest, had wanted Lucy to be a taster for one reason: she was a *bizcochito* virgin. Lucy had never even heard of *bizcochitos* before she moved to New Mexico, and she had yet to taste one. Last Christmas—her first since leaving Florida—she hadn't been in Santa Fe. The holiday season had coincided with her second postbreakup reconciliation with Del. They had decided to take their reunion on tour to Las Vegas. They spent their days drinking pitchers of mojitos, eating shrimp, and talking about what rebels they were for spending Christmas in Sin City. Within a week of counting down to the dawn of a new year, they had broken up again.

This year wouldn't be her first Christmas in Santa Fe either. She was leaving for Florida tomorrow and would be there for the better part of a week. But for now, her lack of *bizcochito* knowledge made her the celebrity judge of this contest. She was given a scoring sheet attached to a clipboard, and stopped at the first plate. The *bizcochitos* were beige, like the Santa Fe desert, and had a thin coat of sugar on top. She took a bite, not sure what to expect. It seemed to be a type of sugar cookie, yet there was something slightly different about it—a hint of nuttiness or caramel. She couldn't tell which. She took another bite, and heard Connie say across the room, "Lucy, you'd better pace yourself. You've got fifty-one more cookies to taste." She looked around, noticing that some of the other testers were biting

down and then spitting the cookie out into a napkin, so as
not to get sick. She tried that with the next cookie, and it
seemed to work. Five plates later, she had a mush of cookies and saliva leaking through a napkin in her hand. Lucy
reached for a cookie from the next batch and took a bite.
This tasted more of chocolate, but it was nothing fantastic.
She spit it out into her soggy napkin. She moved on. The
next one melted in her mouth before she had a chance to
bite down, and there was a sweet taste, but not overly sweet.
She was about to mark it down as the winner when she
noticed Tommy Martinez come in and scan the room, looking for someone. It turned out to be her.

"Hey, boss," he said.

"I'm not your boss anymore," she said while watching
him sneak a cookie off a nearby plate and take a nibble. He
looked over her shoulder to make sure Connie hadn't noticed and took another cookie off another plate. Lucy
grabbed Tommy by the arm and steered him into a corner
and away from the cookies.

"So, I heard something about the fire victims—" he
started to say.

"Tommy," she said, trying to interrupt him.

"Wait, hear me out," he said. "One of my sources said
the men were gay and that it looked like a hate crime."

Lucy must have looked surprised, because Tommy asked,
"You didn't know about that? Interesting."

"Who's the source?" she asked. "Are they with the police?" This time she read his face and could tell his source
wasn't anyone official. Probably one of the many emergency dispatchers he chatted up with his stories of growing
up in the mountain village of Ojo Sarco, the second youngest of nine from a family that had farmed the land for
fifteen generations. Lucy had spent many a night as city

editor marveling at how he worked his female sources, slipping into his best Northern New Mexico accent when speaking English and switching to the old Colonial dialect for the Spanish. In both languages, he stretched out the vowels, making his words sound like a lazy Sunday afternoon.

"All you have is a rumor from one of your groupies," she said. "Are you willing to freak out our entire gay population with speculation?"

"Don't you think the public has the right to know if there is a homophobic killer running around?"

"That is such a stretch," Lucy said, trying to keep her voice down. "You have no proof this is a hate crime outside what one of your little *chiquitas* told you between the sheets."

"You know, you keep pointing out something to me that up until now I've been ignoring," he said, not keeping his voice down. "You aren't my boss anymore." With that, he turned away.

Lucy sighed and looked down at her scoring sheet. She realized she hadn't written down which entry was the melt-in-your-mouth winning cookie. She glanced over to the table piled with cookies. She wasn't looking forward to retracing her taste-test steps.

Gil and Joe were a mile or so outside of Los Alamos when the highway dropped back down toward the desert and the hundred-foot-tall ponderosa pines changed into eight-foot-tall piñon pines. The snow went from three feet deep on the mesa to nonexistent on the southern-facing slopes closer to the valley. They had ended up speaking only to Dr. Goodwin and Saunders. Davis said other lab staff would be made available when and if "the investigation warranted it." He didn't say how that determination would be made, and Gil, for the moment, didn't want to push the issue.

"That entire place felt like a conspiracy theory," Joe was saying. "Do you think they bugged our car?"

"Maybe," Gil said.

"Hey, Davis, I really liked your golf shirt," Joe said into an air-conditioning vent. "I think red is a lovely color for you."

If the lab was overly protective, it was for good reason—because it hadn't been in the past. Gil's great-grandfather used to tell a story about the time he was sitting in a bar in Tesuque, just outside Santa Fe, as a big truck rolled up outside. It had something about five feet high and ten feet long tied down and covered on the flatbed. The driver and passenger, two local men, came into the bar and went into the back room, which was a brothel at the time. A few hours later, they came back out, got in the truck, and went on their way. His great-grandfather would later learn those men were driving to Trinity nuclear test site and that the "something" sitting unguarded in the back of the truck was the first atomic bomb on its way to get tested.

"How did they get our reports?" Joe asked. "Our office sent them? Who in the office even has our reports?"

"It was probably the chief," Gil said. "From now on you should just assume the lab knows exactly what we are doing at all times."

"So I need to stop shaking down the drug dealers and the pimps?"

"Just for the next week or so."

CHAPTER SEVEN

December 21

Lucy was still coming down from her sugar high when her pager went off. Ironically, the call was for a diabetic emergency. She grabbed her coat and headed out the door, glad to have an excuse finally to move her legs and burn off some extra energy.

She drove her car toward the station while simultaneously taking off her blouse and pulling her navy blue uniform T-shirt over her head, ignoring looks from other drivers. She got to the station, kicked off her high heels, grabbed her combat boots, and ran barefoot across the icy parking lot to the ambulance, where Gerald was waiting.

She climbed up into the cab, saying, "I'm in." While Gerald pulled out of the station, Lucy hit the lights and sirens and called Dispatch, saying they were en route to the scene.

She put her boots on while Dispatch gave the address again, "135 Calle Ocho." Lucy started saying aloud, "One-three-five Calle Ocho. One-three-five Calle Ocho." She pulled on her second boot and found the map book.

"Okay," she said to Gerald. "One-three-five Calle Ocho is just across the highway and down near the arroyo."

Gerald hit the intersection of the highway and Lucy hit the air horn, letting cars know they were going to cross. A blue car to their right stopped in the middle of the highway and didn't pull over.

"What does this joker think he's doing?" Gerald asked, as he tried to maneuver the ambulance around him. Lucy hit the air horn again, but the car didn't move.

"How difficult is it to pull off to the right side of the road?" she said. "Why do people freak out when they see us coming? They're like small, furry animals in the headlights."

Gerald finally got around the car, and they headed down the road.

"When are you leaving for your trip?" Gerald asked, during a break in the radio chatter.

"Tomorrow," she said. "Within twenty-four hours I will be on the white, sandy beaches of Florida."

"Is your mom excited for you to come visit?"

"Yeah," she said. "It'll be good to see her. It's been more than a year."

A few minutes later, they were pulling up in front of 135 Calle Ocho, where it looked like someone had thrown up Christmas all over the outside of the house. An inflatable Nativity scene was facing a plastic Santa and reindeer. A trio of inflatable snowmen stood watch over huge glittering snowflake cutouts. And the roof was lined by electric *farolitos*.

Lucy grabbed the med bag out of the side of the ambulance and followed Gerald inside, where the Christmas overload continued. There were not one but three Christmas trees in the living room, each with different colored garland and ornaments. Under each tree was a pile of gifts, and lining the room on every shelf were Nativity scenes— hundreds of them.

An older woman wearing a sweater taken up entirely by a picture of Santa with a bell sewn onto his hat was sitting in an easy chair, her head lolling off to one side. Gerald got on his knees next to her saying, "Ma'am, ma'am. Can you hear me?"

The woman's eyes fluttered open but didn't stay that way. Lucy unzipped the med bag and found the blood glucose machine, while Gerald prepped the woman's finger with alcohol, then stabbed her with a lancet. The woman jumped a little and looked at Gerald with glazed eyes.

"Ma'am," he was saying again. "Ma'am, we're just testing your blood sugar. Sorry I had to poke you."

Lucy put the blood sample in the machine and in a second the number twenty-one popped up on the digital display.

She showed Gerald, and without a word they started getting an IV ready.

"Ma'am," Lucy said. "We need to give you an IV so we can get you some medicine."

While Gerald searched for a vein, Lucy opened up a syringe containing thick, syrupy liquid called dextrose, which was basically liquid sugar.

"I'm in," Gerald said, as he hit the vein with the catheter. "Open it up."

Lucy turned the knob on the IV and let it flow, checking the site where the catheter met skin to make sure there was no swelling. She then took the huge syringe, stuck it in a port on the IV tubing, and started to pump the thick liquid into the woman's veins. As an EMT basic, she was allowed by Santa Fe County to give certain medications, and given the high incidence of diabetes in New Mexico, this was one of them.

It always seemed like a miracle when Lucy gave medicine to a diabetic patient with low blood sugar. They would suddenly go from unconscious, on the edge of death, to fully alert. Within a minute, the woman was sitting up and talking to them as if nothing had happened. And, as was often the case, the woman insisted she didn't need to go with them to the hospital. Diabetics, especially type-1 diabetics, were so used to the rigmarole they had to endure for their disease that a trip to the hospital was not a relief. In fact, it was to be dreaded. The hospital meant waiting around in an uncomfortable gown to take even more uncomfortable lab tests just to have a doctor determine that the incident had been caused by "complications of diabetes," which everyone knew from the beginning. Gerald looked at Lucy and shook his head, so she found a patient refusal form.

Gerald said, "Ma'am, you really need to eat something right now. Your blood sugar is going to crash again and we will be right back here."

"My daughter's coming in to take care of me," the woman said. Still sitting in the easy chair, she carefully straightened her sweater, making the tiny bells jingle.

Lucy could hear the dismissal in her voice, so she jumped in. "How about I find something for you to eat really quick?" She went to find some food, not stopping when the woman protested.

The kitchen was something Mrs. Claus would have considered too Christmassy. There were Santa kitchen towels, Merry Christmas magnets, and red bows on every cabinet doorknob. Lucy went to the fridge and rummaged around, looking for something with protein. She found a piece of cheese and a little bit of leftover chicken, which she put on to a plate and brought out to the woman, saying, "We are a full-service EMS service. Not only do we come to your house, we make sure you eat properly." The woman looked suspiciously at the food.

Lucy said to her conspiratorially, nodding her head to indicate Gerald. "You know, he's not going to leave until he sees you actually eat it." The woman took a bite, while looking at Gerald. He watched as she took a few more. Finally satisfied, he and Lucy said good-bye and went outside to put their equipment back into the ambulance. It had started to snow again; the flakes fell down in big clumps. The snowflakes in New Mexico were not lacy. Growing up in Florida Lucy had always assumed all snowflakes had the pretty patterns she's seen in drawings and books. But New Mexico seemed to have two types of snow: hail snow and fluffy snow. Hail snow looked like tight balls of hail, but since it was winter, it wasn't called hail. Fluffy snow was lighter, less tightly packed. Fluffy snow made it look like God had ripped open a sofa cushion and shaken the stuffing out over the countryside. There were no individual flakes. Instead, they seemed to come together for support as they fell. The absence of lacey flakes was likely due to the snow having much lower moisture content than what was found back east. It was disconcerting to have grown up with an image of snow in her head, and have the reality be so different. One time, when her mom was off her medication, she spent a full day cutting white paper snowflakes with lacy edges and swirls inside. By the time Lucy got home from school, the entire ceiling was covered in snowflakes hanging from strings and seemingly falling onto their heads. It was beautiful and claustrophobic. Lucy's mom hadn't had an episode like that in years, not since she finally accepted she had schizophrenia. But most of Lucy's childhood had been crazy, mixed in with a whole lot of scary. She and her mother had been working on their relationship for the last four months, since the time Lucy last saw Gil and Joe and gave them uninvited advice about a schizophrenic suspect. It had brought up a lot of baggage that Lucy thought was better left unpacked. But it was what finally made her call her mother. It was why she was going home to Florida tomorrow, to see if they could eventually become mother and daughter.

The drive down from the Hill had seemed longer than the drive back. Gil had just driven past the Pojoaque and Tesuque pueblos and was going up Opera Hill when Joe's cell phone started playing "Pour Some Sugar on Me" in mechanical tones. It was Liz. He put her on speaker.

"I don't have much," she said. "The water and smoke at the crime scene destroyed everything. I didn't get any usable prints, but what I do have are more specifics on your burned victim. He's about twenty to thirty years old, five feet, nine inches tall, and a hundred and seventy pounds. His teeth had some orthodontic work done on them, but needed more."

"Any chance for an ID off his teeth?" Joe asked.

"Not unless we get something to match them to," she said. "We won't get any DNA results for at least a week, but I have one last thing. Gil, I know you're a New Mexico history buff, so here's a little fun fact for you: the burned victim was a crypto-Jew."

"He was a what?" Joe asked.

"A crypto-Jew," Gil said. "They were a group of colonists that came over with the conquistadors in the sixteen hundreds who pretended to be Catholic but were actually Jewish. Liz, how in the world did you figure that out?"

"One of the grad students at the university has a grant to study genetic defects in Northern New Mexico. Hispanics, like cerebral cavernous malformation," she said. Gil nodded. He knew a family who had the CCM mutation. A person would seem fine until, one day—when they were in their twenties or thirties—they would start having seizures. Some might respond to antiepileptic medication. Some might die of a brain hemorrhage. Most everyone with the disease was descended from a single Spanish colonist who came over in 1598.

Liz continued, "She got special permission to run the DNA of any John Doe that comes in to get autopsied. The whole process should be secret, but she was so excited that she'd finally found a crypto-Jew that she just had to tell someone."

"What genetic disease affects the crypto-Jews?" Gil asked.

"There is a breast cancer mutation that is found only in Middle Eastern Jewish populations," she said, "but some Hispanic families from the San Luis Valley in Northern New Mexico have their own unique version of it in spades. The defect has been in their families for almost twenty generations. It had to come from a crypto-Jew, since no actual Jews would have been around here back then."

"Thank you, Liz," Gil said. "We'll talk to you later." And she hung up.

"Okay," Joe said. "That is pretty cool. I mean, we don't have an ID on the guy, but we at least know he's a local Hispanic—all from his genes. Is there, like, a crypto-Jew organization in town or something we can talk to?"

"Most of the crypto-Jews don't even know they're

Jewish," Gil said. "When they first came here, they had to practice their religion in secret, otherwise they'd be killed. But some people kept it such a good secret that now no one in the family even knows they're Jewish. When I was a kid a friend of mine, Bobby Lucero, would come over for dinner, and if we had pork, he wouldn't eat it. His grandmother said it was dirty meat." Gil had heard similar stories about families who covered up mirrors after someone died or lit candles on Friday. Even though the descendants didn't know why they did such things, they kept the practices going because it was family tradition.

"So, why did the crypto-Jews come here?"

"They were trying to escape the Spanish Inquisition," Gil said.

"Nobody expects the Spanish Inquisition." Joe said.

"That's from *Monty Python*?" Gil asked.

"Yeah. I have to admit I never thought I'd use it in a conversation about the actual Inquisition."

The Garcia Hardware building had been both a store and a house for the Garcia family until the 1980s, when the last of Mateo Garcia's great-uncles moved to a nursing home in Santa Fe. Now it was just a store. With little hardware, it was more of a general store, with groceries, cleaning supplies, and firewood. It was tucked into the curve of a county road that ran through the mountain town of Chupadero, five miles north of Santa Fe. Chupadero, which literally translated to "the place that sucks," was named for either a sinkhole or a sucking insect such as a tick. Mateo liked to joke that the literal translation was the correct one: Chupadero sucked. But he didn't mean it. Chupadero was home.

The afternoon sun shone through icicles hanging off the

pitched tin roof of the store, throwing light onto the floor next to the cash register, where Mateo stood. No one had come in for a while, so he was checking his e-mail on his laptop. Someone had sent him a link to a video on YouTube of Sapo Trujillo, one of the last of the mountain men, who lived up north near the Truchas Peaks. Mateo clicked on the link and up popped a video of a man in red long johns, wearing a Santa hat and strumming a guitar while walking through a Northern New Mexico field of snow. Sapo sang in Spanish about Christmas and Pancho Claus, while being followed by a baying donkey, who was possibly the better singer.

Sapo wasn't like the traditional mountain men—who forged trails to the frontier in the West and trapped fur. He more closely resembled a free-range hippy. Both types lived off the land as best they could, hunting elk and cooking over fires. But the newer generation was, by necessity, squatters. There was no truly unowned land left in America, so the mountain men set up temporary shelters or built full-blown cabins on public or private land. They would wander the extensive million-acre Pecos wilderness around the Sangre de Cristo peaks and go where no trails went, harvesting wild herbs in the summer and hunkering down in the winter.

Because Garcia Hardware was located at the edge of the wilderness, Mateo had more customers than most who lived in the mountains. He tried to stock basic camping gear for them, such as axes, tarps, flints, and cans of Sterno. He also kept a selection of socks, sunscreen, and ChapStick, which were not so much necessities for the mountain men as comforts that hermit life didn't provide.

Mateo clicked on the video of Sapo again, noticing the handmade shelter in the background, white with snow.

Mateo knew that not all the mountain men would make it through the winter. Many were in their sixties or older and hadn't seen a doctor in years. Come every spring, a rock climber or hiker would find an unidentified body in the wilderness, leading Mateo to do a mental head count, trying to remember when he had last seen each of the half dozen or so mountain men who visited his store. A few years ago, he decided to start a list of their names, and would note every time one came in the store. He glanced over at the clipboard hanging on the wall near the cash register. It wasn't a long list. About half the names were now crossed out. With the winter as cold as it had been so far, he would likely be crossing out more in a few months.

Gil and Joe sat in the conference room at the police station both working on their laptops writing up interview and incident reports from the day. In front of Gil were the pictures of Dr. Price that Chip Davis had given them, plus crime scene photos e-mailed to them from Liz. Joe stopped typing and stood up to stretch. Gil decided he needed a break from staring at the computer. He leaned back in his chair and said, "Okay, let's go over it. We both think this is a home invasion."

"Correct," Joe said.

"Our two victims Price and Jacobson were killed during a burglary."

"Right."

"Then we have Mr. Burns, who is local and, as far as we can tell, doesn't know our victims."

"Yeah and, no offense, Gil, but rich white people in Santa Fe hang out with other rich white people. They don't pal around with the locals."

"Agreed," Gil said. "So who is Mr. Burns?"

"I think the better question is how does he end up at the victims' house?"

"He had to either be invited or a stranger. We can't find any evidence that he was invited, so that . . ."

". . . makes him a stranger who just happens to show up on the one night Price and Jacobson are getting killed? He's either the unluckiest bastard . . ."

". . . or was there on purpose. That means he came with the suspects. He was one of them."

"So Mr. Burns was one of the home invaders," Gil said. He went up to the white Dry Erase board that covered most of one wall of the conference room. On it he wrote: "forced entry; three to four suspects; strong leader, weak followers; strangers to the victims; use extreme force; use weapons; often kill; target more than one home." Detailed demographic information about group dynamics in home invasions was sparse; most states didn't even recognize home invasion as a crime different from regular burglary, so data from one-person robberies mucked up the statistics on home invaders. "Okay," Gil said. "This is the typical profile of home invaders. They work as a group and there is usually one dominant leader."

"And we know two more things about them: at least one of the suspects was local, and they will kill one of their own," Joe said.

"That brings us back to Mr. Burns," Gil said. "If we find out who he is, we find his accomplices."

"That's the good thing about this town," Joe said, "You have family members up in your business all the time. There is nowhere to hide from your relatives. Someone is going to notice that Mr. Burns is missing."

Joe went to his computer and pulled up the missing-persons database. They had already searched for any local missing-person reports, but they decided to expand it nationwide, thinking that Mr. Burns might have been living elsewhere but had come home to commit this crime, as unlikely as that might be. There were a couple of possible matches, but without more identifying information, they might never know who Mr. Burns was.

"His family probably doesn't even know he's gone yet," Joe said.

"The most likely scenario is that Mr. Burns lived in Santa Fe," Gil said. "Our best bet would probably be to put a notice in the newspaper."

"Well, it just so happens we know someone at the newspaper."

CHAPTER EIGHT

December 21

Natalie Martin closed the bedroom door behind her quietly. She'd finally gotten the boys down for the night, after three rounds of reading *Green Eggs and Ham*.

She sighed as she walked into the kitchen, where Nick was cleaning up the dinner dishes. His back was to her as he washed a pan in the sink. She pulled him close from behind in a little hug.

"Hey," he said, turning around and kissing the top of her head. "How'd it go?"

She said in a singsong voice, "I do not like green eggs and ham. I do not like them Sam-I-Am." Her husband laughed and hugged her tight before turning back to the dishes. She started spooning mashed potatoes into a plastic container while her husband moved on to load the dishwasher.

"Don't forget we have that thing the day after tomorrow," Natalie said as she tried to squish the last of the potatoes into the container.

"What thing?" he asked.

"That thing," she said. "You know, the thing . . ."

"You're going to have to be more specific."

"It's on the tip of my tongue," she said, sighing. "Hang on. It'll come to me . . ."

"You mean go get your sister at the airport?"

"Yes," she said. "Thank you. I just could not get that to come out of my mouth—wait, honey, what are you doing?" She walked over to the dishwasher, which he'd opened and was loading utensils into.

"What do you mean?"

"How many times have we talked about the knives?" she said as she picked up a large butcher knife that was sticking, blade out, of the lower basket of the dishwasher.

"What about them?"

"Honey, the knives go point side down," she said, putting the knife back in the basket, tip first. "Remember that man I told you about who died after tripping and falling on the knives sticking out of the dishwasher? That could be one of us—or the kids."

"All right," Nick said. "Whatever."

"I'm serious."

"I know you're serious," he said. "Just like you were serious about the childproof lock on the toilet in case one of them fell in and drowned."

"That reminds me, I got that alarm for the boys' bedroom door," she said. "We need to put that up tonight."

"Let me guess, there was some accident where a kid got out of his room at night and died."

"It's not funny," she said. "That really happened. There

was a little girl in Florida who was able to open her bedroom door and walk outside and they never found her . . ."

"The boys just figured out how to turn a doorknob last week."

"And Devon just learned how to get out of his crib. During his nap today, he got up three times, opened their bedroom door and came running out. If I'd been asleep, I would have never heard him get up, and he could have gotten into who knows what."

"That's why we have the baby monitor in their room," he said.

"That only works when they cry," she said, replacing the last of the knives. "Otherwise, I can't hear what they're doing. If we'd had an alarm on their door, it would just tell us when they opened it."

Nick sighed and kept loading the dishwasher.

"Listen," she said. "Let's just get it done tonight. It should only take a few minutes. Then we can watch a movie. I'll even sit through *Fight Club*."

After clearing it with their boss, Police Chief Bill Kline, Gil called Lucy's cell phone. When she answered on the second ring, he said, "Hello, this is Santa Fe Police Detective Gil Montoya."

"Hello, Santa Fe Police Detective Gil Montoya. This is journalist and firefighter extraordinaire Lucy Newroe."

"Are you making fun of me?"

"For the record, let's just assume I'm always making fun of you," she said. "And by the way, you can just say, 'Hi, this is Gil,' from now on. I feel we have moved past using titles, don't you?"

"I need some advice," he said.

"What kind of advice? Financial? Career?"

"The media kind," Gil said. "We have a missing person that we'd like the public's help in finding."

"How big of a deal do you want to make out of it? A full story or something small?"

"Something small for now."

"Okay," she said. "So, what you want is a news brief. For that, you need to wait until just after ten o'clock tonight and then fax over a short press release with the information about the person."

"Why wait until ten o'clock?"

"Because, my young *padawan,* by ten o'clock, every section of the newspaper has been cleared except the local section. They hold that section until eleven o'clock, in case some other news comes in, like a brief from the police. If you call before ten o'clock they might make a big splashy article about it on page one. After ten o'clock, you are guaranteed it will be only a news brief in the local section. If you call after eleven o'clock, the newspaper will already be on the press, and it'll be too late."

"Should I call you at the city desk after I fax the press release?"

"Um . . ." she said. "Let's just say I'm not working in the newsroom tonight."

"That sounds ominous," Gil said. "Is everything okay at work?"

"It's fine."

"It doesn't sound fine."

"I've just moved to a different department."

"Was it voluntary?"

"Yeah . . . so we're not going to talk about this. Let's get back to your press release."

"Will you be working in the newsroom again?" he asked.

"You're messing with me, aren't you?"

"For the record, let's just assume I'm always messing with you," he said. "So, why did you change jobs?"

"What? I can't . . . hear . . . reception . . . bad," she said, while making staticlike noises.

"Lucy, you just sound like a washing machine."

"In that case, I'll just hang up on you." And she did.

A half hour later, Lucy sat "in the rooms," as they say, listening. They had gone around the circle of chairs, each person saying their name. She'd said, "Tina," however, and she didn't add the usual "and I'm an alcoholic," because she didn't consider herself one. She was an alcohol abuser, sure. But an alcoholic? She hadn't ended up on the street or in the gutter. She hadn't lost her friends or her job. Well, she'd sort of lost her job, but that hadn't been her fault.

She'd stopped drinking two weeks ago and had been coming to AA since then. She had yet to speak at any meeting, not sure what to say. She listened as a man across from her told his "getting sober" story. He had been a pastor at a local church, a respected member of the community. His life was perfect—except he drank. Secretly. Every night. That part sounded familiar to her, but while she was a beer-drinking girl, he was a vodka man. Lucy knew where this story was going. She'd heard it often over the last two weeks. The man would say that, one day, his wife left him or he lost his job and that's when he realized he needed help. Instead, the pastor talked about his kids, especially his bright, gifted, funny seven-year-old son. Lucy wasn't expecting the next part—when a drunk driver hit the wife and son. The wife lived. The son didn't. The pastor fell apart. His secret drinking became less secret. He drove drunk one afternoon and almost hit a school bus. He tried to kill himself, but one of his other children found him.

That's when he decided to go to Mexico. He rented a *casita* on the beach. He called it his suicide shack. He locked the doors, turned off the lights, and sat on the couch—gun in his hand. But he didn't do it. Instead, he stayed locked in the *casita,* thinking he'd kill himself the next day. But he didn't do it. By the third day, the alcohol withdrawal was giving him seizures. He repeatedly woke up on the floor. Ten days later, he left the *casita.* Sober.

Lucy listened to him speak and thought about her own "getting sober" story. It was nothing dramatic. She had just stopped. She wondered if that made her a failure at being an alcoholic. Not that she was one.

Gil stared at the string of Christmas lights he was holding, which had somehow knotted into a ball, and wondered how they had gotten so tangled up. The lights had been sitting in a box since last Christmas, after he carefully wrapped them with twist ties to keep them neat.

Joy, hanging ornaments on the Christmas tree, looked over at Gil and started laughing. "Daddy, we should just buy new ones. I think those are too messed up."

Susan called them to the kitchen, allowing Gil to put the lights back into the box and worry about them later. Therese was already there, standing at the counter.

"Okay," Susan said. "Time for the tamale assembly line."

On the counter was a bowlful of *masa* dough next to one of cooked pork. Susan stood at the sink, where the cornhusks had been soaking for the last few hours. She took a husk out of the water and dried it on a paper towel, then handed the husk to Gil, who spread a thick layer of *masa* on it. He gave the husk to Joy, who added the pork, and then Therese rolled and wrapped the husk tight around the filler. Lastly, Therese stacked them in the steamer pot.

Within a few minutes, they had a dozen tamales steaming over the stove. Gil's grandmother used to say that the reason tamales were cooked during Christmas was because it made the family work together. But Gil thought it might be for a simpler reason—tamales were hard to make, so making them once a year was enough.

"Okay, girls," Susan said, drying her hands. "Go get ready for bed."

Gil's phone vibrated. It was a grave-shift officer calling to confirm that he had sent the fax to the newspaper as Lucy had instructed. Gil grabbed a beer and sat down to watch the NBA highlights. Within an hour, he decided to call it a night. He was still catching up on sleep from the night before. He stopped to check on the girls on his way to the bedroom. Therese, who was already asleep, had kicked her blankets off. Gil pulled them back over her and put his hand on her head. He whispered the same prayer that his own father had said over him each night—*"Angel de mi guardia; dulce companía; vélame de noche; cuídame de día."* He kissed her forehead and went over to Joy's bed. She was still awake and watching him.

"Daddy, can you say my blessing in English?" she whispered. "I want to hear what you are saying."

Gil closed his eyes, put his hand on her head, and said softly, "My guardian angel; sweet companion; watch over me by night; care for me by day."

CHAPTER NINE

December 22

The plastic of Lucy's alarm clock was etched with white lines, which were burns left over from the oven cleaner she had used to try to kill a spider a month ago. She found out the hard way, at the expense of her clock and a large swath of paint on her bedroom wall, that oven cleaner didn't kill spiders. The alarm went off again, and she hit the Snooze button.

"Nathan," she said, pushing him as he slept next to her. "Get up. You need to leave so I can pack."

She got into the shower. When she got out, wrapped in a towel, he was waiting outside the bathroom door with a cup of coffee in his hand. He handed it to her, saying, "Have a good trip. We'll have that talk when you get back." After a kiss on her cheek, he left, and she got down to the business of packing. Her flight was at six that evening, so she'd have to leave the house by 4:00 P.M. Even though her flight was in the afternoon, she had taken the whole day off work. She knew from experience that her packing wouldn't go well. She started the hunt for clothes. She would need her dressy red shirt to wear on Christmas Day, but she couldn't find it on her chair, under her bed, or thrown in the back of the closet. She finally remembered it was in the laundry. She pawed through the basket until she found it, close to the bottom. She took it out and shook out the wrinkles. She had worn it three times before it went in the basket. It had no obvious stains or crusty residue, so it was only sort of dirty, not truly dirty. She looked at it again, considering, then folded the shirt and put it on her bed. She decided that since she'd left it in the laundry basket for more than a week, it was clean again.

Next she searched for her flip-flops. She was looking forward to going home to Florida. She missed the white beaches and palm trees, even though New Mexico was just one big beach, without the water. But she missed her mom and her brothers more. Although as much as she missed them, she knew she'd be ready to come home after the three days. True, she was trying to get along better with her mother, but that didn't mean going insane herself. Her mom could be a bit much, which was a side effect of her schizophrenia. Even on her medication, she was a strange combination of relaxed and intense.

Her brother seemed much less so on his medication. He had inherited the family disease, but had somehow managed to have a fairly normal life. She knew that as a child and sister of a schizophrenic, she had a 30 percent chance of developing the disease. Schizophrenia usually showed up before age thirty, meaning she might still get it. She felt as if she had spent the last ten years waiting to hit thirty so she could finally breathe, knowing for certain she wouldn't become like her mother and brother.

Lucy went to look for her suitcase, which was in the storage closet in the kitchen. She opened the step stool and took the suitcase off the top shelf. As she was stepping down, her foot hit something glass. She looked down. There was a collection of empty beer bottles in the bottom of the closet, where she had put them months ago, intending to recycle them. She picked up the bottles and went out into the cold. She threw them into her neighbors' recycling bin, feeling some satisfaction when she heard each one clink at the bottom. They were a reminder of who she was two weeks ago, not who she was today. It made her feel like maybe she could be sober.

Waiting on Gil's desk the next morning was a copy of the *Capital Tribune*. It was turned to the local section, where one brief was circled in black ink. The newspaper had put in the missing-person information exactly like Lucy said.

As he dialed the office receptionist to see if they had gotten any calls yet about Mr. Burns, Gil flipped to the front page to read the story under the headline THREE DIE IN HOUSE FIRE. The secretary on duty said no one had called. Gil had just hung up when his desk phone rang. Half expecting it to be his mother, whom he usually talked to this time every morning, Gil only answered with "hello," instead of giving his full name and title. But it was Deputy Paul Gutierrez.

"Paul," Gil said. "I thought you were taking time off to spend with your daughter."

"At this very moment, I am sitting at the kitchen table in my bathrobe eating the pancakes she's made me," Gutierrez said. "But I wanted to let you know about a case my cousin with the state police is working on. A call came into nine-one-one a few hours ago, about shots fired out in the county. My cousin was the responding officer and found a busted-in front door and a victim duct taped to a chair and shot in the head."

"Devon, stay still," Natalie Martin said. She was trying to change his diaper while he was trying to roll off the changing table. "Honey, stop moving," she said again as she pulled him back down and fastened the last plastic tab. She put him back on the floor, saying, "All done." Devon toddled off to the living room to find Deacon. She followed after him. The boys began playing near the Christmas tree, which took up a quarter of the room. She had decided to use a red-and-white theme this year. The tree was decked out in a garland of pearl white beads, with red bows holding it in place on the branches. She went to go straighten one of the red bows and, out of the corner of her eye, saw Deacon take Baby Jesus out of the Nativity scene under the tree and lick it. The phone rang. She picked it up as she was still saying, "Honey, please don't lick Baby Jesus. Put him back in his crib." She watched Deacon use one of his pudgy hands to put Baby Jesus back in the manger.

"Did you just say, 'Don't lick baby Jesus'?" her sister asked, laughing.

"Yes. The boys are at that age where everything goes in their mouths," Natalie said, as Deacon again picked up the ceramic Baby Jesus out of his manger. "Deacon, put Baby Jesus down." But he didn't listen. She heard her sister say something, but Natalie was busy grabbing for a nearby plastic dump truck. "Deacon, look at this truck. Isn't it pretty?" Deacon dropped Baby Jesus and came toddling over. He took the truck and put the edge of it in his mouth.

"Is the Holy Family crisis averted?" her sister asked.

"Yes. Baby Jesus is safe."

"It's a Christmas miracle."

"So, when does your plane get here tomorrow?" Natalie asked. "I have to figure out their nap and feeding schedule."

"Ooh," her sister said. "Can you make *me* a nap and feeding schedule?"

Gil and Joe pulled up in front of a house in La Cieneguilla, a few miles outside the city limits. The walls were old adobe. The house probably had been replastered every year for hundreds of years, as the humans tried to keep up with Mother Nature cracking and crumbling the straw-and-mud walls. The home was built as most of the old haciendas were—in a large square with a hollow center, where there was an open plaza with a flagstone courtyard and huge cottonwood trees. Gil got out of the Crown Victoria and stretched his shoulder for a moment, trying to get the stiffness out of an old basketball injury. Through the pencil-thin tree branches up on a nearby hill he could see a one-room *capilla* with a cross on the top. The chapel, one of many scattered throughout Northern New Mexico, likely had been built by the family who owned the hacienda, so they could have a place to worship without traveling into town on horseback.

Gil and Joe walked down a mud-and-ice driveway to join three state police officers standing in front of the house. One of the officers, who had a goatee and shaved head, came over and introduced himself.

"You must be Detective Montoya. I'm Herman Sandoval, Paul's cousin. He called to tell me you'd be stopping by."

They shook hands, and Gil asked, "Can we see the crime scene?"

As they walked toward the house, Sandoval said, "My

family has some Montoyas on my mother's side; they are from Mora."

"My family is from Galisteo," Gil said. "But my grandfather had an uncle from up there." This was part of the usual conversation between Hispanics from Northern New Mexico when they met for the first time. Gil's sister called it "proving your ties." It was an interrogation of sorts, with each person expected to prove their family had been there for hundreds of years. Gil thought it was a way for two strangers to find a connection. Or maybe it had evolved as a way to avoid marriages among people who had too many relatives in common. His sister thought of it as a form of elitism, a way for a stranger to surreptitiously confirm that the other person was of the correct Spanish descent. Gil most often had the conversation with grocery cashiers or bank tellers after they saw his last name on a credit card or check. But he'd also had it after introducing himself to senators and judges. Gil knew he was expected to ask next about the officer's family.

"Are you related to the Sandovals who live near Pecos?" he asked.

"Yes," he said. "Those are my great-uncle's people."

The three of them had reached the front door, and Gil stopped to look at the damage. The door was of polished aluminum—a very modern door for a very old house—but had given way easily with whatever the suspects had used to ram it in.

Inside the foyer, the house opened up into a large living room with viga-lined ceilings. The walls were a stark white and hung with bright modern artwork painted with wide brushstrokes. The furniture, which included a couch and winged side chairs, was also white, and matched the area rug covering the dark Mexican tile floor.

"What did the victim do for a living?" Gil asked.

"He was retired, but he worked from home finding props for movies and TV shows," Sandoval said. Over a glass desk, a wall held a dozen framed pictures of film sets and famous people. One was of the Coen brothers, who had shot *No Country for Old Men* in New Mexico, and another was of John Travolta, who had signed a photo of himself while in town filming *Wild Hogs*.

"You should see the extra bedroom," Sandoval said. He walked down a small hallway and opened the door. Gil followed. Inside, it looked like a cross between a hoarder's house and an antique shop, with furniture and household items overflowing the room. In one corner was an old-looking wooden chair with very straight angles. As Gil got closer, he realized it was an executioner's electric chair. Next to it, on the ground, were a typewriter, a trumpet covered in gold glitter, and a foot-tall statue of Lady Justice. In another corner was an old-fashioned metal hospital bed with a clutter of junk on top. Gil could see a World War II army helmet, a pair of red cowboy boots, a knight's shield, and what looked to be a stuffed housecat.

Gil went back out to the living room to hear Joe, who seemed not have realized that Gil had been out of the room, talking to no one in particular.

"He clearly had money," Joe said, looking over the desk. "His computer setup is amazing. Look at that monitor."

Gil moved toward the center of the room, where one of the white wing chairs had been placed. The state police had already taken the body away, but a large pool of blood remained behind and had worked its way into the upholstery.

"What about the condition of the body?" Gil asked.

"He was shot," Sandoval said. "It looked like a small caliber, maybe a .22. There were lots of shallow cuts on his arms and a few burns; we don't know what was used to make those."

"Was there anything carved in his chest?" Joe asked.

"Yeah, the letter *L*," Sandoval said. "That was messed up."

"Any cuts to his genitals?" Gil asked.

"Nothing that I saw."

"You were the first on scene?" Gil asked.

"Yeah," Sandoval said. He looked more than tired. It was the same look Joe and Gil had had for two days. These cases were taking a toll. "I came to make contact with the homeowner, to check about a shots-fired call, but when I approached, the front door was standing open. I removed my gun from my holster and called it in on my handheld radio. The lights in the living room were on. I saw the victim, Stanley Ivanov, right away. I cleared the house then I checked for a pulse on the victim. When the backup got here, we searched the house and the grounds again."

"What evidence was collected?" Gil asked.

"I'm not sure," Sandoval said. "I know we got fingerprints, at least one off the duct tape used to tie up the victim, but I haven't heard from the investigating detective where they are with that."

"Who's in charge of the case?" Gil asked.

"Gil Montoya?" someone behind them said. Gil turned. It took him a minute to recognize State Police Lieutenant Tim Pollack.

"How the hell are you?" Pollack said with a smile. "It's been, what, like forever?" Gil had first met Pollack a year ago, when they were both working the homicide of a schoolteacher. At the time, there had been rumors that Pollack was leaking information to the press, even though, as the temporary public information officer for the state police, he was supposed to be the one controlling it. Nothing had ever come of the rumors, but Pollack was no longer the PIO. He still had the same intense blue eyes, shaved head, and fast speech.

As they shook hands, Gil introduced Pollack to Joe.

"You finally committed to a partner? Last time I saw you, you were going stag," Pollack said, shaking Joe's hand. "He's like a lone wolf, this guy."

"I guess that would make me part of his pack," Joe said.

"So what's up? What's the deal? Why ya here?" Pollack asked, snapping his gum. "I heard about your victims who got popped in that house fire. You think the same suspect killed my guy?"

"Could be," Gil said. "What can you tell me about your case?"

"I'm sure Sandoval gave you the lowdown," Pollack said. "Pretty much what you see is what you get. Busted-down front door. Dead guy named Ivanov with cuts all over him. Shot in the head. We don't know if anything was taken. We got a bunch of partial prints that we couldn't use, but the rest led back to a guy named Tyler James Hoffman, who's barely eighteen. And Gil, you are going to love him."

"Why's that?"

"He's an escaped inmate from Texas," Pollack said. "Why does every escaped convict in the United States come here? They know we're *New* Mexico and not the *actual* Mexico, right?"

Pollack was not exaggerating. Every week, inmates and wanted felons from all over the United States were caught in New Mexico. It was a mecca for those running from the law. They came to hide in the hundreds of miles of open desert and forested mountains. Maybe they thought they'd be like the Old West outlaws—Butch Cassidy or Billy the

Kid—who'd hid from the law for years, using the deep canyons for their escapes. Most of the captures nowadays were just a footnote in police reports, since the suspects were apprehended without incident, but there were some exceptions. Back in the 1990s a trio of men robbed the Ute casino just over the Colorado border, then headed into Navajo Country, where they ditched their car and went off on foot. It was June, and they had no food or water. With nothing for a hundred miles, law enforcement officers didn't bother to chase them; the men weren't going to come out alive.

"So, why would I love the escaped inmate from this case?" Gil asked.

"Because that automatically makes him a problem for the federal marshals," Pollack said. "Now I just sit on my thumbs until the boys from Phoenix get here. Then you and I get to go home and wait for Santa Claus with all the other good little boys and girls. Like I always say, don't you love it when a plan comes together?"

"Okay," Gil said, hesitantly.

"Tell me about your case," Pollack said.

"It's pretty much the same . . ." Joe started to say, before Gil interrupted.

"I don't think they're related. There are some fairly substantial differences."

"That sucks for you," Pollack said. "If it had been the same guy, you could be sipping on cocoa at home in your pj's by this time tomorrow. Oh well, life is like a rodeo. Sometimes you get the bull by the horns, sometimes the bull gets you."

CHAPTER TEN

December 22

Kristen Valdez tried to stack the cedar wood in the *horno* oven, but she had a hard time gripping the logs through her thick gloves. She managed to push the last log through the small opening of the beehive-shaped oven and then lit a match. The tinder caught easily, and soon a few of the logs started to turn black as the flames reached them. Inside the mobile home, her mother had a modern oven, but the dome-shaped *horno* in the backyard had to be used for the ceremonial baking. Now Kristen just needed to watch the fire for the next hour or so until it burned down to coals.

The back door of the trailer opened and her mom peeked her head out.

"Mom, it's freezing out here. Put a coat on," Kristen said.

"Oh, *hita,* I just wanted to ask if you were going to your cousin's baby naming."

Kristen sighed. Her "cousin" was actually a fourth cousin, and the baby naming ceremony would be at 7:00 A.M. and would require everyone to stand outside for an hour. The naming ceremony was held on the fourth day after birth, when the baby is held out to greet the sunrise and is given her Pueblo name. Later the same day, there would be a baptism Mass, where the baby would get her Christian name for everyday use.

"I think I have to work," Kristen said. That was the excuse she used for everything, but her mother just nodded and went back inside. The family didn't mind that Kristen was a police officer. It was to be expected, since her father was of the Winter People and, since lineage was passed down paternally, so was she. The Tewa pueblos didn't have a clan system like the Navajo. Instead, they had two groups that people were assigned to: the Summer People and the Winter People. The Winter People were associated with the north, masculinity, and minerals, while the Summer People were of the south, femininity, and plant life. Since masculinity was associated with protection, Kristen's job as a police officer, even though it was more dangerous than working as a secretary, was easily accepted. Her mother had been of the Summer People and, as had been expected, changed to her husband's group when they got married. It occurred to Kristen that if she married one of the Summer People, she might not get out of family obligations so easily. "Just another reason not to get married," she thought, as she put another log in the *horno.*

Gil and Joe were back in the car, the tires crunching through the ice on the dirt road as they drove away from the house, when Joe asked, "What was that about?"

Gil didn't answer, and instead said, "We need to start collecting information about Hoffman."

"He's killed multiple people," Joe said. "I think we need to follow the three-name rule and call him Tyler James Hoffman."

"The three-name rule?"

"You know, how you have to use three names, like John Wayne Gacy or Lee Harvey Oswald, for really evil killers."

"As opposed to nice killers?"

"Don't think I don't know what you're doing . . ."

"What about Ted Bundy? He only had two names. Or Jeffrey Dahmer?" Gil didn't wait for Joe to answer, saying, "At least we figured out why the *T* was carved in Jacobson's chest."

"*T* is for Tyler," Joe said. "As in Tyler James Hoffman. But who the hell has the initial *L*?"

"I'm assuming someone in his crew."

"Are you going to keep ignoring me or tell me the deal with Pollack?" Joe asked. "Why did you lie about the cases not being connected?"

Gil waited for a moment, choosing his words, before saying, "The state police have the right to take over any local case as they see fit. If I'd admitted the murders were similar, Pollack could have decided to hand them both off to the marshals, who might not get here for another day or two. In the meantime, no one would be trying to find Hoffman."

"You mean Tyler James Hoffman."

"We'll tell the marshals about our case when they get here, but in the meantime, I want to try to find Hoffman," Gil said. "But that would mean you're not leaving for Las Vegas tomorrow."

"Who cares about that?" Joe said. "I just don't want that Pollack guy in our business. He's a tool."

"I thought you two really bonded."

"He quoted *The A-Team*. Who does that?"

"You quoted *Monty Python* yesterday."

"Do I really have to explain to you the massive difference between quoting from a piece of genius-level British humor and from a 1980s TV show where a bunch of guys drive around in a van? Do you know me at all, Gil?"

Lucy had gone to the store to get travel-size shampoo and conditioner. When she got back to the car, she heard her cell phone beep at her, telling her there was a message. Even though the phone was in her pocket the whole time, she'd missed a call, likely because cell phone reception in the store didn't reach back to the hair products aisle. She listened to her voice mail. It was her brother.

"Lucy, Mom's in the hospital. She got the flu and couldn't keep her meds down for the last few days. She was running around outside naked . . . Anyway, I wouldn't bother coming home for Christmas. She's on the usual seventy-two-hour mandatory hold, and then the doc says they'll keep her locked up for another week or so until her meds kick back in . . . sorry about the trip. We'll reschedule."

She replayed the message, "Lucy, Mom's in the hospital . . ."

Gil and Joe were back in the conference room with their laptops, with evidence logs and crime scene photos spread out on the table like brochures in a real estate office. Joe had run a check on Hoffman, who had been convicted nine months earlier after a series of home invasions in El Paso. He and his accomplices would break in, assault the homeowners, then leave with some small electronics. He was arrested when one of his accomplices turned him in. He was seventeen at the time, old enough to be convicted as an adult of armed robbery and sent to a minimum-security prison in Texas. He escaped just ten days ago when he and two other inmates attacked a guard and then stole a maintenance truck.

"He's been on the run for a little over a week and he decides to come here and not go home to El Paso?" Gil asked. "That seems strange."

"Wait, listen to this," Joe said, reading off his computer screen. "The two guys he escaped with were found dead the next day. Looks like Hoffman has a habit of killing his partners. He clearly has trust issues."

Gil started to say, "He likely learned his lesson after his accomplice turned him in—"

Joe interrupted with a yell that made people sitting at their desks outside the conference room turn and look— "Holy shit, we met him." Joe jumped up from the table and threw his notebook across the room. Then he started to pace, still swearing but no longer yelling. Gil turned Joe's laptop so he could get a better look at the photo on the screen. It was a mug shot showing a young man with sandy hair and blue eyes who was five feet, eleven inches tall according to the page.

"I don't recognize him," Gil said.

"The guy in the SUV outside the burned house, remember?" Joe asked. "He wanted directions to the ski area. Damn it. We fucking had him."

Lucy spent an hour trying to reach her brother, with no luck. He was probably at the hospital, where he'd have to turn off his cell phone. She was at home, her suitcase packed, ready to go. She could still fly to Florida. Even if her mom was in the psych ward, she could visit her on Christmas Day.

The phone blinked on, and she picked it up before it even rang.

"What's going on?" she said as her way of answering. "How's Mom?"

"It's just like I told you on the phone," he said. "She's on lockdown."

"How bad?"

"Bad," he said. "Remember that time when we were kids, and she had the knife? She's talking like that again."

"I can still come . . ." Lucy started to say.

"But Mom won't even remember that you were there," he said. "Just stay home. Maybe you can come next week, for New Year's. But listen Lu, I think Mom would want to get better as soon as possible."

"Okay," she said slowly, not sure what the issue was.

"If they put her on oral medication, it will take another two weeks to take full effect," he said. "But she could get a mega dose shot now, and she'll be better in two days. She'd be able to get back to her life."

"Where are you going with this?"

"I can't authorize them to give Mom the shot since you have her power of attorney . . ."

"Mom hates needles," Lucy said. "You know that. She hates them."

"But that way she'd get back to normal almost right away—" he started to say, but Lucy interrupted.

"I know. I know. I just hate having to put her through that."

"She wants to be on her meds," he said. "Just like I do."

"But the thought of them holding her down and sticking a needle in her arm."

"It's not exactly like that," he said. "They'll put it in her IV. She's already doped up on Ativan and strapped down."

"Strapped down? You're not making me feel any better," she said. "Was it scary when they did it to you?"

"I barely remember it, Lu," he said. "Seriously. It wasn't that bad."

She rubbed her eyes and said wearily, "Hand your phone to the nurse. I'll tell them to give her the shot. What a great Christmas present for Mom."

After Joe had calmed down, Gil suggested they check stolen vehicle reports to see if anyone had reported a missing SUV, but a quick file search was fruitless.

"Do you remember what kind of plates were on the car?" Gil asked.

"New Mexico, I think?" Joe said. "Shit, I don't know."

Gil closed his eyes, trying to picture the man in the SUV, but only the vaguest images would come to mind. "Let's have Dispatch put out Hoffman's picture to patrol plus the description of the SUV."

"Why do you think he showed up at the house again?" Joe asked.

"Maybe he wanted to see what kind of damage the fire had done," Gil said.

Joe's phone rang with the robotic notes of Def Leppard. It was Liz. Before she could mention her reason for calling, Joe told her about Hoffman and the second home invasion.

"Can you run the dental records of the burned victim against any known associates of Hoffman?" Gil asked her.

Liz groaned. "Seriously?" she said. "You're going to make me try to get dental records from Texas? I might as well ask the pope if I can make a dress out of the Shroud of Turin."

Texas, with a population of almost 26 million, was known for officials who strictly adhered to interdepartmental rules and regulations, likely due to the sheer number of people they served. The state seemed to follow the old adage "Do a favor for one and you have to do it for everyone," which resulted in no favors at all. But in New Mexico, with only 1.5 million people, bending the rules to help someone out was not only the norm, but was considered polite. It made interstate cooperation strained. It was likely that Liz would make the dental record request of Texas, only to be told by a specialized department that a dozen or so required forms needed to be completed, and accompanied by signatures and photocopies. If Texas made the same request of New Mexico, whoever answered the phone would just tell them whatever they wanted to know.

"Thank you, Liz," Gil said.

"So why were you calling?" Joe asked. "Please tell us you have good news. We need it."

"I don't know how good it is," Liz said. "I was able to dry out what was left of your burned victim's clothing. In one of the pockets, he had a receipt."

"That might be helpful," Gil said.

"I doubt it," she said. "It was from Baja Taco, dated three months ago. He had a green chile cheeseburger and paid in cash. But on the back, there was a handwritten list."

"I will pay you lots and lots of money if you say it was a list of accomplices," Joe said. "Or addresses of houses to be robbed."

"It looks like a shopping list," she said. "I'll e-mail you a photo."

Joe stood over his computer, hitting the REFRESH button on his e-mail again and again until Liz's message appeared. He read the list aloud to Gil, who wrote it on the white board. There were only six items: beer, box cutters, duct tape, trash bags, pads, and the letters *tpx*.

"Actually, he spelled duct tape wrong," Joe said. "He has it *d-u-c-k* tape."

Gil made the correction as Joe looked at the board. "I have no idea what *tpx* stands for," Joe said. "But everything else is what you would need to tie someone up and torture them." He added the heading MURDER SHOPPING LIST at the top.

Gil knew that coming across a killer's "need to buy" list during an investigation was atypical but not uncommon. Most law enforcement officers had at least one or two cases in their career where a criminal made a list. During actor Robert Blake's trial in 2005 for the murder of Bonny Lee Bakley, the prosecution produced a list allegedly made by Blake's handyman, who also was his codefendant. The list included shovels, a sledgehammer, lye, pool acid, and duct tape, which the defense argued were items any handyman would need for work. Before the 2011 massacres in Norway that left seventy-seven dead, Anders Behring Breivik made an online shopping list that included sulfur powder for explosives and a drill-press vise for making poison-tipped bullets. Mr. Burns's list was, by comparison, fairly unimaginative.

"Maybe *tpx* stands for 'toilet paper extra-large,'" Joe said. He went back to his computer and typed the letters in. "There is a gun manufacturer called TPX. Oh wait . . . they make paintball guns. Here's something. Did you know there is a Louisville Slugger called TPX? That could be it. They could have used a baseball bat to ram down those doors."

"Maybe," Gil said. "But do we really think the same man who spelled duct tape using d-u-c-*k* knows the various brand names for the Louisville Slugger?"

"He could be a baseball nut," Joe said.

"What about the box cutters," Gil said, trying to get them back on track. "Where can you buy those in town?"

"Pretty much at every hardware store and Walmart, I would think," Joe said. "What I don't get is why Hoffman cut these guys. What the hell is that about? You torture someone to get information out of them, like a PIN number or combination. But we didn't find a safe, and no money is missing from their accounts."

"Torture was the goal," Gil said, "Home invaders are a different animal. Most burglars wait for you to leave the house. A home invader waits for you to get home. They aren't doing it for money. They do it for fear. They feed off it."

"A group of homicidal strangers break into your house and all they want to do is torture you?" Joe asked. "Jesus, that sounds like my worst nightmare."

Natalie Martin put the boys down to a nap and fished the keys to the storage shed out of the junk drawer before pulling on her boots and coat. She went outside, noticing for the first time that it was snowing again. In her pocket was the receiver for the baby monitor, just in case the boys woke up during the few minutes she'd be outside. She fiddled with the keys in the lock and pushed the door open against a drift of snow. She was hoping to find another set of Christmas lights in the shed. She could have sworn they had five sets of white lights, but she could find only four. She squeezed herself between some shelves and the Pontiac Tempest, which was sitting snug under its fitted cover. She accidentally pushed up part of the car cover as she slid by, showing a flash of baby blue paint, which looked as smooth as nail polish, and the black cloth convertible top. Nick used to work on the car every weekend when they were first dating.

He'd even proposed as they sat in it watching the stars. But it'd been more than two years since he'd even taken the car cover off. Since before the boys were born. A two-seater convertible leaves little room for baby seats. She smoothed the cover back down and turned to the shelf. After a few minutes of searching, she decided she was too cold to keep looking. She had just gotten back into the house when she heard the front door open and Nick yell, "I'm home." She rushed out to the living room to shush him.

"Hi, honey," she whispered as she gave him a kiss. "I put the boys down for a nap." She looked at her watch and asked, "Why are you home so early?"

"They let us off because some major storm is coming in," he said. "It's really starting to snow. They think we'll get another eight inches."

"It'll be a white Christmas," she said. "How was work?"

"I think half of my experiments are dying," he said. "But on the bright side, that paper I coauthored looks like it's going to be published."

That's when the front door exploded behind them.

CHAPTER ELEVEN

December 22

Joe and Gil were in the conference room, still facing the white board. In red Dry Erase marker, Joe had added "Hoffman behavior profile: likes to torture; rich, male, Anglo victims; on the run; kills accomplices; revisits crime scenes; may like extra-large toilet paper."

Now he was drawing a long horizontal line with hash marks on it. It was the beginning of their time line. The first item on it was the day of Hoffman's escape from prison a week earlier. The next entry was "December 19, 5:47 P.M.: Dr. Price leaves lab." Between the first entry and the next was a large blank space, indicating how little they knew about Hoffman's movements in between his escape and crime spree.

"We know Hoffman had to be in town getting a crew together at least a few days before hitting Dr. Price's house," Joe said. "Or maybe he had the whole crew already from out of town, and Mr. Burns was his only local contact. Hell, I'd usually say at this point we should try to find Hoffman's past known associates, but he kills those people, so that's a dead end. Literally."

"After he escapes, Hoffman makes his way here, for some reason," Gil said. "Let's say it took him three days to get here. That gives him four days to get a gun, find a crew, and determine his victims."

"Now that's something I hadn't thought about," Joe said. "How is he choosing his victims? There might be a connection between them or something."

"Likely several connections," Gil said. "Santa Fe isn't a big town. Most people's lives overlap here. They shop at the same stores or their kids go to the same school."

"Personally, if I want to find rich people, I'm driving around looking at nice houses," Joe said. "But that doesn't make any sense really, because Price and Jacobson lived so far off the street that Hoffman would've had to make a special effort to find their place. Maybe one of the accomplices knew the victims? You know, we still haven't interviewed the snowplow guy."

"How did Hoffman find his victims in the past?"

"Now, that's a good question," Joe said. He tapped the computer a little while and then said, "Okay, it looks like last time, he got a list of names from a buddy. . . . One of the crew worked as a mechanic in a high-end dealership."

"Okay," Gil said. "That's a place to start. Let's look to see if any of our victims had their cars worked on recently."

"Can you handle that?" Joe asked. "I want to check something else."

"What's that?"

"Just give me a second," Joe said, typing another few

strokes on the keyboard. "I read something last night on Alexander Jacobson's Facebook page . . ."

"You stayed up reading his Facebook page?"

"I know you think I just watch porn and drink a fifth of whiskey every night, but that's only on days that end in a *y*, " Joe said. "Anyways, Jacobson wrote something . . . okay, wait, here it is . . . yeah, he says, 'I just got a new gig. Hope I get to see somebody famous.' What does that sound like to you?"

"Like he got a job," Gil said. "Doing what? He was a makeup artist for the Opera, but their season doesn't start for months. It had to be work for another client."

"Exactly—someplace where he'd meet a celebrity," Joe said, looking through some papers on the table. He pulled out his notepad and flipped through the pages until he found what he was looking for. "The state police said their victim, Stanley Ivanov, worked for TV and film companies finding them props. What do you think? Coincidence?"

"You're thinking that they both worked on the same movie or TV show," Gil said. "What's filming in town right now?" New Mexico offered huge tax incentives to studios, and they took great advantage of the discount. At any given time, there were usually two television shows and a half dozen movies filming in the area.

"There's that movie about the state penitentiary," Joe said.

"What movie about the penitentiary?"

"Gil, do you not read anything besides police manuals?" Joe asked. "They're doing this whole big-budget movie about the riot in 1980."

"Why would anyone want to watch a movie about that?" Gil asked more strongly than he'd intended.

Gil's father knew every detail about the riot, even though

he wasn't at the prison that day. Gilbert Montoya Sr. was out of law school only a year when he was named special prosecutor of the inmates who'd started the riot. It happened on a Saturday in February, when the chronically understaffed state pen had only fifteen corrections officers guarding more than a thousand prisoners. When a guard caught two inmates drinking home-brewed alcohol, they attacked him. Other prisoners joined in, and soon four more guards were taken hostage. Using a set of keys left behind by an escaping officer, the prisoners were able to open more cells, including those in solitary confinement, where the deadliest inmates were held. These men led a group armed with blowtorches to Cellblock 4, where the police informants were housed. For five hours, the inmates used the torches to cut their way into Cellblock 4. When police came in later, they found the informants decapitated, hanged, burned alive—and worse. The inmates had full run of the entire prison for only thirty-six hours. In that time, thirty-three prisoners had been killed and more than two hundred injured. For Gil, who was only a kid at the time, the riot wasn't as memorable as when the inmate trials started. State police officers kept twenty-four-hour guard on their house after his father started to receive death threats.

Officer Kristen Valdez stuck her head in the conference room door, asking, "Do you guys need anything? I am just starting my shift."

"I think we're good," Gil said. "Just keep your eye out for this guy." He showed her a picture of Hoffman on his computer. She took out her notebook to write down his details. She glanced at the white board just as she was about to leave.

"Why do you have tampons on your murder shopping list?" she asked.

"What?" Joe said. 'What do you mean?"

"*Tpx,*" she said. "That means tampons."

"Is that some kind of girl code?" Joe asked.

"Sort of, I mean it's the first thing I think of when I see *tpx,*" she said. "You know, like Tampax. But it also is just common sense."

"How's that?" Gil asked.

"See here," she said, pointing at the word *pads* on the list. "That probably means 'feminine hygiene pads.' Since women need both, usually at the same time, *tpx* could mean 'tampons.'"

"Why would Mr. Burns put feminine products on his murder list?" Joe asked.

"Because a woman he knows was having her period and made him go shopping," Kristen said. "I just have no idea how that helps you."

After talking to her brother, Lucy wanted a drink. Instead, she went to a meeting. She sat down in the circle of chairs, waiting for it to start. Next to her, an older woman introduced herself as Karen. "You're Tina, right?" she asked. Lucy nodded. "I can't help but notice you haven't talked yet."

"Nope," Lucy said with a smile. "Not yet."

"You know this is a safe place," Karen said. "It might help to share."

"I don't know . . ."

"Think about it," Karen said, and got up to get some coffee.

Lucy had never spoken to anyone honestly about her drinking, but people had their suspicions. Gerald had talked to her about it a few times. She thought maybe some people at work knew. Joe and Gil definitely knew. She had phoned

Gil drunk before and had gone into the station a few months ago after having spent the night at a bar. But despite her slipups, she had tried to be careful. If she had to leave the house at night after she'd started drinking, she used a Breathalyzer to ensure she never drove tipsy. She kept track of where she bought her beer each night, keeping a set schedule of convenience and liquor stores she would visit, never the same one twice in a week. Lucy had been going to an all-night grocery store, where the automated self-checkout line meant there was no cashier to judge her. But two months ago, she was there one night after work when she saw her managing editor, John Lopez, in the frozen food section. She ducked down the candy aisle and waited, pretending to look at some licorice sticks. She took another few minutes to restack the marshmallow bars and organize the different chocolate Santas according to height. She finally ventured out of the aisle, looking carefully across the store. She didn't want to take a chance of running into her boss holding a case of beer, so she decided to duck out without getting any alcohol. Then there he was, in front of the deli. He caught sight of her and yelled across the store, "Hey, Lucy." She had no choice but to go over to him.

"Did you just get off work?" he asked. "Did we have any breaking news?"

"Not really," she said, hoping this wouldn't be a long chat.

"What did you decide to do about the dead body story?" he asked. He was referring to an article that had made her almost come to blows with the photo editor. A man in Española had driven up to the hospital with a woman in the front seat of his car, and asked hospital staff to help her—only the woman was dead. When police interviewed the man, he said they had been drinking in the car and he didn't notice she'd died at some point. Police estimated he had been driving around town for three days with her dead body in the passenger seat. Lucy pushed to put the story on the front page, knowing people would want to read it. But the photo editor hated the idea, mainly because there was no photograph to go with the piece. A compromise was reached: Lucy could put it on the front page if she found some artwork to go with the story. She left the meeting and called the Española cops, asking for their help.

Now she told her editor, "We were able to get a mug shot of the man, so I put it front page, above the fold."

"Good thinking," he said. "That'll sell some papers."

"Okay, great," she said. "Well, you have a good night." She turned to leave, heading to the front doors, but he called after her, "Aren't you buying anything?"

"Um. You know, they were all out of the cheese I needed to make nachos," she said. "Okay, bye."

Not wanting to repeat that awkwardness, she now drove ten miles out of town some nights, to an Allsup's on Kewa Pueblo, where she wouldn't be recognized as a repeat offender.

Karen came back to the circle of chairs with her own coffee and an extra cup for Lucy. Lucy smiled and sipped the black sludge, trying to figure out what lies she would need to tell when it eventually came her time to talk. And Karen seemed to think the sooner that time was, the better.

The sky was heavy with clouds as Gil and Joe drove out of town and across the white plain to the south, toward the old state penitentiary. Snow was falling across parts of Santa Fe and heading their way. Gil turned off the highway and drove past an unmanned guard post. There were a few trees around, but the old prison itself stood alone, tall and stark.

After the riot, the prisoners had been moved to a new facility just down the road, and the Old Pen had been closed. It became disused but hardly unused. Reality show ghost hunters came to the site and left there claiming that while they were inside the place, radios changed frequencies on their own and cell doors closed randomly. They said they saw shadows of people who weren't there and watched light bulbs glow without electricity. Radio and TV stations held "fear contests" in the prison, locking contestants in cells to see how long they could last in the dark with the ghosts.

Gil drove the Crown Victoria along a tall fence lined by tangles of tumbleweed the wind had blown in from across the plain. Inside the main fence were buildings of long rectangular cinder block with small windows set in them every few feet and a catwalk connecting the roofs. Old semitrailers sat outside along with bags of trash with weeds growing up through the snow. The film studios found the broken-down buildings made good backdrops for movies such as *Astronaut Farmer* and the remake of *The Longest Yard*.

Gil stopped the car by the main gates, which stood open. A surprising number of cars were parked there, with people milling around even in the cold. Most looked to be actors, trying out for parts, including bald-headed inmate types and people portraying law enforcement officers.

Gil and Joe got out of the Crown Victoria and started toward the main building, which was built out of stone and had a large arching doorway.

"This feels really weird," Joe said, adjusting his badge on his belt. "Some of these people look just like police officers."

Gil gave him the once-over and said, "Too bad you don't."

* * *

Lucy sat at the meeting listening to yet another "getting sober" story. This one, like the pastor's from the day before, was an epic tale of woe. She was the next in line to speak, and was getting fidgety, wondering what she would say, knowing Karen expected her to talk. She tried to think. Maybe she did have an epic tale of woe. Maybe something did happen that day she decided to stop drinking. She'd gone to work as usual and then run a call with the fire department. After the call, it was getting dark, but instead of going to the convenience store on Camino Alire, where, according to her schedule, she was supposed to go buy beer that night, she went home. What had made her not go to the store?

The man finished his story and everyone turned to look at Lucy. She took a deep breath and said, "My name is Lucy and I'm an alcoholic." She actually startled herself by giving not only her real name but also saying the word "alcoholic." She decided that being truthful was as good as it was going to get. "And that's enough about me." She folded her hands in her lap and sat quietly while Karen stood and started her tale.

Mateo sat atop Baby, who stomped her hoof on the asphalt and shook her head vigorously. Mateo—decked out in his cowboy hat, chaps, stirrups, and duster coat—shifted in the saddle and wondered again how much longer they would have to be out in the cold. He could almost feel snow coming in his bones. He was doing his duty being out here as a representative of the Santa Fe County Sheriff's Posse. The members were all volunteer and outfitting both themselves and their horses was expensive, especially when it came to the specialized emergency radios and GPS locators they needed. To make money, they worked as mounted parking lot attendants at special museum events or for the annual fiesta. Today was something different. Today they were in front of the old state penitentiary where they and their horses would be working as extras. The movie people had promised to make a large donation to the posse members for their time.

Mateo looked up at the wire mesh fence topped with razor wire. Inside the gate, about a hundred or so rough-looking men stood waiting their turn to audition. They hoped to play inmates in the film, so by necessity, they had to look like they were all murderers and rapists. Some were a little too convincing. Mateo and the other posse members would be playing themselves—or, more precisely, they would be reenacting. Thirty years ago, in this exact place, during the state-pen riot, the Sheriff's Posse had helped round up some of the escaped convicts. Back then, the posse was still part of the sheriff's department, so they, like all other law enforcement officers within a hundred miles, had stood at the gates during the riot. But unlike the other officers—who had had to wait to get inside the prison in order to do their job—the posse's work was on the outside. The walls and fences of the penitentiary, missing their armed guards during the riot, were easy for rioting prisoners to get past. And hundreds tried. The state police jokingly called it the "inmate roundup rodeo." Posse members, sitting tall on their horses, could see a man running across the flat desert plain a half mile away. Mateo's father had been with the posse then, but he never talked about it. Mateo had heard stories, just the same. About a prisoner they chased into the Ortiz Mountains, toward the old turquoise and silver mines, who fell a hundred feet but was still alive when the posse spied him from the cliff above.

The man was impossibly trapped below and hopelessly bleeding. After four hours of listening to his screaming, there had been talk of putting a rifle bullet in him out of sympathy. No one would ever say if it had been done or not. There were also stories about the sounds of the horses' hooves as they trampled over the bodies of prisoners who had frozen to death during the cold February night.

Those posse members had been just regular citizens who volunteered with the sheriff's department. They might have joined with dreams of the Old West, where they would ride off after outlaws, but in reality they mostly wore their revolvers and gold stars as they rounded up loose cows or kept the peace at drunken parties. Then came the riot. What they'd had to do during that time—the acts they'd had to commit—took them very far away from being regular citizens. Afterward, they severed any ties they had to law enforcement. They would still wear the five-point badges, but they would never again carry guns or help catch escaped felons. Instead, they would do search-and-rescue only. What happened during the riot had left its mark. After that, the closest the posse came to doing police work was when they had to pack a dead body on the back of a horse.

Gil and Joe watched workers carefully measure out distances between the inside walls of the prison, use masking tape Xs to mark the floor, then set up large lights on tripods. Space heaters made the cavernous cement room a few degrees warmer than freezing.

An hour earlier, Gil had called a representative with the movie studio, who told him that the assistant preproduction manager could answer all their questions; she was on location at the pen. Joe was the first to bring up the idea of driving the ten miles out to the prison.

"And you aren't suggesting this because every model and actress within a hundred-mile radius will be there trying to get a job as an extra, right?" Gil asked

"That never even crossed my mind," Joe said.

When they arrived, Joe was disappointed to realize that a movie completely taking place in a male prison meant that very few female actors would be involved. Instead, he was surrounded by large men with tattoos.

Now they were waiting for the assistant preproduction manager to get out of a meeting. Ten minutes later, a blond woman wearing snug jeans with knee-high boots and carrying a clipboard came over. She introduced herself as Melody Lithwick.

Not surprisingly, Joe spoke up first, "How are you today?" He got a murmured response of "Fine, thank you," while she watched the workers maneuver the lights.

"How's the movie coming?" Joe asked.

"We aren't making a movie yet," she said. "We're still in preproduction. The assistant director hasn't even finished the shooting schedule."

"Okay, well, I was hoping you could help us," Joe said. "We're detectives with the city . . ."

"Hey, Carl," Melody suddenly yelled across the room, "That fill light is filtering out the shadow from the key light. Move it about a foot to the left."

"Okay," Joe said to her in an overly relaxed tone, trying to get her attention again. "I can tell you're busy, so we'll cut to the chase."

"Sorry, I get too focused sometimes," she said, smiling at Joe, who smiled back at her.

Gil decided to interrupt. "Do you know Alexander Jacobson or Stanley Ivanov?"

"I certainly know Stanley Ivanov," she said. "He gets

props for us. He found me most of the old guns and furniture I'm using."

"When was the last time you spoke with him?" Gil asked.

"Let's see . . . about a week ago," she said.

"Did he mention any problems?"

"No," she said. "He was all business."

"And the other gentleman?" Gil asked.

"What was his name again?" she asked. Gil told her, and she said, "I can't say for sure. I've hired about a hundred people within the last day. How about I have my assistant send you a list of people connected to the set? That's probably the best I can do."

"That will be plenty," Joe said, handing her his business card and smiling again. "That's my personal cell phone number there at the bottom," he added. "Feel free to call day or night. Especially night." Gil walked away, shaking his head, but Joe stayed right where he was.

The men did nothing but yell at them for the first few minutes. Natalie Martin was straining to listen for the twins, but they were silent. She tried to keep her eyes on the three people, watching them move from room to room, but with her hands and arms bound to the chair, she had limited visibility. Instead, she tried to rely on noise, listening to them trample though the kitchen and den. They hadn't yet gone back to the boys' bedroom. She wondered for a moment why they hadn't taped her mouth shut. She could start screaming—but she wouldn't. The twins were silent, and she wanted them to stay that way. She wanted them invisible. Maybe the intruders wouldn't even notice the toys that littered the room.

As soon as they'd smashed their way through the front

door, they had started to punch Nick. One of the men, who had light hair, had hit Nick across his knees with a crowbar, making him stumble to the ground. Natalie had tried to run, but one of them grabbed her around the waist and slammed her to the floor. The light-haired one dragged her over to a dining room chair—part of an antique set that had been her grandmother's—and pushed her into a seat. He grabbed a roll of duct tape out of a pocket and, after ripping off sections with his teeth, wrapped it around her, securing her to the chair.

"You're just like a Christmas present," he said to her, smiling. "All we need is a bow." He went over to the Christmas tree, ripped off a bow, and stuck it to her head. "I can't wait to unwrap you," he said, inches from her ear.

From the kitchen, one of them yelled, "I found the keys to the shed," which made the light-haired man leave the room.

She tried to move, but when she did, the tape only seemed to get tighter.

Nick was seated on a chair next to her. His eyes were closed, his chin on his chest. He looked unconscious. There was blood running down his face. "Honey," she whispered. "Please, honey, look at me." He didn't move.

One of the men came back into the dining room talking on a cell phone, speaking in Spanish. He kicked her chair, saying, "Shut up." The intruders were all dressed in jeans and dark hoodies, but had made no attempt to hide their faces. This worried her. It made her think they were going to kill her.

The light-haired man came back into the room dangling the keys to the storage shed from one finger. "I have the keys to get to the Tempest," he said, putting his face close to hers. "Now I just need the keys to drive the Tempest."

"I don't—" she started to say, but before she could finish, he put his foot on Nick's knee and pressed down, making Nick scream in pain.

"All I want to know is where to find the keys," the light-haired man said, taking his foot off. Nick stopped screaming, but there was a new noise. It was coming from the back bedroom. It was the twins. They had woken up.

Gil was standing off to the side, waiting for Joe to stop flirting with the assistant preproduction manager, when his phone rang. It was Susan.

"What time do you think you'll be getting home?" she asked.

"Honey, I'm working."

"They just said on the radio that the city is sending home nonessential personnel because of the storm," she said.

Gil looked out a window. The snow had gotten so heavy he couldn't see the cars in the parking lot. "I haven't heard anything," he said, while walking over to Joe as he talked. "How bad is it supposed to get?"

"They say at least eight inches," she said. "But the roads are already icy. My mom said she saw three accidents on Cerrillos Road."

"I'll try to leave here in a few minutes."

"Good," she said. "Can you stop at Walgreens on the way home? I need more tape and some boxes to wrap presents." Gil hung up and grabbed Joe's elbow, saying, "Sorry to interrupt, but the city is sending home all nonessential personnel."

"We're nonessential? I feel pretty essential," Joe said. Gil was sure that comment was more to keep the assistant preproduction manager smiling than to entertain him.

* * *

The twins had gone quiet as she walked toward their room with two of the intruders following her. Natalie went over in her head what she was about to do. They reached the door and she took a breath, knowing that if this didn't work . . . but she couldn't finish the thought. It had to work. She reached for the doorknob, bracing herself. She turned the knob—and the alarm she had put on the inside of the boys' door the night before started going off. She had set it to "lullaby" so as not to upset the kids, meaning the noise was soft and singsong; it wasn't loud or intimidating. But she took the opportunity of the men's slight surprise to throw the boys' bedroom door open and slide inside the room. She slammed the door behind her before the men could react. Devon was standing up in his crib looking at her. She pushed the bookshelf in front of the door, so it blocked the doorway, sending books falling to the floor. She could hear the men on the other side of the door, kicking and yelling. She fought with the plastic childproof cover over the doorknob and finally broke it, clicking the lock on the doorknob shut.

"Let's all yell," she called over to the boys. "Come on, yell. Please." They just kept looking at her. She let out a scream and watched as Deacon's eyes started to water. He started to cry. Devon joined in a second later.

She wanted them to make noise. She was counting on it. She grabbed the alarm off the door and switched the setting to "siren" and the volume to high. The sound was a painful screech, drowning out the boys' screams. Maybe if there were enough noise, one of the neighbors would hear it. The men were still pounding on the door, which meant they weren't checking the outside of the house to see if she had escaped. She used a *Dora the Explorer* book to break out the glass in the window, then looked out to the ground be-

low. The distance was five feet at most. She could drop
the boys out first, into the soft snow, then follow behind.
She started to gather up nearby blankets to wrap around
the boys to protect them from broken window glass. She
had just dropped Deacon gently into the snow when she
heard a gunshot come from the dining room.

CHAPTER TWELVE

December 23

The storm had dumped almost a foot of snow by the time Gil went outside just after 4:00 A.M. The sky was a clear dark navy blue with a dotting of stars. He waded toward the street, the snow pushing its way over the tops of his combat boots with each step. He didn't have time to shovel the walk or driveway for Susan and the girls. They might be snowbound for the day. He got to the curb, where Joe had pulled up in a white Ford Explorer with SANTA FE POLICE written on the side in big red letters. They wouldn't be going anywhere undercover today.

While they talked on the phone a half hour ago, it was Joe who had pointed out that the Crown Victoria couldn't make it through the snowy streets. They would need something with higher clearance, since most of the streets, with the exception of the main roads, wouldn't be plowed. Instead, everyone would wait for the inevitable sunshine to melt the snow, clearing the roads within a day or two. Most people didn't even own a snow shovel, since the sun usually did the job for them.

Gil got in the passenger seat, and Joe pulled away from the curb. The streets were unplowed, but he didn't drive slowly.

"There's one good thing about this storm," Joe said. "I finally get to show you how to drive."

They went the rest of the way without talking. The only noise was the police scanner, calling out EMS teams to respond to accidents around town. The streets were dark. The lights from the city bounced back off the new snow, giving everything a soft orange glow.

Joe pulled up in front of a house while Gil called into dispatch, telling them that they were on scene. There were three patrol cars out front, where Kristen Valdez stood backlit by the house. The home itself was the usual Santa Fe family residence with beige stucco exterior and set fairly close to the street. It looked to have been built in the 1940s but had been renovated in the last few years. The neighboring homes were close by. A snowman left over from a previous storm watched them from the yard next door. It was the new snow that had kept Gil and Joe from arriving on-scene sooner. The first ambulance sent to the house more than six hours ago had slid off the road, and a second sent immediately after had almost followed suit. Across town, a patrol car responding to a different call slammed into a telephone pole, sending that officer to the hospital in yet another ambulance that almost crashed. It was enough for the 911 Dispatch Center, which served both the city and county of Santa Fe, to stop all unnecessary law enforcement road travel until the snow stopped falling. It was 3:30 A.M. before the blizzard passed and Gil and Joe could get on the road.

They greeted Kristen, and the three of them walked to the front door, which had been smashed in, most likely with a baseball bat. The living room was a modest size, with a red-and-white Christmas tree off to one corner and a slew of toys cluttering most surfaces. In the attached dining room, two chairs sat in the middle of the floor. They were empty, but there were pieces of duct tape on the carpet, along with a dark, blood-colored stain next to one chair.

Gil almost walked by Natalie Martin as she sat in the dark hospital waiting room. Her head was bent low over her lap. Two small children lay sleeping in makeshift beds she had created with pushed-together chairs. Gil could hear the boys breathing the way children do.

"Mrs. Martin?" he said softly.

She looked up and wiped her eyes. She had dark hair pulled back in a mess of ponytail and an almost gray cast to her face. Her lips were dry, and the skin around her eyes was bluish; in the dim light, Gil couldn't tell if that was due to bruises or exhaustion. She had several small cuts on her lower arms, which were visible where she had pushed up the sleeves of a dark fleece jacket she was wearing. He introduced himself and pulled up a chair next to her.

"How are you?" he asked.

"I'm okay," she said. "I just . . . they're still running tests on my husband . . . they aren't sure how far the bullet went into his brain . . ." She started to cry, and one of the boys shifted in his sleep.

"My partner went to see if there is any new information," Gil said quietly. "Let's go stand in the hallway so we can talk without waking up your sons. We can keep an eye on them from there."

In the fluorescent light in the hallway, he could see how exhausted she was. "I know you already talked with Officer Valdez," he said. "She gave us your statement. I just need to clarify a few points with you, okay?"

She nodded, and he said, "You said there were three people, one Anglo and two Hispanic." She nodded again, and Gil pulled out a small photo of Tyler James Hoffman and asked, "Was this one of the men?"

"Yes," she said, wiping her eyes. "You have a picture of him. You know who he is. That's good, right?"

"We know this is one of the men, but we are still trying to determine who his accomplices are," Gil said. "Did they use any names?"

"All they did was yell," she said. "I don't think . . . no, they didn't."

"Can you describe the two Hispanic men to me?"

"There was only one Hispanic man," she said, wiping her eyes again.

Gil frowned. The description he got from Kristen was "two Hispanic suspects," and she had gotten that information from Mrs. Martin.

"I am sorry," he said. "With this kind of investigation it's easy to get some information mixed up. So, to clarify, there were three people who broke into your home. One man matches the photo I showed you and the second man was Hispanic. Can you tell me the ethnicity of the third man?"

"Hispanic," she said. "But it wasn't a man. It was a woman."

Down the hall behind him, Gil heard the elevator doors open. Something changed in Natalie Martin's face, making

Gil turn to look at who was coming toward them. It was Joe and Kristen Valdez, followed by a doctor wearing a knee-length white lab coat over green scrubs.

"I'll let you talk to the doctor," Gil said.

He joined Joe and Kristen a little way down the hall.

Joe said quietly, "The husband is stable, but they aren't sure how bad it is yet, or if there is brain damage. They're talking about transferring him down to Albuquerque to get trauma surgery."

Gil nodded, then said, "I was just going over what happened with Mrs. Martin. Turns out, one of the suspects is a woman."

"That explains the female-type things on the shopping list," Joe said.

"Gil," Kristen started to say. "I am so sorry. I should have interviewed her more—"

"It's okay, Kristen," he said. "It happens." He saw the doctor put his hand on Mrs. Martin's shoulder then walk back toward the elevators.

"Let me go to talk to her again," Gil said. "I think it's better if I do it alone."

Natalie Martin had gone to sit back down, smoothing the hair on one of the twins.

"Mrs. Martin?" Gil asked. "Can we talk some more?" She nodded, and he sat down across from her, their knees almost touching.

"You said you heard them yell," he said. "Did they have any kind of accent?"

"The Hispanic man had a Northern New Mexico accent. The woman's maybe was more Mexican."

"What makes you think that?"

"When she was on the phone, she spoke Spanish. Really fast Spanish."

"She made a phone call?" Gil asked, getting his note-book out for the first time. That was new, too.

"On her cell phone, when she was telling me to be quiet," she said. "She only talked for a second before the Anglo man yelled at her to hang up."

"Do you know what the woman said when she was on the phone?"

"No," she said, wiping away more tears. "I don't speak Spanish. But she was talking to another woman. I could hear her voice."

"What else did you hear?"

"She said something about her *mija* . . ."

"She said *mija*? Are you sure? She didn't say *mi hita* or just *hita*?"

"It was definitely *mija*," she said. "My friend named her dog that."

"Did you hear the woman on the phone say anything else?"

"No—but there was a baby crying in the background," she said. "It couldn't have been more than a week old. Its cry still had that really high pitch. My boys sounded the same when they were born." She glanced back over to them, curled up in their chairs.

"You told Officer Valdez they had a gun," Gil said. "Can you describe it to me?"

"Uh . . . it had a long barrel that was thinner than most guns you see on TV shows, and it had wood on the handle."

"Okay, good. Is there anything else you can tell me?" He said. "Maybe something you forgot to mention to Officer Valdez."

"There was something weird," she said. "They knew about my husband's 1965 Pontiac Tempest. They were look-ing for the keys."

"Why was that odd?"

"How did they know he had a Tempest?" she asked. "He hasn't had it out of the shed since the summer."

"Maybe they were just looking for a getaway car," he said.

"But we have two other cars in the driveway, out in the open," she said. "And they specifically wanted the Tempest. They said so."

Gil wasn't sure what to make of this. He could tell Mrs. Martin's anxiety was rising, likely due to his questioning, and decided it was time to wrap it up for now.

"I just have one more question," he said. "Do you or your husband have any connection to the movie business or the film that's being shot out at the penitentiary?" Gil asked.

"I don't," she said. "My husband is a scientist, so I doubt it, but you'd have to ask him when he wakes up."

Gil thanked her and went back over to Joe and Kristen.

"I'll stay with her for a little while," Kristen said. "And I'll call a crisis counselor to come talk to her."

"Thank you," Gil said. He watched her go sit with Natalie Martin.

Joe watched them as well, shaking his head. "The Martins don't exactly fit the victim profile," he said quietly. "Neither of them looks like a rich Anglo male to me."

"I guess we need to rethink the profile," Gil said. "But then we need to rethink a lot of this case." Down the hall, they could hear the twins starting to wake.

"The husband's lucky to have gotten this far," Joe said. "Hoffman must have shot him from a little too far away. Kristen said the gun Mrs. Martin described sounded like a Browning pistol. If it hadn't been a .22 . . ."

"He'd be dead already," Gil said.

*   *   *

By 7:00 A.M., Gil and Joe were back at the station. Gil called one of his cousins and asked him to go shovel his mom's driveway, then he called home, just to make sure Susan and the girls were all right being snowbound. They were busy making cookies and watching movies. He spent the next few minutes trying to explain to Joe about how a baby's cry changes as it gets older.

"How could anyone tell the age of a baby by its cry?" Joe asked. "I'm not buying this."

"Susan can. She says it's a part of being a mom."

"If we do find the baby, do you think Mrs. Martin would be able to ID its cry?" Joe asked. "What if we do a crying baby lineup . . ."

"I don't think it works that way," Gil said.

"Then let's call Susan and ask how it does work."

"I'm not going to bother my wife while we're in the middle of a case."

Joe reached over and picked up Gil's phone and hit redial. "Hi, Susan, it's Joe . . . no, Gil's here with me . . . I was calling you"—he paused, waiting for her to finish saying something—"Oh, thanks for the invitation, but I don't know where I'll be spending Christmas at this point . . . I just . . . Okay . . . well, I just have a quick question for you. Can you tell how old a baby is by its cry alone? . . . Uh-huh . . . sure . . . okay . . . all right. Thanks. Talk to you later."

"What did she say?"

"She said it's a mom thing."

Gil tried not to smile, and said, "If Natalie Martin is right about the baby's age, that might help us. If we can track down all the babies born in the last two weeks, it could lead us to the mother."

"And then what?" Joe asked.

"The person with the baby was either the baby's mom

or a babysitter," Gil said. "I actually think our female suspect is the mom."

"Yeah," Joe said. "I can see that. Only a mother would call home to check on her baby while committing a home invasion."

"Plus, Mr. Burns had pads and tampons on the list," Gil said. "After a woman has a baby, she needs those things for a couple weeks. He could have been buying those for his accomplice."

"Then we just need a list of babies born in the last couple of weeks," Joe said.

But an hour later, they were nowhere. The spokesperson for the hospital said she would need a signed release-of-information form from all the patients before she could give out any names. Gil and Joe were about to call the district attorney to see about any legal way to get the names when Gil had an idea. "Maybe there's another way to do this," Gil said. "My mom still reads the newspaper every day. When we go over there on Sundays for dinner, she keeps the obituaries so she can tell Susan and me about who died. But she also reads the weekly baby announcements with Joy and Therese. The girls think some of the names the parents choose are funny."

"If only we knew someone at the newspaper," Joe said, picking up his cell phone. He put it on speaker as Lucy answered her cell phone saying, "Hi Joe."

"Hey, what do you know about baby announcements?"

"When a woman and a man love each other very much they can express that love by having a baby, and sometimes they like to share the news with the entire readership of the newspaper . . ."

"Lucy," Gil said. "Who handles the announcements at the paper?"

"At the moment, I guess I do. What do you need?"

"A list of babies born in the last two weeks," Joe said. They heard her yawn. "Are you still in bed?"

"I know I'm a slacker, but some people don't get up at seven o'clock, especially when they have the day off."

"It's only seven o'clock?" Joe said. "How long have we been up?"

"Sorry," Gil said to Lucy. "We didn't look at the time."

"No problem," she said, with another yawn. "Let me get some clothes on, and I'll call you as soon as I get into work."

"Wait. You're naked right now?" Joe said.

"Thank you," Gil said to Lucy, interrupting Joe and hanging up the phone.

Gil's call hadn't actually woken Lucy up. She had been awake since 6:30 A.M. and just lying in bed, having gone to sleep at 10:00 P.M. the night before. Her early bedtime wasn't because of some new dedication to getting enough sleep. Rather, it was the result of two tablets of Benadryl, which she took at 9:00 P.M., after she became scared she might leave the house to go get beer.

She got dressed and took a step out of her front door and into a pile of snow. She'd forgotten about the storm. She waded her way over to her car and got in. She drove slowly to work, but not as slowly as some of the other drivers who were white-knuckling it down the streets. Every time there was a winter storm, it was like a surprise party had been thrown for the entire city, with lots of white confetti covering everything. No one seemed to ever expect it, even when the meteorologist predicted it. Even when it was all anyone would talk about. It didn't matter. Snow always sent Santa Fe into shock. Not that she was one to talk.

There were many things about the snow she couldn't get used to. One was snow fog. The other was snow thunder. Lucy had only seen fog a couple of times in New Mexico, always just after it had snowed. The sky would be clear and cold, yet fog would come from the ground, giving the snow a ghostlike quality. Snow thunder was something Lucy thought she'd made up one night while sleeping. There'd been a snowstorm as she slept, and she thought she'd heard a rumble of thunder. She dismissed it as impossible, until the next day, when Gerald asked her, "Did you hear that thunder?"

Lucy got to work and, with a swipe of her key card, went into the newsroom. She fumbled for the switch on the wall, and the overhead lights strobed on. Some kept winking, deciding if they wanted to work today. She made her way back to her new office and turned her computer on. Her desk was still barren. She hadn't had time to add any little touches, not that she had many touches to add. She'd never been a picture-of-pet-on-desk person. The computer finished its start-up, and she sat down. Time to work.

CHAPTER THIRTEEN

December 23

Lucy called Joe's cell phone about an hour later, saying, "We only publish the baby names once a week, in the Sunday paper. I have the babies from last week, but the hospital hasn't sent me anything from this week yet."

"How many names are on the list?" Joe asked over the speaker.

"About twenty," she said. "By the way, just to be clear, this is public record. These people all signed waivers that allow us to publish their information. I am not breaking any journalistic ethics by doing this."

"Journalists have ethics?" Joe said.

"If you want, I could make you go find last week's paper yourself," she said.

"Thank you, Lucy," Gil said. "Let us know when you get the information from this week."

The list Lucy sent to them actually contained the names and parental information for nineteen babies. Gil and Joe looked it over for a few minutes. They narrowed it down to female infants only, based on the suspect saying *mija* and not *mijo*. That left nine babies. Gil knew they'd eventually run the names of all the parents through the police database, checking for warrants and former arrests, but for now they'd start with people whose last names were probably Mexican. The assumption that the female accomplice was not from the area was based on two things Natalie Martin had said—that the woman spoke fast Spanish and that she used the phrase *mija*. If the woman had been from Northern New Mexico, she would have said *hita*. Of the nine baby girls born in the last week, only two had last names that were almost definitely Mexican.

"Explain to me how you know Godinez and Escobar are Mexican last names and not New Mexico ones?" Joe asked.

"I only said they were more likely to be Mexican," Gil said. "That's because those aren't really traditional local names."

"You mean, none of the conquistadors who founded Santa Fe were called Escobar or Godinez," Joe said.

"Pretty much."

"What about a last name like Garcia or Lopez?" Joe asked.

"Those could be either Mexican or New Mexican," Gil said. "If Godinez and Escobar don't pan out, we'll look at Garcia and Lopez."

Gil looked over the information. Both Godinez and Escobar didn't have fathers listed, only mothers. He typed the mothers' names into the police database, but only one came back with a record. Guadalupe Escobar, mother to Georgina Rose Escobar, born nine days ago. Escobar, who was eighteen, was awaiting trial for drug possession and resisting arrest. The drug enforcement task force had raided a known drug dealer's house three weeks ago and found Escobar smoking pot in a bathroom. The arresting officer had written in the report, "Suspect is nine months pregnant; ask DA about possible child endangerment charges." Gil doubted the district attorney would file abuse charges in regard to a fetus, but it had been good thinking on the officer's part. Gil next checked if Escobar had a car registered in her name. The search came back saying No Information Found, but there was a recent address.

"And look at this, under aliases," Joe said. "She uses the nickname Lupe. Remember that *L* on Ivanov's chest? Maybe she's the one who carved it."

Lucy knew she could go home. There was really nothing for her to do at work, yet she stayed at her desk. She cleaned the computer monitor and keyboard and was now trying to hunt down a mouse pad. She was considering stealing one. She went into the newsroom, which was still empty, and started looking in drawers to find a mouse pad and any other office supplies she might need. The police scanner on top of her old desk jumped on and Dispatch called Pecos ambulance out to an Echo call, which meant it was bad. The dispatch system used codes to let the responding EMS crews know how serious the call was. Alpha meant it was minor. Delta meant it was major. Echo meant the patient was dead. She listened to the Pecos crew call into service. She wished there was a way for her to do a column about being an EMT. It would be a great excuse for her to constantly be out in the field. But that would never happen. Strict federal law would prohibit her from revealing anything about a medical call—except maybe in the case of a dead patient. Lucy wondered about that. Maybe there was a way for her to combine both funeral announcements and a column. She could do an obituary on a dead person then interview the EMT or police officer who'd responded. It could show how interconnected everyone was, even in death, that when a community member fell, there was someone there to catch him. And how a person who died impacted the person who found him without the two people ever knowing each other.

The more Lucy thought about the idea, the more she liked it. But she knew it would be a hard sell, both to her editor and to the Santa Fe County Fire Department. She would be walking a fine line, but it was a line she had been walking since she joined the fire department. She didn't walk the line well—in fact, she stumbled often—but she always tried to do what was right by both sides. Maybe, just maybe, this column would be a way for her to finally merge both parts of her life. She might have to make some journalistic concessions that could be potentially problematic, such as keeping the name of the EMT or victim anonymous. She wasn't sure it could be done, but if it worked, she might finally be free of the constant moral dilemma that was her life. As the saying went, a person cannot serve two masters. But she had been doing just that since she joined the department almost a year ago.

She would have to have a sample column to show both Lopez and the Santa Fe County fire chief. Luckily she had just run a call where she'd found a dead patient. For her sample column, she could do an obituary on Dr. Price and write about her own experience in the fire. Her sample column would never go in the paper, mainly because it was a conflict of interest, but it would show Lopez and the fire department what she was hoping to do.

That was enough to make her pick up the phone and call Los Alamos National Laboratory, hoping to talk to Dr. Price's co-workers. She talked with two public information officers, explaining what she wanted. They both told her the same thing: she needed permission for an interview. There had to be forms signed and approvals made. One of the PIOs said he would get back to her.

She waited by the phone for a half hour. The longer she waited, the more convinced she became that the PIO would use the excuse of tomorrow being Christmas Eve to stonewall her. She was getting anxious. She called the hospital to check on her mom, but the charge nurse wouldn't put her call through, saying her mother needed rest. She tried to call her brother, but it went to voice mail. What Lucy needed was to get out of the office. She could go over to the hospital to pick up the birth announcements from this week and e-mail the names to Gil. At the same time, she could introduce herself to the maternity ward staff, maybe bring them doughnuts. She needed to be in their good graces since she'd have to rely on them to pass out the baby notice forms to the new parents. The parents were not required to fill out the forms that gave the newspaper permission to print the names, but the vast majority did. In the past, it had been known to happen that if the nurses didn't like the reporter doing the birth announcements, the forms didn't get passed out. She was out the door a minute later.

Gil and Joe sat in their white marked SUV in the snow outside a two-story brown apartment building with a blanket hanging from one of the bottom windows in an effort to keep out the cold. They had already gone to knock on the Escobars' door and that of the neighbors, but no one had answered. They now were waiting for a call back from the district attorney to see if they could enter the premises. Their evidence was no slam dunk, based as it was on Natalie Martin's account of hearing a baby cry and some fairly loose ties to a birth announcement, but it might be enough for a warrant, given the severity of the crimes. In the meantime, Joe called Kristen Valdez, asking her to check on the whereabouts of the drug dealer whom Lupe Escobar had been arrested with. With that done, he used his phone to look through the e-mail they had been sent by the film's assistant preproduction manager. He was checking a list of names of extras, cameramen, and work crew members against the police database, while keeping up a running commentary on the pictures the manager had attached. He nicknamed one man with a thick mustache "70s porno movie guy" and a tough-looking bald man "Mr. Clean Goes Ghetto." Joe let out a yell when he found Alexander Jacobson's last name.

"It looks like Jacobson was hired to do makeup," Joe said. "Specifically, he was going to do the fake prison tattoos on the extras. Hey, it looks like there's a link to photos of some of his practice work." Up popped pictures of arms, backs, and necks etched with intricate fake prison tattoos.

"Jacobson really knows his stuff," Joe said. "Some of these tattoos look totally real." He handed his phone to Gil, who flipped through the pictures.

Gil stopped on one photo of a man's arm. The predominant tattoo was a circle in blue ink, drawn like the Zia sun. Inside the circle was a large *S* with a smaller *n* and *m* nestled in its hooks. Something about it was bothering him.

"You staring so hard at . . .?" Joe asked.

"This tattoo," Gil said. "It's from the New Mexico Syndicate."

The New Mexico Syndicate was the biggest and most violent prison gang in the state. It was a Hispanic and Native

American group. The most respected inmates in the gang formed the "Panel," who handed down orders to generals and lieutenants on the outside about what actions to take and whom to kill. They were mostly into the drug trade. When a gang member was released, he was expected to go back into his district to make sure the local drug dealer gave the gang a percentage of the cut. The syndicate was currently at war with the Barrio Azteca gang in southern New Mexico over the methamphetamine trade.

"But why is the tattoo making your face constipated?" Joe asked, looking at Gil's expression.

"The inmates started the syndicate as a result of the state pen riot," Gil said. "They said the riot proved that the only true protection in prison was to be part of a gang."

Joe seemed to get his meaning. "So if the movie is trying to be true to life, then that tattoo needs to go," he said. "What about—hold on. You think this tattoo is real?"

"It could be," Gil said. "And it makes me wonder why a member of the New Mexico Syndicate would be working on a movie set."

When Joe called, Kristen Valdez had been on her way back to the station, already looking forward to getting out of her uniform and off to the dances. She listened while he told her about their suspect, Guadalupe Escobar, and that they needed someone to check out a drug dealer's house where she had been arrested smoking pot. For a change, Kristen had started to say no. She was just coming off her overnight shift, and there was no foreseeable sleep in her future. She was simply too tired. But before she could object, Joe said, "Just drive by and see if the drug dealer or, even better, Escobar is there. If he is, call us and we'll do the heavy lifting." She hesitated, which Joe heard, so he added, "I am bored out of my skull just sitting here in front of Escobar's house waiting for her to show up. I would so much rather be shaking down her drug dealer. Please, please, please."

He gave her the address, 1241 Camino Dulce, and said she was looking for Johnny Rivera, which Joe said sounded like a 1950s gangster name. Kristen got the impression she was supposed to laugh, but she didn't. She was just too tired.

Now she was driving out toward the city limits, where the map book indicated she would find Camino Dulce. She pulled off Old Pecos Trail and onto a dirt road that curved toward the mesas to the north. The road itself didn't have any signs giving its name, and there were no mailboxes or house numbers—or even any houses to see, for that matter. She passed two more nameless dirt turnoffs that could have been either roads or long driveways. She guessed by the map book that she needed to turn down the third dirt road on the left. She drove her patrol car over the washboard ruts, bouncing and jarring with every turn of her tires.

Two dogs—both medium-sized Labradors combined with at least two other breeds—came running out from some bushes, barking and chasing her car. She took the dogs as a sign that there was a house ahead.

She pulled up in front of an old mobile home and called into Dispatch, telling them her location, as was procedure. She got out of the car and pushed her gun belt down, which always rode up as she sat in the car. The two dogs had stopped barking and, instead, came up to her, tails wagging and tongues hanging out. She let them sniff her hand before they went trotting off toward an old flat-topped adobe house about sixty yards away. She went up three metal steps to the front door of the trailer and knocked.

As she waited for someone to answer, she looked around. From her perch slightly above the ground, she could see there was no car in either the driveway for the trailer or the dirt area nearer the house. Between the trailer and the house, she could see a few family graves, the tombstones sticking out of the snow.

She knocked again, but it was quiet. She could hear the wind but nothing else. She tried to look in the window next to her, but all she could see was the reflection of the sky behind her. She went down the steps and headed over to the house, and the dogs appeared again, to escort her. She looked off toward the mesas, which served as a backdrop for the family cemetery, just off the road. She noticed that some of the burial plots had foot-tall wrought-iron fences around them with plastic flowers intertwined between the bars. On other grave markers were placed a few egg-sized rocks.

She got to the house and knocked, not really expecting anyone to answer. She wasn't disappointed. She waited another minute before she walked back out toward the road, the dogs keeping her company. She went to the mailbox and checked a few bills inside to make sure she had the right address. Then she got back into her cruiser and called Joe, telling him that no one was home.

Holding tight to a box of doughnuts and holding tighter to the coat wrapped around her, Lucy tried to make her way through the hospital parking lot without slipping on the ice. The sun had melted much of the snow from the storm last night, leaving only slippery patches behind. She walked past a Ford F-150 that looked just like Tommy Martinez's truck and even had a *Capital Tribune* parking pass hanging from the rearview mirror. She dialed him as soon as she got inside.

"Are you at the hospital?" she asked, purposely not mentioning their last tension-filled conversation.

"Yeah," he said. "I'm in the ER. There was another home

invasion last night. A family was taken hostage, and the dad got shot in the head."

"That's awful."

"I know, and they have two little twin boys," he said. "From my count, that makes three home invasions in the last few days."

"Really?" Lucy asked.

"There was the one last night, one out in La Cieneguilla," he said. "And the one you went to with the fire department."

"Stop fishing, Tommy," she said. "I'm serious."

She hit the button for the elevator, trying to balance the box of doughnuts in one hand while taking off her coat and cradling the phone between her cheek and shoulder. She decided something had to give.

"I have to go," she said, "or I'll twist my neck off."

She got out of the elevator at the maternity ward. In the waiting room were groups of people: stressed spouses, screaming siblings, sleeping grandparents. There was no way to tell if they were all related or waiting for the arrival of different babies. Over the loudspeaker came the chiming of a bell. Either an angel had just gotten its wings or a new baby had arrived in the world. Some greeting cards might say they were one and the same. When Lucy had first visited the hospital, she had no idea the chimes meant a baby had been born. She thought maybe the chimes were a stealthy yet relaxing way for administration to communicate with the security guards. One chime meant a stabbing in the ER. Two chimes meant a body dumped at the front door.

Lucy went over to the front desk and waved to a woman on the phone, making sure the nurse saw her leave the doughnuts on the countertop. Not that Lucy was bribing the nurses. She went over to a basket labeled BIRTH AN-NOUNCEMENTS FOR NEWSPAPER and took out a stack of forms, filled out by the proud parents. She waved good-bye to the nurse, who was still on the phone.

She went back into the waiting room and took a seat, wanting to go through the announcements right then and there, in case one of them might be of help to Gil. Next to her, a family was celebrating its newest addition. The grandfather was handing out plastic cups to everyone in the waiting room, while an uncle popped a bottle of champagne. The grandfather tried to give Lucy a cup. She started to say no, but the uncle was there, pouring champagne into her cup.

"Attention, everyone," the grandfather said to the room. "Let's all raise our glasses to my daughter and my beautiful new granddaughter, Emma Victoria Romero." They all drank, except Lucy, who went as quickly as she could to the elevators, still holding her cup. She dumped it in the trash, not caring if the family saw her, only feeling the need to get it out of her hand.

CHAPTER FOURTEEN

December 23

Kristen Valdez walked toward the Nambé tribal plaza, which was made of dirt like all the roads in the area. Here, the dirt was more for ceremonial reasons than economic. The dances in the plaza were supposed to be a connection to the earth—not asphalt. The plaza was surrounded on three sides by two- and three-story flat-topped adobe buildings dating back to the 1400s. The Pueblo people were here for thousands of years before that. On the fourth side of the plaza were the religious buildings: the church and the kiva. As was the case for every pueblo, when the Spanish came in the 1600s, they built a church on the plaza and renamed the tribe. Most tribes, such as Santa Clara or San Felipe, were renamed in honor of a saint. The Nambé had been one of the few tribes able to keep a version of its actual name. Nambé Pueblo's real Tewa name was Nanbé Owîngeh, which meant "People of the Roundish Earth." Recently, some of the other tribes had started reverting back to their true names. San Juan Pueblo had changed to Ohkay Owîngeh, which in Tewa meant "Place of the Strong People," and Santo Domingo Pueblo, which spoke Keres, switched its name to Kewa Pueblo.

Kristen wondered if the trend of the tribes reverting back to their origins would include religion. The Catholic Church, as much as it was not an original part of Pueblo life, had become enmeshed in tribal customs over the centuries. Kristen glanced up at Nambé's church, which had been built by the Franciscans in 1613, been destroyed during the 1680 revolt, been rebuilt, fallen down, and been rebuilt again. Within ten feet of the church was the tribal kiva. The only part visible aboveground was its circular roof with a hand hewn wooden ladder leading underground. The kiva predated the church by at least two hundred years. It was a single, round underground room about twenty-two feet in diameter with whitewashed walls covered in pictographs of rainstorms and snakes—on one wall hung a crucifix. The kiva was a junction between the underworld and the above world. The underworld was where humans and animals lived, until they crawled out through the kiva and went aboveground. As she walked closer to the plaza, Kristen could hear drumming from the kiva, where the dancers were preparing.

Around the snow-covered dancing ground in the center of the square, a crowd had gathered, with *emo* girls in black jeans and men in Harley Davidson shirts. Most of the people were tribal members, but there were also plenty of Anglos and tourists. A half-dozen Buddhist monks, wrapped in saffron robes, stood nearby. They came every year from the monastery in Santa Fe to offer their blessings to the celebration.

Kristen nodded to Emmet Ortega, the tribal officer, who was deep in conversation with a well-dressed Anglo woman holding an expensive camera. As Kristen passed by, she heard the woman say, "I want to play by the rules, but people are giving me dirty looks." The tourists always wondered why the pueblos didn't allow photos or videos to be taken of the dances. Some of them thought it was because tribal members believed that having their photo taken was akin to having their soul stolen. But that had never been true. It was more about protection of the tribal culture and respect for the sacredness of the dance. Just as people are discouraged from taking pictures during Mass, so it was the same during the dances.

Kristen made her way over to her mom and sat down in a lawn chair next to her. Her mother, covered in a fleece blanket with a cup of coffee in her hand, sat next to Kristen's uncle, grandma, and a half dozen other relatives. They were catching up on news of the tribal members who had died in the last year. "Then Martine lost Elisa in a car accident up on Opera Hill," her mother was saying as Kristen surveyed the crowd, watching couples huddle together for warmth and two little girls play on the dancing ground. She decided to practice some of the skills she'd learned while watching Detective Montoya. He was always studying people, trying to interpret their behavior by their body language and word choice. He usually caught small indications from suspects that everyone totally missed. It was why she was constantly offering to help him on cases—because she wanted to learn how to do it, too. She glanced around the crowd, looking for someone to study. Over near the church were a couple of boys who looked to be about sixteen years old, in hoodies and low-slung jeans with tattooed names wreathed around their necks. They looked like they were going to cause some trouble. Kristen wondered why she thought this. She kept watching them and realized that they seemed to shift their stances a lot, which usually was a dominance display. They could be anticipating a fight. One of them, who stood a good foot above the others, kept looking over at another group of teenagers nearby. At that age, she reasoned, height meant power, so the taller boy was likely in charge. She tried to determine by his body language why he kept glancing over at the other teenagers. He looked nervous. That meant fear. She wondered what was scaring him. It took Kristen a moment to notice exactly where he was looking: at a girl standing with the other group of teenagers. The fear and dominance display finally made sense. The boy wasn't looking for a fight. He was looking for a hookup. Kristen knew that Detective Montoya would have determined this within a minute of watching the boys. He would have known not to waste his time observing them when someone else in the crowd was likely up to something much worse. Kristen continued watching the boy, who, a moment later, went up to the girl, who smiled.

The tribal governor passed by wearing a dress coat over his suit and tie, his long hair pulled back in a braid. A chorus of "Hello, Governor" and "Hi, Governor" went up, as did a few "*Hola, jefe*s." The governor went to join the other elders standing next to the church. Kristen could hear them talking in their heavily Tewa-accented English, staccato and halting. The war chief stood with them, seemingly part of the conversation, yet he looked only at the crowd. It was part of his job to keep an eye on the tourists and watch for witches, who were known to use the dances as a way to disseminate their curses. There was a time, when Kristen was sixteen and wearing a lot of black and skull-and-bones jewelry, that her family thought she might be becoming a witch. but it was just her Goth phase.

Joe was dialing the number for Melody, the preproduction manager, when there was movement from the Escobar apartment on the first floor. A woman wearing slippers with a coat over her bathrobe opened the front door and came out carrying two trash bags. She looked to be about sixty-five—too old to be Lupe Escobar—possibly a grandmother. They got out of the car, and Gil called over to her, "Excuse me, ma'am." She turned to look at them without interest. They introduced themselves, giving their names and titles. She said her name was Connie Lopez. Gil asked, "Do you know the Escobars?"

"No," she said, not stopping on her path to the garbage can at the curb.

"But you're coming out of their apartment," Joe said. She said nothing as she got to the trash can and struggled to open the lid, which was covered in snow. "Ma'am?" Joe said again, hoping for a response. There was none.

Gil decided they needed a different approach. "You said your last name was Lopez?" he asked, thinking the "proving your ties" conversation might make her more likely to talk to him. With the sleeve of his jacket, Gil brushed the snow off the top of the trash container and then opened it for her. "My mother's cousin has a wife who is a Lopez. Her family is from Los Trampas."

"My husband's last name is Lopez," she said. "He has relatives up in that area. You're a Montoya?" she asked him as she put the bags in the can. "Do you know the Montoyas from over by Old Pecos Trail?"

"That's one of my aunts," Gil said. "But my father's family is from Galisteo."

Joe, seeing that a connection had been made, jumped in, "Were you related to the Escobars?"

"Related? No. I'm just their landlady. Or I was their land-lady."

"They moved?" Joe asked. "When?"

"Yesterday," she said as she started to walk back to the apartment. Joe and Gil fell into step alongside her. "Blanca may have finally just had enough."

"Who is Blanca?" Gil asked.

"Blanca Escobar," she said. "Lupe's mother. It was just the two of them. And then the baby."

"What makes you say Blanca had finally had enough?" Joe asked.

"They got into a big fight yesterday, yelling and scream-ing at each other," she said. "I live in the apartment above them. I could hear most of it. Blanca said she was leaving because of the crazy *guero*."

"*Guero?*" Joe asked

"It means a white guy—sort of," Gil said. It was a term Mexicans used either to describe a fair-haired white person or to call them a name akin to "whitey." "Did she say any-thing else?"

"Not that I heard," the landlady said. "Blanca seemed like a nice enough person. As soon as that baby came home from the hospital, she took good care of it. That's more than I can say for Lupe."

"You didn't like her?" Joe asked.

"She was always bringing home fancy things, but as far as I could tell she didn't have a job," the woman said. "And she left that baby with her mom at all hours of the day and night. My guess is drugs." When they reached the front door, she said, "You might as well come in the apartment to get out of the cold."

She opened the door and stomped her feet on the welcome mat. Gil and Joe did the same, and then followed her inside.

"They didn't really leave anything here," she said. "But you're welcome to look through it."

A futon couch covered with a floral sheet stood in front of a fake, undecorated Christmas tree. In the bedroom, the bed was stripped bare and the dresser drawers were empty. The only things in the bathroom were a half roll of toilet paper and a half empty shampoo bottle.

"How well did you know them?" Joe asked.

"Not at all," she said. "I learned a while ago that my tenants' problems aren't my business."

"How long did they live here?" Gil asked.

"Not long," she said. "They got the place right when she was eight months along, so really, only a month or so."

There was no sign that the baby had been there. No crib was set up, and no mobiles hung from the ceiling.

"Did Blanca have any family in the area?" Gil asked.

"No, Lupe was from El Paso, I think, but Blanca was from someplace in Mexico," she said. "My guess is that Blanca took the baby and went back home."

"You don't think Lupe went with them?" Gil asked.

"That would mean she'd have to give a damn about someone other than herself," she said. "Besides, I saw her get picked up by some Anglo guy in one of those big dark cars. He was probably the crazy *guero*."

"Had you ever seen the man before?" Gil asked. She shook her head. "Did they give you any contact information when they signed the lease?" he asked.

The woman laughed and said, "What lease?"

"Just some quick cash under the table and Uncle Sam is none the wiser," Joe said, winking at her. "I don't blame you in these hard times." The woman smiled at Joe, and he gave her his card. Before he and Gil left, he told her to call them if anyone came back to the apartment.

Lucy was just stepping into the emergency department, thinking she'd find Tommy, to see if she could smooth over the rough edges of their recent conversations, when her phone buzzed. It was the PIO from the Los Alamos lab calling her back, confirming she was being allowed to talk to Dr. Price's immediate supervisor. Lucy found a pen in her pocket and wrote the number of the supervisor, Dr. Laura Goodwin, on her hand. It was the next number she dialed. Dr. Goodwin picked up on the second ring.

"Hi, my name is Lucy Newroe. I'm a reporter for the *Capital Tribune,* and I am looking to do a story about Dr. James Price, who I believe worked in your department. Would you be able to talk with me today?"

"Yes," came the response. The woman sounded hesitant and almost disinterested.

"That's wonderful. Thank you. I know this is a difficult time."

According to the laws of communication, Dr. Goodwin should have responded to that statement with a "Thank you" or "Yes, it is." But she was silent.

"So, how long did you work with Dr. Price?" Lucy asked.

"Not long."

"What was he like?"

"I don't know."

Lucy sighed. When a journalist starts an interview, she already knows exactly what kind of quote she is looking for from the subject. A good reporter is never surprised by what an interviewee tells her. And if a subject isn't saying what the reporter wants, an experienced journalist will craft the interview in such a way so as to get the person to say the desired phrase. Sometimes, a reporter may have to ask the same question several times to get what she needs. If worse comes to worst, and the interviewee just won't give a good quote, the reporter will say the exact quote she wants and just add at the end, "is that right?" Lucy could tell that Dr. Goodwin was one of those rare people who, for whatever reason, didn't follow the customary social interaction rules. This meant Lucy couldn't predict how Dr. Goodwin would respond to a question, and therefore she would have to work much harder to craft the interview correctly. Lucy also knew Dr. Goodwin wasn't going to give her what she needed, at least not over the phone.

"Hey, you know what? I'm actually on my way up to Los Alamos right now," Lucy said. "How about I buy you lunch?"

"I'm not . . ."

Lucy heard the beginning of a denial and said quickly, "I have cleared everything with your public information office, and they are really happy that you're talking to me." Lucy knew that the implication that the PIO office expected Dr. Goodwin to talk to her would smooth the way. Lab employees were government employees, and they did what they were told. She heard a feeble "okay" and arranged to meet Dr. Goodwin in Los Alamos in an hour.

The dances were supposed to start at 12:00 noon, but of course they never did. Kristen Valdez thought that was a result of a difference in the concept of time between natives and the outside world. Tribal members would say, "We'll meet when the sun goes down," or "after I put the sheep in their pen." The concept of noon was very precise and considered almost rude to natives, since it didn't allow someone to go about his day in a smooth manner. People who paid close attention to time were always rushing to make their next appointment and not leaving time for everything that needed to be done.

It was almost 1:00 P.M. by the time Kristen heard the drummers. They were in a procession with the dancers being led out of the kiva by a Catholic priest, who was there to bless the dancing grounds. Each drummer went to the center of the plaza and came up to a fire ring, which surrounded only the cold remnants of an old fire. They dropped in ash taken from the kiva fire, making the sign of the cross after they did so. Then they stood in a line and began drumming.

The dancers—about two dozen men and women—stood in three lines in the center of the plaza. The male deer dancers wore white shirts over white wraparound leggings tucked into ankle-high moccasins. They had straps of bells tied around their knees that jingled with each step. They wore headdresses of deer antlers and evergreen, with feathers hanging down that almost completely covered their eyes. Some of the men held canes about three feet high in each hand and used them to walk, making them look like they moved on four legs—like deer.

Another group of men, portraying the hunters, raised their feet up high, tomahawks in hand. All the female dancers wore black one-shoulder pueblo dresses with white wraparound leggings and turquoise squash blossom necklaces. The female steps were daintier, more like a shuffle on tiptoe. There was little noise except for the drummers and the sound of the dancers moving their feet to the beat across the unpaved plaza. Kristen watched her mother's brother patrol the dancing grounds, picking up any lost feathers or evergreen branches. All were a sacred part of the dance and had to be disposed of properly. Kristen had performed in the dances when she was younger. The drumming and the jingling bells were rhythmic, almost trancelike. If she had the time, she would still be dancing, but her job took up most of her time. For a dancer, there were always ceremonies to prepare for, and eagle feathers or deerskin to hunt down for costumes.

Over near where the elders were standing, Kristen watched as the war chief, in his cowboy hat and bolo tie, pulled the governor off to the side for a private conversation. A moment later, the governor looked up and surveyed the crowd before his eyes rested on Kristen. He signaled for her to approach.

She walked around the outside of the dancing ground as the men watched her. "Good morning, Governor," she said.

He nodded at her and, as was traditional, waited for his thoughts to settle before he spoke. When he did, his Pueblo accent, with its low pitch and quick stops, was thick. It was an accent Kristen had never had and one that was dying out. "There is something which we need your help with," he said. "George Gonzales has not called his wife in some days. She is worried."

"Yeah, he's probably just down in Albuquerque trying to buy some heroin," Kristen said too quickly, without using the right amount of deference or formality. She would probably hear about it from her mother. The men showed no reaction, but she flushed and said, "I am sorry, Governor." Kristen had spoken like a police officer—like an outsider—when she was supposed to have spoken like a pueblo member. "This must be a distressing thing to the family, going such a long time without hearing from him," she said. When speaking to an elder, it was considered polite to restate what had already been said. It was a way of showing agreement and acknowledging that there was common ground.

He nodded and said, "That is true."

Kristen nodded as well but didn't speak right away; instead, she did as was expected—she stopped to consider her words. After a few moments, she said, "It would be a good thing to help the family to ease their worries."

The governor nodded and said, "This would be a good thing."

With the matter decided, she said good-bye. As she turned to walk away, she wondered if George Gonzales was the missing man Joe and Detective Montoya had been looking for.

Lucy was getting antsy during the drive to the lab, so she distracted herself as she usually did—by looking at the sky. It was sunny, as always, however, this was not the strong, confident sun of summer, but the weak, thin sun of winter. This was a run-and-hide sun, which couldn't overpower any cloud. The desert gave way to forest as she got closer to Los Alamos. The two-lane winding highway was lined by signs that switched from warnings of elk crossings to others listing the designation numbers of the various laboratory tech areas—16, 51, 10—all in seemingly random order. Lucy drove past structures that made no sense; they were in the middle of New Mexico forest: domed black huts with antennae pointing in every direction and cement buildings with no windows or doors.

She approached the center of the town, with its wide streets neatly plowed. In the sixty years since the city of Los Alamos had been founded, the hard edge of newness had worn off, but it was still unmistakably modern—at least by Northern New Mexico standards. Here, there were no faux adobe homes or any effort at painting everything in earth tones. The houses could have been picked up and set down on any Midwest street and not seemed out of place, but then, everyone from Los Alamos was from somewhere else. They were from back east or farther West, such as California or Oregon. Under the snow, most of the houses even had real grass in their front yards, something that was frowned on in Santa Fe.

When Lucy had first started working at the newspaper, she quickly realized that the lab was a different kind of government organization. Most federal and local agencies have at least one worker who will talk to the newspaper off the record, telling them innocuous information along with headier stuff. It was very common, almost a monthly occurrence, for government employees to call the newsroom with stories about corruption or bad bosses. It was why journalists were called watchdogs, because they kept officials in check. But the lab was different. The information released came only from the PR department and it was all fluff about workers building the fastest computer in the world or creating a new walking, talking robot. The only time Lucy had heard of the lab releasing information it shouldn't have was when, several years ago, it sent out a fax saying it was going to spray a harmless bacterial agent into the air over Los Alamos in order to track how a biological weapon might disburse. When the public found out, there was an uproar, and the experiment was called off. However, a lab spokesperson later said the lab would only conduct the experiment later, but not tell anyone the next time. They were the federal government, after all, and were not required to inform the public about everything.

Yet even though lab employees didn't approach the media with the usual tidbits, that didn't mean there wasn't rumors out in the general public. People still brought up the human radiation experiments the lab had supposedly helped conduct on unknowing subjects back in the 1950s. And people whispered about the Cerro Grande forest fire that thirteen years ago burned more than four hundred homes in the town of Los Alamos but supposedly spared the lab. Why were the Los Alamos firefighters told to expect to get cancer from residual radiation, even though the lab insisted that the fire didn't reach any of its buildings?

Lucy parked her car at the restaurant and got out. Inside, she went up to the only woman sitting by herself. Dr. Laura Goodwin had blond hair tucked behind her ears and a sharp face. She was not the dowdy female scientist from the movies, where some magic makeover would suddenly make her more attractive. Instead, she was pretty, with an almost elfin look. Lucy shook her hand and sat down, hoping for the best.

Fifteen minutes and some spinach dip later, Lucy had written a total of eight words—Dr. Laura Goodwin's full name and title, Primary Structural Biosystems group director.

Mateo Garcia looked up from the cash register as the door to the store opened. Willie walked into the shop, a sleeping bag over his shoulders and snow on his woolen cap. Unlike everyone else, he didn't stomp his feet when he came in, so a trail of melted snow followed behind him on the floor. Likely that was because he was used to living outdoors, up in the mountains, alone. He walked straight up to the counter.

"Tobacco," he said. His eyes looked a little yellow and his long, gray beard was like a squirrel's nest.

"How are you doing with the cold?" Mateo asked. Willie said nothing. Mateo reached for a pouch of loose tobacco and asked, "Rolling papers?" Again Willie said nothing, so Mateo put the tobacco in a plastic bag. "Consider it a Christmas present."

Mateo took a shoebox from under the cash register and thumbed through some papers until he found the check he was looking for. Every month, someone from Charlotte, North Carolina, sent a check, in care of Garcia Hardware, made out to Willie for fifty dollars. Since it had opened more than a hundred years ago, the store had been serving as a bank and post office for locals. Mateo would cash their checks and hold on to their mail. The customers had different reasons for wanting Garcia Hardware to be their bank and post office. Some didn't want to have to go into town to get cash. Others didn't want the government to know where they were. Mateo gave Willie a pen and watched as his hand shook as he endorsed the check.

"Do you want any cash back?" Mateo asked. Willie moved his lips as if he were saying something, but no sound came out. It was something a few of the mountain men did. They were unused to talking, and sometimes forgot that they had to speak the words aloud.

The bell on the door rang again and Josh Cordova came in with his oldest son, who was around ten. They called hello to Mateo and went over to the DVD rentals, which Mateo tried to keep stocked with about a hundred or so movies. The bell on the door rang again, and Shorty Anaya came in yelling, "Jesus, it's cold."

Mateo kept an eye on Willie, who had shuffled over to the bread aisle, most likely to get away from the newly arrived customers. The bell rang again, and Mrs. Valdez came in, dressed in her work clothes. She was an HR manager for the tax and revenue department in Santa Fe. Shorty called hello to her. Their properties were next to each other's. She came up to the counter and handed Mateo forty dollars, while she yelled over to Shorty, "I think your dog tried to eat my chickens." Mateo grabbed another shoebox under the counter and looked through a collection of jewelry, iPods, and watches. He pulled out Mrs. Valdez's silver bracelet, handed it to her, then put the forty dollars in the register. He also sometimes was a pawnshop for customers he knew were reliable.

Shorty came over to the counter and spoke to Mrs. Valdez. "Aaron Dominguez, who lives down the road from you, said he saw mountain lion tracks yesterday. Could that be what ate your chicken?" They both looked at Mateo, assuming he would know about the mountain lion incident.

"I haven't heard that," he said. "But one of the Pacheco kids saw bear tracks last week."

"Which Pacheco?" Shorty asked.

"The ones who live up by the canyon, not the ones near the river," Mateo said. He heard the bell on the door ring again and watched Willie move back out into the night. He pulled the shoebox out from under the counter and wrote the date on a scrap of paper, then added: "Tobacco pouch, $5; Check cashed = $50; amount owed = $45." He wrote "I owe Willie" at the top and thumbed through the box once more, pulling out a small white envelope with Willie's name on it. He put the scrap of paper in it with the others. If Willie ever decided to collect on all the IOUs he had piled up from over the years, Mateo would be out thousands.

CHAPTER FIFTEEN

December 23

Lucy was ready to accept that the interview had tanked. None of her journalist tricks was working. Dr. Goodwin answered open-ended questions with one word and looked confused by Lucy's attempts to be friendly. Even the most basic of small talk left big silences.

"So, I know I already asked this," Lucy said, "but is there anything you can tell me about Dr. Price? Even the tiniest thing could help with my article."

"Not really," she said, again. But this time, after a pause, Dr. Goodwin asked a question of her own, "Why are you asking about Dr. Price?"

"I thought I explained that," Lucy said. "I want to do an article about Dr. Price and then interview the EMT who went to help him when he passed away." Lucy thought that mentioning that *she* was that EMT would have been unprofessional.

"Yes, I understand that," Dr. Goodwin said. "But why do an article specifically about Dr. Price?"

"What do you mean?"

"Why not do one on Dr. Ivanov?" she asked. "He's dead, too."

"Who's Dr. Ivanov?" Lucy asked. "I'm not familiar with that name."

"He died the day after Dr. Price," she said.

"Really?" Lucy said, finally having a reason to take the cap back off her pen and get ready to write in her reporter's notebook. "And how did he die?"

"I shouldn't talk about it," Dr. Goodwin said. "I'm sure it's against lab policy."

"You know, I totally respect that," Lucy said, purposely smiling and softening her face. "But it could be a real relief to talk about it."

"I don't know," Dr. Goodwin said.

"I understand," Lucy said. "But it might help."

"I'm not sure."

Lucy knew the best way to break through Dr. Goodwin's reluctance. She raised her hand, getting the attention of the waiter, and said to him, "We'll have two margaritas."

As Joe and Gil sat in the SUV still parked in front of the Escobar apartment, Joe called Melody, the preproduction manager, and asked her about the tattoos. She said the arm in the photo belonged to a consultant hired by the studio.

"We wanted someone who knew the system and who was there during the riot," she said. "He's able to give a sense of realism to the whole thing. He's been a great resource."

She told Joe the consultant's name: Pat Abetya.

To which Gil said, "Holy shit."

Within minutes, Gil and Joe had gotten Abetya's address from Dispatch and driven to his house, which was actually a mobile home. With off-white paneling and a tin roof, it looked to be at least thirty years old. A four-foot-high cinderblock wall surrounded the property. Part of it had fallen into the driveway and had yet to be moved out of the way. Joe tried to hide their vehicle behind some juniper bushes as best he could while still keeping an eye on the house, but they were hardly inconspicuous with SANTA FE POLICE clearly written on the side of the SUV. They had circled the block before parking, looking for the dark SUV they'd seen Hoffman driving, but there was only one car nearby and, according to a records search, it belonged to Abetya.

Gil and Joe got out of the car and went up to the trailer. A tawny pit bull chained in the yard of the house next door started to bark and snarl. Gil knocked and waited for someone to answer. He knocked again, louder. He tried to hear if the television or radio was on inside, but it was impossible to tell over the sound of the barking. Joe walked around the trailer, looking in windows. He came back shaking his head. "Nobody home."

They went back to their vehicle and settled in to wait as Joe looked up Abetya's record on his phone. "Wow, this guy has been in the system for, like, forever. He was convicted of robbery of an occupied residence back in 1973. He was given eight years for that. He was at the state pen during the riot . . . that's weird. He should have gotten out in 1981. But he served a full life term of thirty years on top of the eight. His file doesn't explain why. How do you know him?"

"I don't know him," Gil said.

"Yeah, but you've got some kind of issue with him," Joe said. "You look pissed."

"I'm fine," Gil said.

"No, you're not."

"Last I heard, Abetya was one of the bosses of the New Mexico Syndicate," Gil said to change the subject. "He could even be a general by now or a don."

"That still doesn't explain your problem with him," Joe said. "Come on. Just tell me or I'll be really annoying about it."

Gil sighed. "After the riot, my father was the prosecutor in charge of convicting the inmates. Abetya was one of them."

"And? Something else had to have happened."

"During the trial, Abetya started to organize the syndicate, and he sent death threats to my dad to get him to stop prosecuting the inmates."

"So, there is some extra-special hate for this guy," Joe said. "I get it. Anything else I should know?"

"That's it," Gil said, as he settled down into his seat, watching the trailer. A woman walked by with her toy poodle, barely glancing at them. An hour later, there had been no activity other than the sky becoming darker.

Joe yawned. "This sucks. Can we please go to the hospital to see if Natalie Martin can ID a picture of Abetya? At least then we'd have probable cause to get a search warrant." They had first discussed the idea of going to see her a half hour ago, but Gil had dismissed it. They had bothered Natalie Martin enough. Plus, he felt in his gut that the sooner they found Abetya, the sooner they'd find Hoffman. And the best way to find him was to stay where they were.

Gil didn't answer, and instead said, "I have to stretch my shoulder out." He got out of the SUV and walked a few feet away before dialing his mom's number. She picked up on the fourth ring.

"Hey, Mom," Gil said. "I just wanted to make sure that Tomas came to shovel your driveway."

"Yes, *hito*," she said.

"When is Elena coming?" he asked. His younger sister, who worked as a lawyer for the state attorney's office in Albuquerque, was supposed to come up so she could drive their mom to midnight Mass.

"Not until tomorrow morning," she said. "What time are Susan and the girls going to church?" His entire family would be at the Basilica in Santa Fe tomorrow night, just like they were every year, to listen to the choir and see the decorations. Then they would go home and open presents. The next morning would be the party at his mom's, and it would last all day.

"I'm not sure," he said. "You have to call Susan." He waited a second before saying, "Listen, Mom, can I ask you about something?"

"Of course, *hito*," she said.

"When Dad was prosecuting the inmates from the state pen riot, why did he have to have the police protecting him?"

His mom didn't answer right away, but she also didn't completely brush his question off, which was what he had expected. Instead, she said, "That was a bad time. Why are you asking about it?"

"Dad told me that an inmate named Pat Abetya had said some things to him," he said. "I think Abetya is involved with a case I'm working on."

"That man—he wasn't a good man," his mom said. "You were too little back then. Your father and I didn't want to worry you or your sister."

"Mom, I was ten," Gil said. "I was old enough to know something was going on. There were officers all over the house. What happened? Was Abetya the man Dad needed protection from?"

"Oh, *hito* . . ."

"Just tell me, Mom, please." Gil said.

She answered quietly, "The protection wasn't for your father; it was for me and you and your sister."

"What?" Gil said, loudly enough that Joe, still sitting in the SUV, turned to look out at him. Gil paced a few feet away and struggled to keep his voice level as he said, "I really need you to explain this to me, Mom."

"That man . . . he sent someone to the house," she said.

"What do you mean?" Gil asked. "Pat Abetya sent someone to threaten you?" His voice started to rise at the end, his anger coming out.

"I was putting your sister down for her nap and you were at school when he broke in. He had a gun."

"What happened?" Gil asked. His eyes were closed, his jaw clenched, the phone tight against his ear.

"Before he could do anything, your grandpa heard me scream and came running over from the old house with his shotgun."

"Did they catch the man?"

"No," she said. "Your grandpa shot at him, but he ran away. They followed him as far as the Mexican border, but they never caught him."

When Gil was ten, Judge Gilbert Nazario Estevan Montoya insisted on teaching him how to shoot a shotgun. They stood out in the field for hours, while Gil took aim and the judge yelled at him when he missed. They repeated this over and over, until Gil could hit his mark perfectly. Now he knew why.

"How did they know Abetya had sent the man?" Gil asked.

"They were cousins," she said. "But your dad couldn't prove that man, Mr. Abetya, was involved. All your dad could do was prosecute him as best he could for the riot. Mr. Abetya was supposed to be released that year, but your father got him sentenced to life."

Lucy's margarita sat in front of her, untouched. Dr. Goodwin's was the same. Lucy was still trying to maneuver around Goodwin's reluctance.

"It must be hard having two employees die like that," Lucy said. Dr. Goodwin didn't answer. Lucy decided if an appeal to human emotion didn't work, she'd have to try something else. "It must have really increased your workload."

"Yes," Dr. Goodwin said. "It really did."

Lucy kept going. "That must be difficult. I'm sure you were already working long hours."

"I'm always there after everyone else has left for the day," Dr. Goodwin said, taking a sip of her drink. Lucy smiled. She had finally found a topic Dr. Goodwin cared about.

A half hour later, Lucy sat sucking from her fingers the salt that had once lined the rim of her margarita glass, which was now empty. Dr. Goodwin was really chatty now, going on about her work while never revealing what kind of work she did. She would just refer to generic experiments and procedures.

"With Dr. Price gone, I'll have to interview for new employees," Dr. Goodwin said. "I don't have the time for that. I was already doing the work of another employee who's on maternity leave."

"That's hard," Lucy said, taking a final hit of spinach dip, scraping the bottom of the bowl. She signaled for the waiter to bring them another round of drinks.

"She was supposed to come back to work six months ago," Dr. Goodwin said, finishing off her margarita. "But she said she needed more time, since she had twin boys. Is having twins really that much harder than having one baby?"

Gil, still standing out in the cold, called his sister and told her the whole story about Pat Abetya. Her first response was much like Gil's, only with more swear words. Her second response was "I'll be at mom's in an hour." They had no reason to think Abetya would want to revisit an old grudge. But then again, he already had committed three home invasions. How easy would it be for him to kill two birds with one stone—go out to Gil's mom's place for another home invasion while simultaneously getting back at the family of a man who'd helped get him sentenced to thirty years in prison? Elena called back ten minutes later to tell him their aunt Yolanda and cousin Tomas, who was a corrections officer at the state pen, had volunteered to go over and help make tamales until Elena arrived. Next, Gil called Susan, just to check on her, but he got only her voice mail.

Gil got back into the car and tried to warm up his hands in front of the heater.

"Everything okay?" Joe asked, looking at Gil intently.

"Yeah," Gil said, rubbing his hands together.

"Not that I believe you in the slightest," Joe said, "but I'll let it go for now."

"Thanks," Gil said. "Hear anything new?"

"Nope," Joe said. "Just to be clear, we still think Escobar and Hoffman are involved, right? And Abetya was using his consulting work to get names and addresses of the people connected to the movie so he and Escobar and Hoffman could go pay them a visit?"

"That's about it," Gil said. He leaned back in his seat and tried to concentrate on the job before him: surveilling Abetya's house

Hours later he was still in the same position. Joe sat next to him, occasionally looking up from the movie he was watching on his phone. There had been no movement inside the house; despite the fact Abetya's car was in the driveway. Joe and Gil had debated the idea that Hoffman had turned on Abetya and the latter was lying dead inside the trailer, which wouldn't be the worst news Gil had heard. The other possibility—which was Joe's favorite—was that Abetya was Mr. Burns and had been dead all along. But they couldn't be sure either way and didn't want to swarm the house too early and possibly scare off Hoffman. So they stayed put.

They had police cars in front of the Escobar house and more officers looking for the SUV Hoffman was driving. Now they just had to wait. They debated putting SWAT on standby, just in case Abetya showed. But they decided there would be time for that when they knew exactly where Abetya was.

The phone on Gil's belt vibrated. It was Lucy. He let it go to voice mail.

The drive down from the Hill had many pockets of cell phone dead areas. The mesas and canyons were stingy with what signals they let get past.

Lucy called Gil again as soon as she had a signal, saying, "Gil, I found something that might help you. Call me." She had tried him once from the restaurant and left a similar message, but he hadn't gotten back to her. But then, that was only twenty minutes ago.

She was passing Pojoaque Pueblo when she thought to call Joe's cell, but one look at her signal told her she'd have to wait until she topped Opera Hill. The waiting was making her anxious.

Lucy heard the siren before she saw the police cruiser. At first she thought he was going to pass by, off to some car accident or bank robbery. She was surprised when she pulled off to the right to let him pass and he pulled up behind her. She was positive she hadn't been speeding, careful to keep it one point under the limit. Maybe her taillight was out. Maybe the men in black SUVs were coming for her because she'd interviewed a lab employee. The sheriff's deputy got out of his car and walked up to her door, his right hand covering the butt of the gun on his belt. Lucy rolled down her window and was hit with a blast of cold air. She tried to smile nonetheless.

"Hi there, officer. How are you tonight?" she said.

"Ma'am," he said. "I need to see your vehicle registration and driver's identification."

"Okay. Let me get it out," Lucy said. She was careful not to obstruct the deputy's view of the emergency radio installed in her car, hoping he might give a firefighter a break. But he said nothing. She handed over the documentation, which he took, saying, "I'll be right back. Stay in your car."

He sat in his patrol car behind her, calling in her information. She had no speeding tickets. Not even any for parking. She thought at most she would get a warning. As she waited for him, she watched the passing cars and their occupants, who craned their necks to look at her, everyone wondering just what kind of criminal she was. The deputy came back, knocking on her window before she had a chance to roll it down.

"Ma'am," he said. "You need to step out of the vehicle."

She got out of her car, smiling and said, "Geez, it's cold out here."

The deputy didn't smile. Instead he said, "Ma'am, I need you to come over here and walk a straight line."

That was the first time it occurred to her that she was being pulled over for drunk driving.

CHAPTER SIXTEEN

December 23

Gil was resting his eyes when Joe's phone rang. He zoned out Joe's conversation and instead went back over the home invasions in his head. They had passed the list of a hundred or so people connected to the movie on to Chief Kline, who was deciding whether to alert them to the possibility they might be targeted for a home invasion. Gil was thinking about calling the chief to check on his decision when Joe got off the phone.

"That was one of the guys from county jail," Joe said after hanging up. "Lucy's been arrested."

"For what?" Gil said, less surprised than he probably should have been.

"DWI," Joe said.

Gil sighed. Lucy was always very good at causing problems—and her drinking had become one huge problem. She had called him drunk a few months ago, during a missing-child case and had even come to the station one night after a few beers. "Does she want us to come get her out?"

"All they said was that she was waiting to talk to you."

"She can keep waiting," Gil said. Somehow Lucy was able to frustrate him more easily than anyone else he had ever met. When it came to her, his emotional meter seemed to have two settings: amused and annoyed, with nothing in between.

"You sound mad," Joe said.

"No, I just don't care right now," Gil said, lying.

Her jail cell wasn't that bad. She was in a group pod with three other women, all of whom were asleep. There were bunk beds attached to the walls and benches to sit on. The cell wasn't overly grimy or scary, and the red jumpsuit she was wearing was comfortable enough for her to stretch out in.

She was in a Santa County detention center after having been processed at the sheriff's department, which included a mug shot and fingerprinting. She had passed the field sobriety tests—sort of. Bad footing or icy pavement could explain her minor stumbles. But there was no arguing with the Breathalyzer test. She'd known that if she refused to take it, she could be charged with aggravated DWI, so she blew into the instrument—as she had so many times at home to ensure that she never drove drunk. The Breathalyzer had registered a .09, just above the .08 limit. She would be held in lockup until arraignment in the morning, at which point she could post bond and get out. In the meantime, she was trying to figure out a way to get in touch with Gil.

A corrections officer came by, and she called over to him, saying, "Did you call him? What did he say?"

"He didn't answer," the officer said.

"Call him again."

"Give it up. He's not coming to get you out of here," the officer said.

"What about his partner, Joe?"

"I talked to him. He didn't say anything. Sorry."

"What time is it?"

"Just after nine thirty."

Mateo Garcia stood at a glass-and-wood counter with a calculator in his hand. He had locked the store's doors at 9:00 P.M. and turned the red-and-white sign on the door to CLOSED. Now he had the shoebox containing all the IOUs in front of him. Willie's visit that day had made Mateo curious about just how much money he would owe the mountain man when the time came. Mateo had spent the last ten minutes pulling out receipts and typing numbers off the IOUs into a calculator. Willie came in only four or five times a year, but the fifty-dollar checks came in every month.

There was a knock on the door and Mateo looked up. Mr. Anaya, Shorty Anaya's father, waved at him through the glass. Mateo went to unlock the door, and Mr. Anaya came shuffling in, leaning heavily on his cane.

"What can I help you with tonight, sir?" Mateo asked him.

"Oh, I need candy," he said. "It's almost Christmas. I need candy to hand out to the kids when they come to the door."

While Mr. Anaya made his way over to the candy aisle, Mateo went back to the counter to use the store phone. A few minutes later, Shorty Anaya drove up and came into the shop, stomping the snow off his boots.

"Thanks for calling," he said to Mateo. They both watched

as Shorty's father took a Hershey bar and put it in his coat pocket. Shorty shook his head, laughed, and yelled across the store, "Dad, put the candy back. It's not yours." Mr. Anaya didn't listen and put a bag of Skittles in his pocket next.

"Don't worry about it," Mateo asked. "I'd rather *he* shoplifted from me than some teenager. How's he doing with the Alzheimer's?"

"He's good," Shorty said, "until he goes wandering off like this. How he manages to walk in the dark up that icy road . . ." He didn't finish the thought.

"It's no problem," Mateo said. "At least he always comes here and doesn't head off into the woods."

"I think he comes here because he remembers it from when he was a kid," Shorty said. The Anaya family had been shopping at Garcia's Hardware since it first opened in 1910. The Anayas still lived in the house where generations of children had grown up.

The wood floor creaked as Shorty went over to the candy aisle. "Dad, it's time to go," he said, taking his father's arm to lead him out of the store.

"I don't want to go," Mr. Anaya said, sounding like a whining child. "I need to get candy for when the kids come to the door."

"He's been saying that since he got here," Mateo said. "I think he's remembering *Mis Crismes*." Mateo's mother had told him stories about *Mis Crismes* from when she was a girl in the 1950s. On Christmas morning she and her brothers and sisters would each take a pillowcase and go door to door to neighbors, yelling, "*Mis crismes*." When the neighbors opened the door, each child would get a treat in his bag. Mrs. Quintana had popcorn balls. The Archuletas gave out candy canes. The Ortegas down the hill made *bizcochi-*

tos. His mother could come home with a pillowcase full of cookies, apples, and oranges. Mateo wondered why the tradition had died out. He and his friends had never celebrated it. As best he could tell, his mother's generation was the last one that did, unless the practice still survived in the tiny mountain villages.

"Is that what you're talking about, Dad?" Shorty asked him. "Are you remembering back when you celebrated *Mis Crismes*."

"*Mis Crismes, Mis Crismes*," Mr. Anaya said in a little high voice, making Shorty and Mateo laugh.

"Those were good times," Shorty said as they reached the door. Mateo opened it for them. "Back then you got Christmas candy for free just by asking for it and you didn't have to shoplift." Mateo told them good night as he closed the door behind them. He decided to leave the IOUs for another day and instead made a sign that read, CLOSED UNTIL DECEMBER 26, which he put on the door that he locked behind him.

One of Lucy's cellmates had woken up, and Lucy had gone into interview mode, talking to the woman as if she were a subject of an article, asking her question after question yet never offering any information about herself. The woman, who had four kids, two ex-husbands, and only $14.02 in the bank, had been arrested on her third DWI, which meant jail time. Lucy was just about to ask the woman if she was scared to go to jail when the corrections officer came past again and Lucy asked, "What time is it?"

"It's twenty minutes later than the last time you asked," he said.

"That would make it after eleven, right?"

"Why do you keep asking me about the time?" he asked.

"It's after eleven, right? That's all I need to know."

"Fine, yeah. It's officially"—he looked his watch—"eleven-oh-nine and fifteen seconds."

"Thank you. I want to make my phone call." He shook his head and opened the cell door, leading her to the guard station, where the phone was. She dialed Tommy Martinez's cell phone.

"Hey, boss, what's up?"

"I'm in jail," she said.

"For what?" he asked, sounding like he didn't believe her.

"DWI, but that's not why I called. I need a favor."

"I can come bail you out—" he started to say.

"No, I need you to do something for me," Lucy said. "Do you have a piece of paper and a pen?"

"Yeah, okay, go ahead."

"Do you know who Detective Gil Montoya is, with the Santa Fe Police?"

"Sure . . ."

"Can you get a hold of him right away?"

"No problem."

"I need you to ask him something," she said. "Write this down. I need you to ask him if it's true that all the victims of the recent home invasions worked in the same department at Los Alamos National Lab."

"Really? Is that true? Do they?"

"I don't know for sure," she said.

"Now you're fishing."

"I'm hoping he'll look into it after you call him," she said. "I can't seem to get him to call me back."

"So you were at the fire where the two bodies were found?"

"Yep," she said. "I was there." She thought of the joke

she'd made with Gil at the fire scene, when she'd teased him about giving her his trademark don't-tell-anyone-at-the-newspaper-about-this-crime-scene speech.

"This will go great in the story I'm writing tonight about the newest home invasion," Tommy said. "Wait. . . . damn. It's past eleven o'clock. Copy desk probably put the paper to bed already. Hang on." In the background, Lucy heard Tommy calling over to the night editor. She couldn't be sure of what they said to each other, but she was completely sure of what the answer would be. In journalism, some deadlines were absolute.

"Damn," he said back into the phone. "They said there's no way to stop the presses."

"Yeah. I know," she said. "It's a bitch how those deadlines work. If only I'd called a half hour ago." She could hear how tired she sounded. Not sarcastic, just tired.

"I guess I can get it in the day after tomorrow," he said. "That sucks, though."

Lucy sighed. "Yeah, it sucks, but that should be fine. It'll be a big scoop." The story wouldn't hit the paper—or any other media—until Christmas Day. It might give Gil enough time to do something with the information she was sending him through Tommy.

"But you still have to make the call as soon as we hang up."

"Okay. I will. Promise," Tommy said. "What else can you tell me? What's the name of the department they work in? When did the home invasions we're talking about happen? Do they include those people killed in the house fire and the family that was hit last night?"

"Nope. That's all you're getting from me."

"Okay. I'll figure it out."

"I know you will."

"But what do I say when Montoya asks how I got the information?"

"Tell him the truth," Lucy said, laying her head against the wall near the phone and closing her eyes. She had promised Gil only three days ago that she wouldn't tell anyone at the newspaper about the fire or the bodies. Seventy-two hours was all it took for her to renege. She felt worse about breaking that promise than about her DWI. She had been drinking and driving; she deserved to be arrested. It was embarrassing, but she could make a joke out of it that would make everyone laugh, including herself. But her promise to Gil wasn't as easy to make light of. She knew Gil had taken her promise seriously—and would take her breaking it just as seriously. She might just have lost one of her few friends. "Tell him I told you—and please tell him I'm really sorry."

Joe was asleep against the passenger-side window. His breath had caused condensation to build up on the windshield. It was hard to see outside the SUV, but the heavy vapor also served as a tinted window, making it hard for anyone to see in. They had been sitting outside of Abetya's house for more than seven hours. Gil was reconsidering having SWAT go in when his phone rang. He didn't recognize the number, but thought it might be Chief Kline calling him back.

"Detective Montoya, this is Tommy Martinez from the *Capital Tribune*. How is your evening going?"

"Can I help you with something?"

"Yes, sir. I was hoping you could confirm that all the victims from the three home invasions you've had this week are connected."

Gill thought for a second before saying, "What do you mean connected?"

"I mean they all worked in the same department up on the Hill."

The ringing phone had woken Joe up, and he was staring at Gil, trying to understand only one side of the conversation.

"The Hill?" Gil asked, confused. "I don't—where are you getting your information?"

"From my boss . . . I mean my old boss, Lucy Newroe."

"Lucy told you to call me," Gil said. It wasn't a question. Next to him, Joe swore loudly. "And she said the victims all worked up on the Hill." Joe swore again.

"Yes, sir, and she told me to tell you that she's sorry."

"May I ask what she said she was sorry for?"

"She didn't say," Martinez said. "I assume she thought you'd know." Gil did know—she was sorry for breaking her promise.

Gil hung up the phone after saying "No comment," but not in response to a specific question, just the conversation in general. He looked over at Joe.

"We missed something."

CHAPTER SEVENTEEN

December 24

It was early morning when Kristen Valdez pulled up in front of the Gonzales mobile home. For the last half hour, she had been watching from her house up the street, waiting for the telltale smoke coming out of the Gonzales' adobe oven in the backyard. Everyone would be cooking today, and the first thing that had to be done was to make the fire in the *horno* before sunrise. While she'd waited, she spent her time trying to get a good enough Internet connection to research genetics on her phone. She had been thinking about the man who had burned in the house fire. If she understood the Wikipedia entry about genetics correctly, it seemed possible that George Gonzales was the missing man. Joe had said that genetic testing proved the burned man had been a crypto-Jew, which meant he was a descendant of the conquistadors. For more than four hundred years, the pueblo tribes had been intermarrying with the Spanish, to the point that it was no longer possible to determine based on looks alone who was Northern New Mexico Hispanic and who was Pueblo Indian. If a Gonzales' ancestor had married a crypto-Jew, George might have the gene.

Now Kristen got out of her Mitsubishi Eclipse, which looked almost doll-like next to the black Ford F-150 truck already in the driveway, and walked up to the Gonzales' door. She felt the wind cut through her jeans and creep up under her T-shirt. She pulled her coat around her tighter as she knocked, then glanced back at her own house, just up the road. She could swear she saw her mother peeking out from behind the kitchen curtains. Her mother had been none too happy when Kristen had told her about the governor's request to help locate George Gonzales, because it meant going into the witch's home. Kristen touched the turquoise stone hanging from a heavy silver chain around her neck. Her mother had made her wear it because the blue color warded off spirits that might wish to do her harm. She also was carrying a loaf of bread wrapped in foil, which her mother had sent in the hope that it might keep them in Josephine Gonzales's good graces.

Mary Gonzales, George's wife, answered on the second knock. She was a large woman in her twenties with acne-marked skin and smooth, straight black hair.

"Hello, Mary," Kristen said. "How are you?"

Mary didn't answer. Kristen said, "The governor told me you were worried about your husband. He wanted me to look into it."

Mary didn't move the door, which she had pulled open only a few inches.

"That's okay," she said. "We don't need any help. We heard from him yesterday. He's fine."

"I understand," Kristen said, a little disappointed. That meant George wasn't the burned man. It would have helped the case if he had been. "I'm glad it all worked out." Mary wasn't looking at her and instead watched the road, as if she were waiting for something, which made Kristen curious. She said, "Would you mind if I came in? My mom made some bread for your mother-in-law."

Mary hesitated, but someone inside spoke in a low tone that Kristen couldn't hear, and Mary opened the door. As Kristen moved past Mary, she noticed the other woman had her coat on, keys in hand, and was holding her purse. Inside the trailer, a dark brown shag carpet and a wood stove churning out heat gave the place the feel of warm dirt. A baby about six months old sat in a bouncy swing, while a toddler around two years old hit some wood blocks with a plastic hammer. George's mother sat on a brown-plaid sofa next to a Christmas tree loaded with tinsel.

Kristen nodded at Josephine Gonzales, who was so petite she seemed in danger of being sucked into the couch. "Merry Christmas, Mrs. Gonzales," Kristen said. "My mother wanted you to have this." She handed the foil-wrapped bread to Josephine Gonzales, who looked at it with suspicion, causing Kristen to say, "It's just pumpkin bread." They hadn't offered Kristen a seat or anything to drink, making it clear they wanted her gone. She took another moment to glance around the room, but nothing seemed out of order. She said Merry Christmas to them again and turned leave. Next to the front door were a rolled-up sleeping bag, a camp stove, and a box of granola bars. Without commenting on the camping gear, she went back outside and got into her car. She pulled away and drove down the street to her own house. But instead of getting out, she parked where she could see the only road leading out of their neighborhood. And then she waited.

About five minutes later, the Black Ford F-150 drove past, with Mary Gonzales at the wheel. Kristen watched until the truck was almost out of sight before she started to follow it.

The hospital was dark and quiet as Gil and Joe walked through the hallways. Natalie Martin was still in the same waiting room, but the sleeping children were gone, replaced by a woman sitting next to her, holding her hand. Natalie Martin introduced them to her sister, who had flown in for the holidays. Natalie Martin said the medical team had decided to do the surgery at the hospital instead of flying her husband down to Albuquerque. So, after her boys had been picked up by her friend Julie, she was still doing what she had been for the last twenty-four hours: waiting.

Since the reporter's phone call last night, Gil and Joe had been going over all the threads of the case, checking everything that might indicate a connection between the victims and the laboratory. Gil kept officers in front of the Escobar house, and he sent a car to Abetya's to keep up the surveillance. Gil called Chief Kline to update him, and Gil suggested they hold off alerting the movie people until they had either verified or debunked the reporter's story.

"We should just call Lucy," Joe said. "She's the one who figured out the laboratory connection. She might know more about it."

It was a solid suggestion, but Gil didn't want to call her. At the moment, he never wanted to talk to her again. "I think she's proven she cannot be trusted as a resource," he said.

"Come on, Gil," Joe said. "We should at least ask her."

"That's not an option," Gil said. It must have been his tone, because Joe let it drop.

They kept sifting through all the papers at the office for another fifteen minutes, until Gil finally accepted there was one sure way to find out the truth. That was how he ended up in the hospital. He hadn't wanted to bother Natalie Martin again, but the only other choice was to go to Lucy, and that was something he wouldn't do.

"Mrs. Martin, we do have a few more questions for you," Gil said, pulling one of the upholstered chairs closer to her and sitting down. "Do you know this man?" He showed her a picture of Abetya. She shook her head, and Gil asked, "He isn't one of the men who broke into your home?"

"No," she said. "I haven't seen him before." Gil looked at Joe, who nodded. It seemed more and more likely that Abetya was the burned man.

"Can we ask more about what kind of work your husband does?" Joe asked, trying to get an answer to their other question—how Hoffman and his team had found their victims. During the car ride over, Gil and Joe discussed the idea that maybe the home invasion crew worked off two victim lists: one from the movie studio and one from the lab.

"He's a biochemical engineer," she said.

"And where does he work?" Gil asked.

"He does water safety testing for the state," she said.

"He doesn't work for the lab?" Joe asked. "Not even doing contract work or something?"

"No," she said. Joe looked over at Gil. It looked like Lucy's tip was wrong; the victims were tied to the movie after all, not the lab.

Then Natalie Martin added, "But I did."

"You did?" Joe asked.

"That's where I worked before the boys were born two years ago," she said. "Actually, I guess, technically, I'm still employed there. I took a leave of absence after my maternity leave was up."

"In what department did you work?" Gil asked.

"Primary Structural Biosystems," she said. Joe swore and went pacing off a few feet. "But I can't tell you what kind of work I did. It's classified."

"And do you know Dr. Jim Price and Stanley Ivanov?"

"I know Dr. Ivanov," she said. "I've heard of Dr. Price. I think he might have been the one who replaced Dr. Ivanov when he retired."

"But you've never met Dr. Price."

"No," she said. "I was on maternity leave when he transferred over."

"Do you know if Dr. Ivanov and Dr. Price knew each other?" Gil asked.

"I don't know," she said. "But I kind of doubt it."

"Why's that?"

"I barely knew Dr. Ivanov, and we worked together for ten years."

Gil stood thinking for another second. Something was nagging at him. It took him a moment to realize what it was. "You've never met Dr. Price," Gil said again, more to get his thoughts in order than as a question. "So there would be no way that he would know about your Pontiac Tempest?"

"No," she said. "But Dr. Ivanov might have known about it. I kept a picture on my desk of my husband and me standing in front of the car the night he proposed. My husband's big proposal idea was to take me out for a ride after finally getting the car redone and then ask me to marry him as we looked at the stars."

She started to cry, and her sister, who had been silent for the entire interview, hugged her tightly and said, "I think it's time to take a break."

"I'm sorry, Mrs. Martin, I know this is hard, but I have just a few more questions," Gil said. The sister sighed heavily and leaned back in her chair.

Gil took this as a sign he could continue. "Can you think of anyone at work who had a problem with you, Dr. Price, and Dr. Ivanov specifically?"

She shook her head, then added, "But the people in my office . . . it wasn't a happy work environment."

"What do you mean by that?"

"Everyone there is brilliant, but they do better working by themselves," she said.

"Can you elaborate?" Gil asked. She didn't answer for a moment. He could tell she was reluctant to talk about it. He tried a different tact. "You've been on leave for two years, Mrs. Martin. You haven't returned to work, but you also haven't quit. Why is that?"

"I love the work," she said.

"But you haven't gone back."

She shook her head and closed her eyes. "It was my dream job," she said, opening her eyes at looking at Gil again. "But those people . . ."

"Your co-workers were competitive?" Joe asked.

"It was more than that," she said. "In every lab it's expected that your co-workers will take your chemicals or make sure your experimental protocols are out of date. That kind of stuff happens all the time. People get envious of others moving ahead and want to slow them down. But in our department, it went beyond that."

"How so?" Gil asked.

"I had my own lab, which I kept locked, but I would come in and find alcohol dumped in my cell cultures, killing months of work. Or whole sections of papers I was going to publish would somehow get permanently deleted from my computer. It finally got bad enough that I told my boss, Dr. Goodwin."

"What happened?" Joe asked.

"She said I was doing it myself because I wanted someone to blame for my mistakes," Natalie Martin said. "She made me take a lie detector test, and the security officers kept pulling me in for interviews. After that, I kept my mouth shut."

"Did you ever find out who was behind it?" Gil asked.

"No. And by the end, I didn't care; all I wanted was to get out of there," she said. "The last straw was right after I found out I was pregnant. One of the first things I did was get rid of all the chemicals in my lab that could cause birth defects. A week later, I was running some DNA when I noticed that the agarose gel I was using had a blue tint. I ran some tests and found someone had put ethidium bromide in the gel."

"That sounds bad," Joe said.

"Ethidium bromide is a teratogen," she said, her voice angry. "It intercalates double-stranded DNA. They were trying to expose me to it to give my babies birth defects. What kind of person does that? I took maternity leave the next day."

Lucy was asleep on her bunk when a corrections officer opened the cell door. "Lucy Newroe, you have a phone call."

She followed him to the guard station and picked up the phone. She recognized Joe's East Coast accent instantly.

"How you holding up?" he asked, surprising her with his concern.

"Fine," she said. "I'm thinking about getting a prison tattoo while I'm in here, to add to my street cred."

"I can't get the charges dropped, but I can get you out of there."

"No, I think I'll stay," she said. "I have arraignment in a few hours, and I'll get out then."

"Seriously?"

"Yeah, I don't want any special treatment. I'll work my way through the system like everyone else. I screwed up, and I need to pay the price. But thanks anyway." Clearly, hearing the AA dogma over and over about taking responsibility for one's mistakes had made an impact on her, she thought.

"You did the crime so you'll do the time?"

"Something like that, but, really, I just don't want to go home. There's a pile of laundry there I want to avoid as long as possible."

"We got your phone call, or rather the one from your co-worker," he said. "Thanks for the tip, even if you kind of screwed us in the process."

"If you had just called me back, we could have avoided all this unpleasantness," she said. "But aren't you going to ask me how I found out the lab connection?"

"I kind of feel like I don't have the right to ask," he said. "Not after everything. Plus, I kind of think you'll claim some journalist ethics crap and not tell me."

"That was the plan, but you had to go and ruin it."

"Let me know if you need anything."

"What does Gil have to say about my being in here?"
Joe hesitated. "Not much."

"Yeah, right," she said. "Dad's too busy to worry about

the screwed-up kid in jail. Does he even know you're calling me?" Joe didn't say anything. She said, "So, he doesn't.
That must mean you'd think he'd get mad if he knew we
were talking."

"Something like that."

"Well, thank you for checking on me, Joe. I really appre-
ciate it."

"Okay," he said, reluctantly about to hang up.

"Hey, Joe," she said, catching him before she heard the
click ending the call. "Merry Christmas."

Gil sat in the passenger seat of the marked SUV parked il-
legally outside the hospital. Since Joe was driving today, he
had been taking full advantage of the perks of having a
marked police vehicle—the main one being they could park
where they wanted; Gil was trying not to complain about
it. Joe had stepped outside to make a phone call, shivering
in the morning cold. Gil assumed the secret call was to a
woman, maybe someone Joe was supposed to meet in Las
Vegas before the case got out of control. Now Joe was back
in the driver's seat with the car idling, typing in the names
of the employees who worked in Primary Structural Biosystems from a list given to them by Natalie Martin. The list
was two years out of date, but it was a place to start. Joe
ran the names through the DMV database to get home addresses. There were six who lived in Los Alamos, three to
the north, in Rio Arriba County, and seven in Santa Fe
County, two of whom had been Dr. Price and Dr. Ivanov.
Natalie Martin was the only one who lived in the city of
Santa Fe. All in all, there were fourteen people who needed
to be notified about Hoffman.

Joe called the Rio Arriba and Santa Fe county sheriff's
departments, asking them to put patrol cars in front of the

workers' houses in their jurisdiction, while Gil called Chip Davis up in Los Alamos to let him know. Davis said he would send security officers to the employees on the list who lived up on the Hill, and offered to make sure the list Natalie Martin had provided contained the most recent information. Before Davis could hang up, Gil told him what Natalie Martin had said about the sabotage at the lab.

"Did you ever find out who was behind it?" Gil asked.

"It was an internal matter," Davis said.

"Whom did you suspect?" Gil said.

Davis hesitated before saying, "We only conducted a minimal investigation."

"Why was that?"

"What happened to Dr. Martin was unfortunate but not unusual. It wasn't a priority."

"Is it normal for employees to be given a lie detector test when they complain they are being harassed by a co-worker?"

"I'm afraid I can't discuss our security policies," Davis said. That was the sound of the famous Los Alamos wall of silence going up. Gil knew he wasn't going to get any more answers, so he hung up. As he waited for Joe to finish his call, he watched in the side mirror as the exhaust from their SUV swirled around the bumper. Something about it seemed peaceful.

"What are we thinking here?" Joe asked after he hung his phone. "Where did Tyler James Hoffman get this employee list from?"

"Dr. Price's house was the first one they robbed, so it makes the most sense they got the list from him," Gil said.

"Except Natalie Martin says she didn't know Dr. Price, so he wouldn't have had her address."

"Maybe they went to Dr. Price's house and he gave them

Dr. Ivanov's address," Gil said. "Then they went to Dr. Ivanov's house, and he gave them Natalie Martin's address."

"But according to Natalie Martin, Dr. Price didn't know Dr. Ivanov," Joe said. "The simplest answer would be that lab employees are given the names and addresses of all their co-workers, and Dr. Price had the newest list, with Dr. Ivanov's information on it, and gave that list to the killers."

"Even creating a list like that would be a huge breach of security." Gil said.

"I'm sure their boss knew them all," Joe said. "What was her name? Dr. Goodwin? And she would have their addresses. We should talk with her again."

Joe's phone rang, and he answered it with a "Yo." The person on the other end of the phone spoke, and as he listened, something in Joe's demeanor changed. He said a final, "Okay, thanks," then hung up.

"That was Dispatch," he said. "There's been another one."

CHAPTER EIGHTEEN

December 24

Kristen Valdez had followed Mary Gonzales out of Nambé Pueblo and toward Santa Fe. She had an easy time blending in with traffic on the highway with her little car. She wondered why she was following Mary. The governor had basically asked Kristen to do a welfare check—which police officers often do—on George Gonzales. If she had been doing it in an official capacity, she would have had a commanding officer tell her how to proceed now that the family said they no longer needed help. Instead, she wasn't sure what to do. According to the family, George Gonzales was fine. She could just take them at their word and head back home in time for breakfast. But she kept following the truck.

At the first traffic light, Kristen was two cars behind the truck when Mary turned left, down a dirt service road. Kristen slowed and watched the bumper of Mary's truck bounce over the ruts frozen into the mud. Kristen waited to turn onto the road, knowing that as soon as she did, Mary might catch sight of her. The truck drove another twenty feet, then stopped next to a mesh fence. Kristen knew exactly what that fence protected—the now-closed St. Catherine Indian School. It had been built in the 1890s by the Sisters of the Blessed Sacrament to serve as a private Catholic school, one of dozens of government and religious facilities created to "assimilate" native children into mainstream society. The students had to cut off their braids, take new English names, and stop speaking their tribal languages. There were horror stories from those schools: forced removal of children from homes, widespread beatings by teachers, and worse. But Kristen had never heard any such stories about St. Catherine's. Maybe it had always been a progressive school or maybe it had only been so since the cultural revolution of the 1960s, but St. Catherine's let its students not only keep their traditions, but celebrate them—as long as they still participated in the Catholic rituals. It became a place where kids wanted to go. In 1998, a hundred years after it opened, the Sisters found the school just too expensive to maintain. The last class graduated that year.

Kristen turned her car down the dirt road and drove until she pulled up behind the truck. Mary, who had been getting a baby's car seat out of the extended cab, turned to watch with a hand on her hip as Kristen got out of her car.

"What are you doing here?" Mary asked, clearly annoyed. The baby in the car seat blew bubbles and made smacking noises.

"I'm just trying to find George," Kristen asked.

"I told you we don't need your help," Mary said, as she

set the car seat down and started pulling the sleeping bag and camp stove out of the bed of the truck.

"I am only doing what the governor asked me," she said.

"It's not your business," Mary said, closing the doors.

"Is George in some kind of trouble?"

Mary didn't answer as she struggled to hold on to the camp stove and the sleeping bag while picking up the car seat.

"Listen, Mary," Kristen said. "If George is in trouble, do you really want to be taking your baby in there?"

Mary still didn't answer, but she had stopped trying to gather everything into her arms.

"As far as I know, he hasn't done anything wrong," Kristen said. "I can just go in there and get him, while you and the baby can stay in the warm car." Mary didn't respond, but she was listening, considering. Kristen continued, "We'll be back out in two seconds. Then he can go home so you can all celebrate Christmas together."

Mary finally nodded. Kristen helped her put the car seat back in the truck and tossed the camping gear in the truck bed. Kristen went back to her car and fastened her gun belt around her waist, under her coat, thinking she might need the flashlight hanging off it but not thinking about the gun. She had been able to get Mary to promise that she wouldn't call George to tell him Kristen was coming, since it would likely make him run.

Kristen walked down the dirt road, looking for a place either to scale the fence or crawl under it. The school itself consisted of dozens of abandoned buildings—some made of low cement brick, others of actual brick, and still others of stucco painted a burnt orange. As she walked, she took a long look at the cemetery across the road. It struck her as odd that the Indian school was built next to a graveyard.

The Navajo kids, with their strict prohibition against being near anything dead, must've had a hard time convincing their parents to let them attend. She once had a Navajo friend who tried out for a local modeling job. When her friend didn't get the part, a medicine man said it was because she had driven past a cemetery on the way to the audition. Her friend had to have a four-hour long ceremony to take the curse off her. It made Kristen glad that pueblo tribes didn't share the same belief.

Kristen found a small gate that made it easy for her to squeeze past the fence. The snow crunched under her feet, as did some shell casings. After the school had been abandoned, the city's SWAT team got permission to use some of the old buildings for urban rescue practice. They would set up training scenarios for rookies, recreating hostage situations and riot conditions, sometimes even using live ammunition. Kristen had heard that the Sisters of the Blessed Sacrament had hoped to sell the school to developers, which made her wonder how much the value would be depreciated due to the hundreds of bullet holes pockmarking the walls.

She walked up a slight hill, scaring a dark red cardinal, which flew out from a chamisa bush. The only things that still lived on campus were the animals. She could see their tracks in the snow—jackrabbits, sparrows, and raccoons—weaving in and out of the brush. On top of the hill, she stopped in front of a native-themed mural whose colors were still bright. In it, a young man with flowing hair reached up toward a bird. She turned the corner and found another mural, this time in a more geometric, petroglyph style, lining an archway. The nuns clearly had encouraged the students to express their world in art.

Through the arch, she noticed a path that had been

beaten down in the snow by someone. She followed it toward what looked to be an old-fashioned schoolhouse with a small belfry on the roof. She climbed the steep stairs up to the school and tried the door, expecting it to be locked, but it opened silently. The inside hallway had drifts of snow in it as well as a continuation of the tracks from outside. Someone had walked through here.

She went in slowly, not wanting to surprise anyone who was making the building his home. She turned into the first doorway on her right. It was a classroom with the chalkboard still on the wall and a few basketball jerseys thrown across some long wooden tables. A gust of wind made the windows rattle in their wooden frames. She went back out into the hallway and into the next room, where dozens of old desks were pushed up against the chalkboards lining the walls. She was turning to leave when she noticed someone sitting in a dark corner, away from the light of the windows. She unzipped her coat and thought about pulling out her flashlight, but instead unsnapped the leather latch holding her gun in its holster and put her hand on the butt. "Hello?" she called. The person didn't move. She called "hello" again. She thought she saw movement, and took a step back, tightening her grip on the gun. The person had shifted out of the shadows, but kept his face in the dark. She could tell it was a man, crouched down. He shifted position again, and she thought she saw a long dark braid of hair going down his back.

"George?" she called out.

"George Gonzales," she said. Still no movement. "George Gonzales. It's Kristen Valdez. I live down the street from you. Your wife, Mary, sent me here to find you. She's worried."

He raised his hand against the wall and stood up from his crouching position. He was mostly in shadow again, but Kristen could clearly see him. It was definitely Gonzales. She also could see his hands; neither held anything. She released her grip from her gun; her hand felt cramped from holding on to it so tightly.

"I need you to come out of the dark so we can talk."

He moved slowly into the sunlight falling through the crisscrossed windows. He wore jeans, wet up to the knees from the snow, and a green parka.

"George," she said, intentionally saying his name again to keep him centered—and to keep him mindful of their connection. "Can you do me a favor and unzip your jacket?" He wordlessly did as he was told. Kristen noticed a wide streak of something dark across the front.

"Is that blood on your shirt?" she asked, her hand automatically going back to her gun. Before he could answer, she said, "I need you to put your hands on your head." He lifted his arms up. As he did so, his T-shirt rose up as well, showing the top of his underwear peeking out from beneath the waistband of his jeans—and something else.

"Get down on your knees," Kristen yelled. Almost before she knew what she was doing, her Smith & Wesson was out of its holster and leveled at him. "Keep your hands on your head and get down on your knees, now!"

With his hands laced behind his head, he awkwardly got on one knee and then the other, as she kept her gun pointed at him, watching for the slightest movement he might make for the pistol tucked in his waistband.

Gil and Joe walked back into the hospital and asked the triage nurse where they could find the gunshot victim. They were sent back into the ER and found the right room. The door was closed. The commotion inside told them things weren't going well. Gil asked one of the passing nurses if the paramedics who'd brought the man in were still around. She pointed toward the break room where two men in dark blue uniforms and military-straight haircuts sat sipping coffee. Gil introduced himself and asked the paramedics to describe what had happened.

"We were dispatched to a heart attack call out in Tesuque," one said. "We got to this big-ass house, and the front door was wide open. We could see this guy laying in the living room. He was unconscious, with a bullet wound in his upper arm, so it was a load and go, and we hauled ass out of there and called police while we were en route here."

"Was he duct-taped to a chair or anything?" Joe asked.

"Not that we saw," he said. "He does have bruises on him."

"Did he wake up during the ride in?"

"Not really," he said. "Just some moaning."

"Do you know who made the nine-one-one call?" Gil asked.

"You'd have to ask Dispatch," he said. "But as far as we could tell, he was alone in the house."

"Did you get a name?"

"His driver's license said it was Brian Mazer."

Joe pulled out his notebook and flipped through some pages before saying, "He's on the list."

Lucy stood in line, waiting her turn to talk to the judge via video. She didn't quite know what to expect. New Mexico didn't mess around with drunk driving; it had learned its lesson. The state used to have more alcohol-related deaths than anywhere in the country. In 1982, 65 percent of all crashes involved alcohol. In 2009 that number had been reduced to 36 percent, thanks in part to tough new laws that required every person convicted of DWI to install something called an ignition interlock on his car. Lucy would have to get one put in and then blow into it, proving she was sober, before her car would start. And she'd have to do that for the next year. But she wasn't sure what else getting a DWI entailed. She had told Joe not to get her out because she didn't want to circumvent the system; she wanted to be treated like everyone else. And like everyone else, she'd plead not guilty when it was her turn to face the judge and he would set bail. After that, who knew?

Gil sent a city patrol officer to go secure Mazer's house as a crime scene and to back up the Santa Fe County deputy who had already been dispatched to the address. He and Joe stood outside Mazer's hospital room. Gil watched hospital staff members scuttle in and out, carrying gauze, bottles of medication, and IVs, while Joe was busy texting on his phone.

"What are you doing?" Gil asked.

"I'm asking that assistant preproduction manager, Melody, from the movie, if she knows Natalie Martin, her husband, or Mazer."

"That's a good thought," Gil said.

"Why do you sound so surprised?" Joe asked.

After another half hour a tall, dark-haired doctor came out pulling a pair of latex gloves off.

"The trauma surgeon is coming in for a consult. Most likely they'll do surgery to get the bullet out," she said.

"How's he doing?" Joe asked.

"Not too bad, considering," she said. "He sustained a gunshot wound to the upper arm and was beaten pretty badly. He's lost a fair amount of blood, but we pumped him full of fluids and he's stable now. I'm waiting for some test results to see if he'll need a blood transfusion."

"Has he said anything?" Gil asked.

"He was unconscious from the blood loss until just a few minutes ago," she said. "He's still pretty out of it, but you're welcome to talk to him until the surgeon gets here."

Gil and Joe went into the room, where a medical aide was picking up medical trash that had been thrown on the floor by staff as they worked. Mazer, who looked to be in his late forties, with a dark beard and a balding head, lay on the bed with his eyes closed. He was hooked up to an IV and heart monitor, with tubing winding its way to his body and back. His right arm was immobilized, and the upper part was wrapped in layers of gauze and tape. He had a black eye and heavy bruising on one side of his face, with a large cut on his temple that had been stitched up.

Mazer opened his eyes at the sound of the door closing behind Gil and tried to focus on them, confusion apparent across his face.

"We're police detectives," Gil said, keeping the introductions to a minimum for now so Mazer could understand the information in his deteriorated condition. "Can you tell us what happened?"

Mazer shook his head and whispered, "Didn't see him."

"Did someone break into your house?" Gil asked.

"They broke down the door."

"They?" Joe said. "There was more than one person?"

"I . . . don't know," he said, closing his eyes again.

Gil took out the picture of Abetya, "Have you ever seen this man?" Gil asked, raising his voice, making Mazer pop his eyes open. He looked at the photo for a second and licked his lips before saying no.

"How about this man?" Gil asked, showing him a photo

of Hoffman. Mazer looked at it, but closed his eyes again before he could answer.

"Mr. Mazer?" Gil asked, raising his voice, trying to rouse him again. But this time Mazer's eyes stayed closed.

George Gonzales was belly down on the floor of the school-house, his hands handcuffed behind his back.

"This is just a precaution," Kristen said. "I'll take them off you as soon as we have things straightened out." She had heard Detective Montoya say much the same to his suspects. It always seemed to have a calming effect.

"Are you injured?" she asked. "Where had the blood come from?" George didn't answer, so she snapped on some latex gloves she had stashed in another compartment in her belt and searched him. She found a lighter and some old tissue in his pockets, but no wounds on his body. The blood wasn't his.

Using the handheld radio clipped to her gun belt, she called for a patrol unit to transport George, since she had come in her personal car. Keeping the gloves on, she pulled an evidence bag out of a small zippered compartment on her gun belt and dropped the gun she had taken out of his waistband inside. She pulled George's wallet out of his back pocket and found his driver's license. As she was taking a picture of it, she noticed it listed an address in Santa Fe and not Nambé Pueblo. She took a picture of the gun as well and texted both photos to Joe, along with the message, "Found during welfare check. Suspect has blood on his shirt. Bringing him to station."

She took a moment to look out the windows of the schoolhouse, both to check if the patrol car had arrived and to see if Mary had decided to come find out what was going on. At her feet, George was making sniffling noises while sweat fell off his face onto the hardwood floor.

"Are you sick?" she asked. "There's something going around."

He didn't answer, but his face looked gray. Something occurred to her. "When was the last time you fixed? Has it been more than eight hours?" If so, then he wasn't sick in the usual sense. Instead, he was dope sick. When heroin users go into withdrawal, they get body aches, runny noses, and intense fatigue. In essence, they feel like they have the flu, only ten times worse.

"Two days," he said, so low that she had to strain to hear it. "Almost three." It was the first time he had spoken.

"You must really be hurting," she said. "I will get you some water as soon as we get to the station." They both went silent again. She knew she should be taking advantage of the fact that he had finally spoken, but she wasn't sure what to say. She decided to make small talk.

"I talked to your mom and your wife," she said.

He turned his head as best he could to look up at her and asked, "How are they?"

"They are really worried about you." He didn't respond. "I saw your kids, too. The baby is adorable." His face softened, and she knew she had found the right tack, but then heard the sound of the patrol car pulling up outside.

She got George up to his feet and escorted him outside. Another patrol car pulled up, and she heard a yell, and turned to see Mary Gonzales running awkwardly up the hill, toward them, hauling the baby's car seat with her. Kristen put George in the backseat of one of the patrol cars and closed the door just as Mary reached her, out of breath.

"What is going on?" Mary asked, as she tried to push

her way past Kristen. "You said you were just going to talk with him."

Kristen put her hands up to stop Mary from approaching the car. "There are just a few things we need to sort out."

"He hasn't done anything," Mary said, setting the car seat down while the baby inside it slept.

"That might be true, but he has blood on his shirt," Kristen said. "We have to figure out where that came from." What she didn't add was that the pistol she had taken off George had a long, thin barrel and a wooden grip on the handle—just like the Browning Natalie Martin had described.

The surgeon had gone into the room to exam Mazer, which meant Gil and Joe were back outside in the hospital corridor, standing around. As the surgeon came out, Gil waylaid him, asking about Mazer's prognosis.

"We're taking him up to surgery now," the doctor said.

"When can we have another chance to talk to him?" Gil asked, as Joe moved away to answer his ringing phone.

"Not until after the procedure," the doctor said. "The bullet hit his right radial collateral artery and possibly the middle collateral. I won't know for sure until I get in there. Give it about five hours, then check back."

"Is he in danger of dying?" Gil asked.

"Not if I can help it," the surgeon said, not actually answering the question.

Joe came back over to Gil, snapping his phone closed and saying quickly to the surgeon, "Can we have just another second with him? We just need to ask him two more questions." Gil looked at Joe, not sure what he was talking about. Before the surgeon could answer, an orderly brushed past them and went into Mazer's room. Joe was right behind him—through the door to Mazer's bedside. The surgeon made an exasperated sound but didn't move to stop him. Gil went into the room, too. Joe was showing Mazer, who had his eyes closed, the screen of his phone.

"Dr. Mazer," Joe was yelling. "I just need you to open your eyes. Open them . . . just open your eyes."

"Joe—" Gil had started to interrupt, needing an explanation from Joe, when Mazer opened his eyes.

"Good," Joe yelled. "Now look at the picture. Have you seen this man?"

Mazer nodded slightly.

"Who is he?" Joe asked.

"The man who shot me," Mazer said, groggy but audible.

"And is this the gun he shot you with?" Joe asked, sliding his finger over the phone's screen and holding up another picture on it for Mazer to see.

"Yes," Mazer said, closing his eyes again, then adding, "That's it."

"Thank you, sir," Joe said, almost joyfully. "Thank you."

Joe went back out of the room and said to Gil, "We need to go back upstairs and see if Natalie Martin can make a positive ID, too."

"What is going on?" Gil asked.

"We have a suspect in custody and the murder weapon," Joe said.

Gil stood in the observation room, looking through one-way glass at George Gonzales, who sat uncuffed in the interview room occasionally wiping his nose on his sleeve. Because they were needed as evidence, Gonzales had changed out of his bloody shirt and his jeans and shoes. He now sat in an orange inmate jumpsuit, although he was not under arrest—yet. It was a gamble, but Gil had decided to wait until after he'd interviewed Gonzales to give him a Miranda warning. Until Gil said the words "you have the right to remain silent," he wouldn't be able to use in court any statements Gonzales might make. Instead, he could use the information only to further the investigation. Joe had read over Gonzales's arrest record during the drive to the station. There were plenty of minor drug possession charges and a DWI, but nothing that reached the level of severity and brutality of the home invasions. As Joe had said as he read the reports, "Gonzales is a criminal, but he doesn't seem like a bad guy." Gil decided to use that as the premise of his interview—Gonzales as victim in the classic "wrong place, wrong time" situation. That would be the story Gil would spin. With any luck, Gonzales would pounce on that idea, agreeing that he wasn't a bad person, just in a bad situation. Having established this, Gil could then suggest to Gonzales that because he was a good guy, he would want to help set the record straight and tell his side of the story. The object of all of this was to give Gil what he sorely lacked at the moment: Gonzales's cooperation. Without it, they would never find Hoffman.

"How did he seem when you first found him?" Gil asked Kristen, who stood next to him in the observation room with Joe on her other side.

"He was quiet," she said. "The only time he spoke was when I told him his family was worried."

"What did he say?" Gil asked.

"He asked how they were," she said. "Oh, and he did say he was dope sick. It's been two days since he last fixed."

"Good job," Gil said, smiling at her so she would know he meant it. "Why don't you watch from here?"

"Actually, sir, I wanted to check on his wife," Kristen said. "She was on scene and followed us to the station. I just want to make sure she and her baby are somewhere out of the way."

"No problem," Gil said.

He went out to his desk, where he unclipped his gun holster from his belt and locked it in his desk drawer. He then grabbed a notebook and went into the interview room. Natalie Martin had identified Gonzales as well; he had willingly participated in the attack of the young family, yet Gil was about to make him believe he was a misunderstood hero—but it was the game Gil had to play.

Gil sat in the chair opposite Gonzales and started with his usual question. "Why do you think you're here today?"

Now that Gil was this close to him, he could see that Gonzales was having a hard time focusing his eyes, the lids half closed.

Gonzales didn't answer.

"You don't have any ideas why you are here?" Gil pressed. Gonzales just shrugged. His body language could have been interpreted to mean he was apathetic or relaxed, but he had his arms wrapped around him and didn't look up when he talked. He was scared—very scared.

"All right," Gil said. "Well, I think you should know, George, that our investigation will uncover all the details regarding the case. In light of that, if you know anything about it, you should tell me now."

Gonzales said nothing.

"Look," Gil said, leaning in. "I know some bad stuff has happened in the past couple of days. Things that anyone would have a hard time with. And I know you want to tell your side of the story."

Gonzales didn't answer.

"I know you were just a good guy who found himself in an impossible situation," Gil said.

Gonzales stayed quiet.

"Things probably just got out of control and you were stuck, right?" Gil asked.

Gonzales still didn't answer.

Gil leaned back. Gonzales wasn't taking the bait, which was unusual. This type of interrogation, which was used by investigators across the country, had a high success rate. As part of the tactic, Gil had specifically not asked Gonzales about the gun or the blood on his shirt. The idea had been for Gil to talk in generalities until he had built a rapport with Gonzales. A mention of specific evidence could shut the conversation down before it started. Gil needed to switch methods. He needed to shake him up a bit. He decided to see how Gonzales would react to a more concrete question. "Why don't you tell me about Tyler Hoffman?"

Gonzales's right foot began to bounce and he pulled his arms tighter around him, but he still didn't answer.

Kristen Valdez found Mary Gonzales out in the waiting room, near the receptionist desk, the baby asleep in her arms.

"Where is he?" Mary asked.

"He is being interviewed by some detectives," Kristen said.

"What?" she asked. "Why?"

"They just think he has some information about a case they are working on," she said. "We are trying to figure out as quickly as possible what is going on, I swear."

Mary shook her head and looked away.

"I just had a question for you that might help clear something up," Kristen said. "Why does George's driver's license list an address in Santa Fe when he lives in Nambé?"

"What? How does that matter?"

"I'm just curious. I need to tie up a few loose ends."

"He's had the license forever," she said. "Since before we were married. He lived in the city for a while a few years ago. I guess he just never changed it." New Mexico driver's licenses were good for eight years. It was a safe bet that many New Mexicans no longer lived at the address listed on theirs.

"Why do you care where he used to live?" Mary asked.

"Like I said, just tying up some loose ends," Kristen said. She told Mary good-bye, but instead of going back in the station, she went out to her car. She got in the front seat and fished her phone out of her pocket. She pulled up the screen listing the photos she had taken with the phone and found the picture of George Gonzales's driver's license. She took a second to look at the address—1267 Camino Dulce—before starting her car and heading to the outskirts of town.

Mentioning Hoffman's name had rattled Gonzales. He was more scared now. His eyes, which he'd had a hard time keeping open a few minutes ago, were focused on the wall behind Gil, unblinking. He had pulled his arms tighter around his body and was bouncing both legs. Gil needed to bring him back to safe ground. Kristen had mentioned that Gonzales was worried about his family. This was something Gil could use.

"I heard your wife is here," Gil said. "Do you want to talk to her?"

The effect was instantaneous. "She's here?" Gonzales asked, unwrapping his arms. "I don't want to see her." That was good news for Gil, who had been lying. There was no way he could let the two of them talk.

"Tell her not to go home," Gonzales said. "She has to go to her mother's."

"Why?" Gil asked. Gonzales didn't answer. "Are she and the kids not safe at home, George? Are you worried Hoffman will go after her?"

Gonzales didn't answer and kept bouncing his leg.

"We can protect them, George," Gil said. "I know you're worried about them. I saw what Hoffman did at the house up in Montaña Verde. I saw how he tortured those men and what he did to Pat Abetya."

"Who?" Gonzales said, turning to look at Gil, a slight frown in his forehead.

Kristen Valdez pulled her car off Old Pecos Trail and onto an unnamed dirt road that curved toward the mesas to the north. She knew where she was going but still kept count of the number of dirt roads she passed anyway, just to be certain she didn't make a wrong turn. She took a left and went over the washboard ruts, her little car jumping like a kid's bouncy inflatable castle at a carnival. The two Labrador-mix dogs came running out, barking and chasing her car. She pulled up in front of the old mobile home and put her gun belt on before going up the three metal steps to the front door and knocking. She didn't expect anyone to answer. There were still no cars in the driveway of the trailer, but she saw an old truck parked nearer to the house. She went down the steps and headed over to the old adobe home, the dogs at her heels. She walked past the cemetery and got to the house. She knocked, not really expecting anyone to answer. But this time someone did.

* * *

"So," Joe said slowly to Gil, who was back in the observation room looking at his notebook. "I think now is as good a time as any to bring up what is sure to be an unpopular topic."

"Which is what?"

"Do we still think that Abetya is involved?" Joe asked. He continued quickly, before Gil could interrupt. "Maybe he's not Mr. Burns. You saw Gonzales's face when you said his name. He had no idea who you were talking about."

"He was probably faking it," Gil said, still staring at his notebook, trying to figure out where to go next in the interview.

"But I think . . . I just don't feel like we are considering all the options," Joe said.

"How so?" Gil asked, flipping the page, debating whether to tell Gonzales about Dr. Mazer's identification of him as the shooter. Gil hadn't wanted to do that for the same reason he didn't want to mention the gun or blood—he needed a rapport with Gonzales, which he wouldn't get if he accused him of attempted murder.

"We started looking at Abetya because he, Jacobson, and Ivanov all worked on the movie set," Joe said. "And we thought that was how Hoffman and his crew were finding their victims. But now we know that all the victims are from the lab; it might not have anything to do with the movie. Plus, Gonzales has no idea who Abetya is. Maybe Abetya isn't involved."

"We aren't at a point to make that decision," Gil said as he flipped to another page.

"We still have a car outside Abetya's house," Joe said. "We could at least consider . . ."

Gil turned to look at Joe, and said in a low voice, "He had his cousin go threaten my mother with a gun to stop my dad from prosecuting him."

"Okay, I didn't know that," Joe said, speaking more slowly. "He's definitely a son of a bitch, and if we can send him to hell, I'm all for it. But, look, that girl Melody, on the film, texted me back. She's never heard of Natalie Martin, her husband, or Mazer. It's just really unlikely that Abetya's involved."

"We don't know that yet," Gil said. He had turned back to his notebook.

"You said it yourself, Santa Fe is a small town," Joe said. "People's lives overlap again and again. Maybe this is just an overlap that doesn't matter."

"You need to drop this," Gil said. He tried to say it as casually as he could, but it still sounded like a threat.

"Okay," Joe said. "Okay. No problem. Sorry."

They sat in silence. Joe tapped his hand against his leg, while Gil kept going over his notes.

Joe lasted only a minute before saying, "What if we just talk in generalities about how Abetya fits in the whole thing? Is that okay?"

Gil rolled his eyes. "Seriously?"

"Just listen for one second," Joe said. "So Tyler James Hoffman, Lupe Escobar, Pat Abetya, and George Gonzales somehow meet up with one another and say, 'Hey, you're evil. Let's do crime together.' Then they somehow get the addresses of all the laboratory employees who work in the Primary Structural Biosystems department and decide to kill them off one by one."

"When you put it that way, it sounds like they were working from a hit list rather than finding houses to rob," Gil said.

"Okay, that wasn't my point at all," Joe said. "I was trying to draw your attention to the fact that we don't know how all these bad people met each other."

* * *

The woman who opened the door was in her late sixties. She wore polyester pants with a floral blouse and her long gray hair pulled back in a bun. She stepped out onto the porch and shooed at the dogs while Kristen Valdez identified herself.

"I have a driver's license from George Gonzales, and it lists this as his address," Kristen said.

"Oh, George hasn't lived here in years," the woman said.

"He lived with you?"

"No, he lived in the trailer over there, with Johnny," she said. "They moved in together for a little while after high school." Kristen knew she looked confused, mainly because she hadn't expected to find anything here, least of all that George Gonzales had once lived with Lupe Escobar's drug dealer. Both men had Camino Dulce listed as their addresses, but Johnny Rivera's records had him living at 1241 Camino Dulce, while George Gonzales was at 1267. At first glance, it had seemed to Kristen that the different numbers would obviously belong to different houses. But the Rivera family likely owned the only property on the road, so any number combination listed as being on the street "Camino Dulce" would have ended up in their mailbox. When it came to deciding on addresses in the rural areas of the state, it often came down to guesstimating, leaving the mailman to deliver mail based more on the receiver's name than anything else.

"They went to St. Catherine's together?" Kristen asked.

"Yes," the woman said. "Well, mostly. Johnny got suspended his senior year, but he and George stayed friends. Johnny's mom had Santa Clara Pueblo blood, which is how he could go to an Indian school."

"So, are you related to Johnny?" Kristen asked.

"I'm Mrs. Rivera," she said. "His grandmother."

"When was the last time you saw him?" Kristen asked.

"Oh, let's see," she said. "He borrowed my car about a week ago, when his friends came over."

"Do you remember exactly what day that was?" Kristen asked, trying not to rush the words out.

"Let's see, it had to have been December nineteenth," she said. "I remember thinking it was my older sister's birthday. She's passed away now."

"I'm sorry," Kristen said automatically before asking, "Did you see his friends?"

"I only saw them from a distance as they got into the car," she said.

"How many people were there?"

"It was hard to tell," she said. "I think four. One of them was a girl. I heard her laugh. That kind of sound always carries. It made the dogs bark."

"Could one of the other friends have been George?"

"I guess," she said. "Although it would have been nice if he'd come over to say hello."

Kristen got a description of the vehicle—a 1998 Honda Civic—and wrote it down in a small notebook she'd fished out of her pocket. She thanked Mrs. Rivera and hurried back to her vehicle to call Joe, the dogs following along. She was about to open her car door when she turned to look at the graveyard. Tall brown weeds poked up from under patches of snow, and a few fake flowers, bleached almost white, were twisted among the fences around the graves. She put her keys back in her pocket and walked toward the cemetery. As she got close, she stopped to look at the egg-sized rocks that had been placed on the headstones. Kristen had never known anyone who wasn't Catholic. In grade school, high school, and even at the police academy, everyone she knew was a member of the Church. But she had seen *Schindler's List* and she remembered how, at the end of the movie, the Jewish families put small rocks on Oskar Schindler's grave. Her mother had said it was a Jewish custom, a way to remember and honor the dead. Kristen stopped next to the nearest headstone, which was a stone cross with two small rocks balancing on top of it. Hand-carved into it were the years 1885–1942 and the name Adonay Moises Rivera. She walked through the snow to the next tombstone and looked at the inscription: BELOVED WIFE AND MOTHER YSAAC RIVERA. Below the name, a cross had been carved into the stone, and on either side was etched a faint Star of David.

Gil sat across from George Gonzales. He held his notebook in his hand, but it was closed. Next to him on the floor was a covered file box with Gonzales's name on it. In front of him, between his chair and Gonzales's, was another box. This one was empty and uncovered. Since getting Kristen's call, Gil had stopped trying to figure out an interview strategy. Joe had been wise enough not to say "I told you so" within Gil's hearing afterward, but that didn't stop Gil from feeling momentarily adrift. He started to doubt his motives in pursuing Abetya, wondering if all he had been after was old-fashioned revenge, but he stopped himself mid-guilt. There would be time for that later. Now his only priority was finding Hoffman before he moved on to his next target.

Kristen's phone call had crystallized everything for Gil. He had all the pieces he needed. That meant he could do a soft interrogation. It was the method preferred by security firms when interviewing employees suspected of stealing. But it worked only when a strict time line of the crime could be established. It was simple enough: the interrogator presents all the evidence without asking the suspect for input or even allowing him to talk. The interrogator makes it clear that the investigation is wrapped up and that the person is completely guilty. This puts the suspect on the defensive and ready to listen.

"George, we are almost done," Gil said. "We have all the information we need to make our case. We know that you, along with three accomplices, committed four home invasions within the last week. I can guarantee you, George, that our investigation will uncover all the details regarding these cases. In light of that, if you know anything about it, you should tell me now."

Gil didn't wait for Gonzales to respond. He was done playing games. "On December nineteenth, you, Tyler Hoffman, Guadalupe Escobar, and Johnny Rivera met at Rivera's house to plan a series of home invasions." He spoke matter-of-factly, with little intonation, as if he were reading the weather report on the radio. "At some point that day, you went to the store and, using a list that Ms. Escobar had written out, bought the following items." Gil took the cover off the closed box and took out an evidence bag containing the handwritten murder list. He read out loud: "Beer, box cutters, duct tape, trash bags, pads, and Tampax." Gil took the evidence bag and threw it in the empty box in front of him. It wasn't the real list. That one was still down with Liz, in the Albuquerque crime lab, in an evidence locker where it would stay until the trial. This one had been written by Joe, who had forged it as best he could.

"On December twentieth you went to the house of James Price and Alexander Jacobson. Both men were tortured. Someone cut off Alexander Jacobson's genitals and put them into James Price's mouth. My guess is that was Tyler Hoffman, and he also was the one who carved the letter *T* into Alexander Jacobson's chest." Gil pulled an evidence bag containing the slightly bloody duct tape that had been used to tie down Dr. Price and looked at it a moment before throwing it into the empty box.

This duct tape had actually come from Gil's desk drawer. Joe had dripped some ketchup over it then dried it using the hand dryer in the men's restroom. Gil would never have used the real evidence in an interrogation. There was too much of a chance it would get damaged. Plus, the more people who handled the evidence, the more likely a defense lawyer could get it thrown out for contamination.

"At some point, Johnny Rivera was tied up and hung from the ceiling in the back bedroom, where he was tortured and then burned. We know it was him because genetic testing matched the body to someone of his ancestry." Gil pulled out an evidence bag with some ash in it. He wasn't sure what Joe intended the ash to be. In actuality, it was just some burned paper and white pieces of broken plastic. Gil thought maybe Joe had intended it to look like human flesh and bone. "On December twenty-first, you went to Stanley Ivanov's house. Mr. Ivanov was tortured as well, and someone carved an *L* into his chest. I am assuming that was Ms. Escobar." Without waiting for Gonzales to respond or defend himself, Gil continued, "On December twenty-second, you went to the Martins' house, where you tied up Natalie and Nick Martin. You tried to get the keys for their Pontiac Tempest, but before you could, Natalie Martin was able to get away. As you were leaving, someone shot Nick Martin in the head. I am going to assume that was you," Gil said, as he took out an evidence bag containing a generic car key—Joe's, actually—and threw it in the box.

For the first time, Gonzales started to speak, "Wait that wasn't—" Gil could see the glint of sweat on his forehead.

Gil continued, ignoring him. "That brings us to today, when you went to Brian Mazer's house and beat him up. At some point, Brian Mazer was shot. And this time we know it was you who shot him because he identified you before he went into surgery, and we found the gun on you." Gil reached into the box next to him and took a picture of the Browning he had printed out, throwing it into the box in front of him.

"Hold on—"

"Just as I was coming back here to talk with you, I got a text from my partner." Gil took out his phone and read the text from Joe. "Brian Mazer pronounced dead at 1430 hours." Gil held up the phone so Gonzales could see the text. "So that means you will be charged with murder." Gil put his notebook into one of the boxes and started to pack them up.

"Wait . . . wait," Gonzales said, trying to stop Gil from leaving. "I didn't murder him. It was self-defense. I swear."

Gil stopped for a second, but then opened the door and walked out.

Gil stood in the hallway holding his two boxes of fake evidence and looked at Joe.

"We need to let Gonzales go," Joe said. "He was just doing what any of us would have done when threatened by a beaten man tied to a chair. It was clearly self-defense."

When Gil didn't react, Joe sighed and said, "Fine, I will go put the word out to patrol to be on the lookout for the Honda Civic Johnny Rivera borrowed." Joe took the boxes from Gil, who went back into the room with Gonzales.

"Tell me how you met Hoffman," Gil said, sitting down.

"I just want to make sure that nothing I tell you will come back on me . . ."

Gil stood up and started to walk out the door. His hand was on the knob when Gonzales said behind him, "Okay, okay. Just tell the lawyers that I am helping you."

"How did you meet Hoffman?" Gil asked again, sitting down.

"It was just like you said," Gonzales said, wiping his nose. "I went over to Johnny's place, you know, just to hang out." The pitch of his voice was a little too high, which probably meant "hang out" was code for something illegal, such as buying drugs. "I was just sitting on a couch when this guy comes out from the back room and says his name is Ty. We have some beers and I say how I need some cash. Ty says he knows of this ripe house where the man just has money laying around. He said it would be a quick in-and-out. So we get in Johnny's car. On the way, Ty says we need a fourth person, so we pick up Lupe at her place."

"Johnny was Lupe's dealer, so that's how he met her and Ty?" Gil asked.

"Yeah," Gonzales said. "I guess. So we pull up to this big-ass house and Ty grabs this baseball bat that Johnny kept in the backseat. He goes right up to the door, turns the knob like he knew it would be open, and yells, 'I'm home.' This guy comes out in his bathrobe and Ty just swings at his head with the bat. And then there's blood everywhere, and he drags the guy over to this chair in the dining room and just starts tying him up with duct tape then cutting on him with a box cutter. I'm freaking out, and I want to get the hell out of there—"

"Hold on, there was one guy at the house, not two?" Gil asked, knowing that the house Gonzales was talking about had to be Price and Jacobson's.

"Nah, just the one guy," Gonzales said.

"What day was this?"

"I dunno," he said. "The first day."

"On December nineteenth?" Gil asked. "And where was this house?"

"In Tesuque."

That meant that the first house hit wasn't Price and Jacobson's. It was Mazer's.

"What happened next?"

"Ty was like 'This is my house. Make yourself at home.' Then he turns a TV on and sits on the couch and starts watching a game. We drank the guy's wine and had some leftovers. I passed out. I don't think Ty slept at all. Next thing, it was morning and Ty says we have another job to do."

"What happened to the man in the chair?"

"I don't know. The chair was still there in the dining room, but he was gone. I didn't see him. I just followed the guys outside."

"What happened next?"

"Ty gets in the man's SUV and hands this paper to Johnny and tells him we're going to the house owned by these gay guys because they'll have better stuff than most people."

"What was on the paper?"

"It was a list of names and, like, their addresses and what kind of stuff they had." Gil nodded. So it was Mazer who had given the home invasion crew his co-workers' addresses. But given the circumstances, he'd probably thought he had little choice. "What else can you tell me about the list?" Gil asked.

"It was a printout, like from a computer," Gonzales said. "There was, I think, like, five names on it."

"Five names? Do you remember any of them?" The crew had already hit three houses on the list, not including

Mazer's. They had to find out where the other residences were in case Hoffman and Escobar decided to keep at it.

"No. I didn't really see it. I just remember Ty saying that doing five houses was good, that it was enough to have some fun and not so much that we'd get caught."

"What happened when you got to the next house?"

"The same thing," he said. "Ty goes and busts down the door and ties the guys up."

"What did you do?"

"Nothing, really," he said. "We just hung around and watched TV and, you know, I took a nap and Lupe and Johnny were playing pool. They had a really nice Xbox."

"What happened to Johnny?" Gil asked.

"Ty was going kind of crazy," he said. "It was bad ... worse than before. Ty—we were just sitting there, and he gets up and starts cutting on the gay guys, but not like before, with the other guy. He's cutting one guy's junk, and there's all this blood and screaming." Gonzales shifted in his chair, then crossed his arms over each other in an act of self-comfort. "I just had never seen anybody do anything like that. And Johnny—he couldn't take it. He said he was leaving, and Ty hits him from behind, drags him to a back room, and ties him to the ceiling."

"What did Ty do to Johnny?"

"I can't—he made us cut on him ... not for any reason; just to make a point," he said. "Johnny—he and I were tight ..." His eyes started to tear up, his face lined in grief.

Gil interrupted, asking, "What happened next?" He couldn't let Gonzales dwell on his friend. He needed to hear the rest of the story. Gonzales didn't answer right way, wiping a tear out of his eye. "What happened next?" Gil asked again, more firmly, less caring.

"Ty went back out into the living room," Gonzales said,

after a moment. "Seconds later, I hear two shots. And I realize he's shot the gay guys. Then Ty comes back in the bedroom, takes a bottle of vodka, and dumps it on Johnny and lights him on fire. He's on fire in front of me—holy shit, his screams . . . and that smell." Gonzales stopped, shaking his head, tears in his eyes. "But then the fire went out, and Johnny was still alive and just kind of moaning. So Ty goes out to the garage and comes back with gasoline and lights him on fire again. He went up so fast, and then the ceiling caught fire, so we booked it out of there."

"Where'd you go?"

"Back to the first house."

"You went back to the house in Tesuque?"

"Yeah," he said. "We kind of just hung out there all week. Last time I saw Ty, he was still there."

CHAPTER NINETEEN

December 24

Lucy had already had her turn in front of the judge, and was watching the other women in her cell block take their turns, when a corrections officer came over to her and said, "Your bail has been posted."

"Really?" she said. "By whom?" But the corrections officer said he didn't know. He led her out of her cell and over to the locker where she had stored her clothes and purse. As she got changed, she wondered who her savior was. Most likely Tommy, since she had been pretty clear with Joe that she didn't want any help. She tied her shoes and headed toward the front of the building, collecting her court appearance paperwork along the way. She went through the heavy metal door and into the glass-and-tile lobby.

And there was Nathan.

* * *

Joe was waiting for Gil when he left the interview room. With him was Kristen. Before Gil could thank her for her help, Joe started ranting.

"Those bastards held Brian Mazer for a week," Joe said, pacing the hallway. "Jesus. That guy will need more than surgery. I'm thinking sessions twice a week with a shrink. We saw what Hoffman did to Price and Jacobson, and he had them for only a day."

"The best thing we can do for Mazer is find Hoffman," Gil said.

"Yep," Joe said. "So I ran down Mazer's car, thinking that was what Hoffman was driving, since when we saw him he sure as hell wasn't in no Honda Civic."

"Let me guess, it's a dark SUV," Gil said.

"Yup. A black Lexus RX, and I am embarrassed as hell that I couldn't remember that. You'd think a Lexus would stick in my mind more."

"We saw it for only a second."

Joe continued, "I called the officer we put in front of the house, but he says no one has come in or out. We should send an unmarked unit over to replace him. If Hoffman happens to drive by, I don't want him to get spooked by a police car."

"Good idea," Gil said. "But we really need to know if Hoffman is there or long gone."

"I say we activate SWAT and let them figure out if he's there or not," Joe said as he stopped pacing for the moment.

"Is the Lexus in the driveway?" Kristen said, speaking up for the first time. "Or the Civic?"

"Uh . . . I'm not sure. Good question," Joe said. "Let me call the officer who's been in front of the house." A minute later, Joe hung up, saying, "Okay, the thing is, the officer can't see the house from the road. It's another one of those long driveways like at Price and Jacobson's house."

"So, he's really just watching the front of the property," Kristen said. She turned to Gil. "We don't know what's going on up at the house. I can take my car and go relieve the guy out front. Then I can just go take a walk to go see if the Lexus is even there."

Joe muttered, "That's not going to happen."

She ignored him. "We have to know if Hoffman is in there before SWAT goes in. If they go in and he's not home we've just blown our chance to get him." SWAT, by necessity, was not known for their stealth. They made a lot of noise when they went into a house, and they left behind a lot of boot prints, broken doors, tire tracks, and shell casings when they cleared out. Hoffman would take off as soon as he saw someone had been there.

"We can just send the officer in front of the house—" Joe started to say, but Kristen interrupted.

"He's in uniform. If Hoffman sees him, he'll run. I'm already in street clothes. If Hoffman sees me, I'll wave and pretend to be a neighbor." She turned to look at Gil. "I know exactly what kind of suspect we are dealing with."

He knew why she was stressing her last point. When a police officer got shot on the job, a department would spend countless hours determining if there was a precipitating event or one avoidable reason it happened. In the majority of cases, it came down to one simple thing: officers get shot when they don't know what they are walking into. Gil could prep the officer sitting in front of the house, telling him about Hoffman and giving him a rundown of the crimes Hoffman had committed, but the truth was Kristen knew better than anyone—better than Gil himself—what

Hoffman was capable of. She had seen it as the first arriving officer at the Martin house.

Gil thought for another second before saying, "Our priority has to be finding Hoffman, so Kristen, you can go over there. But you will wear a vest at all times and take every precaution, do you understand?" She nodded. Gil said, "Grab some paper and a pen and come with me."

Kristen followed Gil into the interview room.

"George," Gil said. "Officer Valdez here has some paper, and she'll help you draw a map of the outside of the house in Tesuque. Show her where there are any outside buildings or trees. Then draw a floor plan of the house." The floor plan would be for SWAT, while the map of the outside would be for Kristen. And they'd print out another map for her, from Google Earth, for comparison, just to be safe.

Gil went back out to where Joe was waiting, looking annoyed.

"Listen," Gil said to him. "I know you want to be the one going out there and gathering intel. You hate waiting here, but we have to figure out the other two names on that list Mazer gave Hoffman, because if Hoffman isn't at the house . . ."

". . . He might be at someone else's house duct-taping them to a chair," Joe said. "I get it." There had been seventeen employees in the Primary Structural Biosystems department before Hoffman started his spree. Minus his four victims so far, that made thirteen employees who could possibly be the last two names on the list Mazer had given Hoffman. Joe and Gil had asked patrol cars from the various county and city districts to their keep an eye on those thirteen people, but there was no guarantee how that had panned out. Hoffman might be outside his next victim's house right now.

Gil looked at his watch. "Mazer will be out of surgery in

a few more hours. We can ask him then who else was on the list he gave Hoffman."

"And when we get into Mazer's house, we can check his print job history and reprint it," Joe said.

"That's good," Gil said. "It will most likely take Kristen half an hour or so to go over to the house and check about the car. Then we call SWAT."

"It'll be at least an hour or hour and a half until we can get in there," Joe said. He started to pace. They had to find Hoffman.

"What if we call Natalie Martin?" Gil said. "Maybe she can tell us why, out of seventeen co-workers, Mazer put her name on that list."

Natalie Martin's phone went to voice mail, so Gil left a message. He was starting to catch Joe's nervous energy while they waited for Kristen's call. He left Joe to his pacing in the hallway and went back into the interview room with Gonzales.

"We need to talk about the blood on your shirt," Gil said. "So what happened?"

"I dunno, I just finally decided to get out of there."

"What made you decide that?"

"Ty had let Lupe go home to see her family, but he wouldn't let me leave," he said. "That made me nervous, like maybe he's not letting me leave because he wants to kill me. I just made a plan to get to the front door, open it, and get the hell out."

"What went wrong?"

"The guy from the chair started screaming."

"He wanted you to take him with you?"

"No, he starts screaming at the top of his lungs for Ty to come."

"He was yelling for Ty to come and stop you?"

"Yeah," Gonzales said. "I went for the front door, but Ty came running out with the baseball bat, so I tried to get to the back door, and the guy in the chair, he tackled me."

"He wasn't tied to the chair?"

"No. Ty had let him go a while before. He grabbed at me, and he had the gun in his hand and we fought for it."

"*He* had the gun? Not Ty?"

"No, *he* had it. I grabbed it from him, and Ty swung the bat at me, and I took a shot, but I must have missed and hit the guy instead. I didn't see what happened. I got to the back door and I just hauled ass. Even when I hit the snow, I just kept going."

"The blood on your shirt was from when you shot the man who'd been tied to the chair?"

"It must have been, yeah."

Back out in the hallway, Joe was pacing again. "What the hell?" he said to Gil the second he closed the interview room door behind him. "Mazer tried to help Hoffman? What is that about?"

"Maybe Mazer had Stockholm syndrome," Gil said. "He was kept there for nearly a week, and Hoffman was probably beating him and threatening to kill him. Maybe the only way for him to survive was to convince Hoffman he was on his side. Maybe he bought into his act too much."

"Maybe," Joe said. "But no matter how you slice it, that is fucked up. But that isn't the only thing."

"What do you mean?"

"I started thinking about how EMS just happened to show up at Mazer's house," Joe said. "We never did find out who called them."

"Maybe Mazer did before he went unconscious."

"That's what I was thinking," Joe said. "I also was

thinking that maybe Mazer told the nine-one-one operator who shot him or something. So I called Dispatch. They're sending me the audio file of the call."

A few minutes later, Joe was at his office computer downloading the file. "It looks like the call came from the house phone, so it was probably Mazer. Good. Give me a second." A moment later, Joe hit the SPACE bar on his computer to play the recording.

The operator's voice said, "This is nine-one-one. What is the nature of your emergency?"

A young male voice said quickly, "He's having a heart attack."

"Okay, can you tell me your address?"

"He's not looking very good. He's calling me . . . I have to go."

Then the line went dead.

Kristen crouched in the snow, her jeans getting wet and cold. She had parked her car down the street from Mazer's house and gone through the piñon and juniper forest on foot. The nearest neighbor was two acres away, so she was able to skirt easily around the Mazer house and then behind it. The house, like all the neighboring houses, had no landscaping or cultivated yard. Instead, it was just stuck in the middle of the forest, which made for easy cover.

She moved slightly to the north, hoping to get a better glimpse of the driveway, but a small rise and a thick tree stand meant she'd have to get closer. The shining sun made a bright white patchwork mosaic in the snow. Kristen kept out of the light and stayed with the shadow of the trees. She heard a door open somewhere nearby and froze. The deep snow both muffled and deepened the sound, making it hard to determine where it was coming from. She stayed crouched where she was for another few minutes, then carefully made her way up the hill to the driveway, which curved around the back of the house. There was no garage or shed. But in the driveway was a Honda Civic and a dark Lexus SUV. Hoffman was home. Kristen stayed where she was, surveying the one-story house for another few minutes before retracing her steps back down the hill.

After Joe listened to the 911 call, his pacing only got worse. "Was that Hoffman?" he asked. "That sounded like Hoffman." Gil let Joe keep talking. Interrupting him to point out that they'd met Hoffman only once and that neither of them could remember what his voice sounded like would have been useless. Besides, Gil agreed with Joe: it seemed likely that the voice was Hoffman's. "Why would Tyler James Hoffman call an ambulance for Mazer?" Joe asked. "Hoffman's killed, what, a half dozen people, yet he calls the ambulance? For Mazer? What the fuck."

"He's a sociopath," Gil said.

But Joe kept talking. "Does Stockholm syndrome go both ways? Could Hoffman have been feeling all soft and fuzzy for the guy?"

"The only reason he'd have called an ambulance for anyone is if he was going to get something out of it," Gil said.

But Joe wasn't done. "Maybe Hoffman is feeling some goodwill-toward-man Christmas crap."

Gil's phone rang. It was Natalie Martin calling him back. "I'm sorry to bother you," he said. "How's your husband doing?"

"He squeezed my hand when he got out of surgery," she said. "The doctors said that was a good sign."

"That's great news," Gil said. "I know you probably want to get back to him, but I have a few quick questions for you."

"Okay."

"We think that Hoffman got the list of you and your co-workers from Dr. Brian Mazer," Gil said.

"Brian?" she said, surprised. "We've worked together for years. He's one of the few people who everyone liked."

"Did he have any problems with you, Dr. Price, or Dr. Ivanov?"

"I'm not sure about Dr. Price," she said. "But Brian and Dr. Ivanov were friends. They carpooled every day before Dr. Ivanov retired."

"So Dr. Mazer knew where Dr. Ivanov lived?" Gil asked.

"Yes," she said. "Actually, come to think of it, there was one little thing between Brian and Dr. Ivanov. Brian wanted to move into Dr. Ivanov's lab when he retired, but his request was denied. Brian said Dr. Ivanov was the one responsible. They had both been working on the same demethylation protein code sequence for years, and I guess Dr. Ivanov didn't want Brian to break the code when he hadn't been able to. At least that's what Brian said. They weren't really friends after that. I'd heard that Dr. Price moved into Dr. Ivanov's lab instead."

"How was your relationship with Dr. Mazer?"

"Brian was the only person from work who came to my baby shower."

"And your baby shower, was it held at your house?" Gil asked.

Natalie Martin hesitated, then said, "Yes."

"So he knew where you lived?"

"Yes," she said slowly. "And Nick showed him the Tempest. They went out to the shed together . . ." Her voice trailed off.

"Mrs. Martin what else—" Gil started to say, but she interrupted him.

"Brian was the only person who knew I was pregnant," she said in the same urgent voice of realization. "I didn't tell anyone else at work, because we didn't share those kinds of things, but Brian . . ."

"Mrs. Martin?"

"He was the only one who knew I had cleaned out all my chemicals." She stopped, but Gil waited for her to continue. When she spoke again, her voice was high. "*He* put the ethidium bromide in the gel. Why would he have done that? Why would he have tried to hurt my babies?"

"Mrs. Martin, I am so sorry."

"I just saw him three days ago. How could he—and he smiled and he asked about the boys . . ."

"You saw him three days ago?" Gil asked. "Are you sure?"

"Yes, it was the day before the attack," she said. "I bumped into him at Whole Foods."

"He was shopping?"

"Yes," she said. "He said he had family over, and he asked me about my Christmas plans."

"How did he look? Did he act nervous?"

"He seemed fine," she said. "He had a couple of bruises, but he said that was from slipping on some ice."

"What time of the day was this?"

"Um, it must have been close to dinnertime. I remember the kids were acting crazy because they were starving. He told me about the Christmas party they'd had that day at work and said he was there buying food for a relative he had staying with him."

"He'd been at work that day?" Gil asked.

"He must have been," Natalie said.

CHAPTER TWENTY

December 24

Gil and Joe both sat in the conference room. Gil stared at the white board while Joe rubbed his eyes.

After hanging up with Natalie Martin, Gil had gone back into the room with Gonzales, who mapped out as best he could Mazer's whereabouts for the past week. After a few minutes, it became clear that Mazer was tied up only on the first day. And Gonzales saw Hoffman hit and cut Mazer only a little, in the beginning. After that, the knife and fists stayed out of it. Gonzales saw Mazer a few more times, and each time he was untied, walking about the house. Gonzales never thought to ask Hoffman why their hostage was being allowed to walk free.

"Gonzales is lying," Joe said. "He has to be lying."

"Why would he lie about it?" Gil asked. They were waiting for a call back from Chip Davis at the lab. He was checking to see if any surveillance equipment had caught Mazer at work that day.

"Maybe Mrs. Martin is wrong about the date," Joe said.

"She seemed pretty sure," Gil said.

"Maybe Mazer cut a deal with the devil," Joe said. "He would give Hoffman the names if Hoffman didn't kill him."

"That makes the most sense," Gil said as his phone rang. It was Davis. Gil put the phone on speaker, knowing Joe would just breathe heavily at his ear trying to hear the conversation if he didn't.

"Dr. Mazer was at work all week," Davis said. "He left early for the past few days, but it's almost Christmas, so most people aren't even at their desks."

"No one mentioned anything strange about him or saw his bruises?"

"No," Davis said. "But they all have separate labs and offices. He could easily have come and gone without seeing anyone."

"You don't happen to have his personnel file handy, do you?" Gil asked. "The least we can do is tell his relatives that he has been hurt." The real reason Gil wanted the name of a family member was to ask them about Mazer's state of mind. But there was something else, something in the back of Gil's mind. Something he couldn't quite get at.

"Hang on," Davis said. Gil heard him typing into a computer. Davis came back on the line. "I don't really have much. He's divorced, but it looks like they had a child a while back."

"Do you have a name?"

"Sorry," he said. "Whoever compiled this information did it before my time. They didn't follow the same procedures when filling out the forms that we do now. It's hard to tell. I'll keep looking though this, but all I can really tell you is that Dr. Mazer hasn't had any contact with his child or his ex-wife for a long time, otherwise they'd be on our radar."

"Do you have anything about the ex-wife? Did she remarry? Is there a stepdad in the picture?"

"Hold on . . . hold on. Yeah, it looks like she remarried. His name is Philip Hoffman."

As the investigating officers, Gil and Joe needed to be there when Hoffman was arrested. But Hoffman was armed and dangerous. That meant there also needed to be a coordinated assault on the house, which was a SWAT specialty. SWAT would handle the entry and timing of the mission. The schedule had the team arriving at Mazer's house in twenty-five minutes, since they wanted to make entry before it started to get dark and sunset was in forty-five minutes. It would take Gil and Joe fifteen minutes to get to Mazer's house in Tesuque from the hospital in order to meet them before the raid. That left exactly ten minutes for Gil and Joe to question Dr. Mazer, who had just gotten out of surgery.

The surgeon warned them that Mazer would be groggy and likely wouldn't remember any of the conversation, since he'd been given midazolam for sedation, and the drug's side effects included amnesia.

"Sounds good to me," Joe said to Gil. "If we add a few more bruises to his collection during our interrogation, he'll be none the wiser." Maybe it was the lack of sleep coupled with the level of violence in the case, but Gil no longer much cared how he got the information he needed. In the five days since he had given Hoffman the list of names, Mazer had gone to work, the grocery store, and any number of other places. He could have warned Price, Jacobson, Ivanov, and the Martins. He could have called the police. He could have stopped Hoffman. He could have done anything—but he'd chosen to do nothing. Gil knew that this was because Mazer got something out of keeping quiet. He got to get rid of people he'd thought had wronged him while simultaneously gaining the trust of his long-lost son.

Mazer lay in his bed in the surgery recovery suite. His eyes fluttered open when Joe called his name.

"You're not going to remember any of this," Joe said. "So let me just get this out of the way. You are nothing but a motherfucking—"

"Joe," Gil said. "Knock it off. We don't have time for that."

"I never get to have any fun," Joe said in a pretend pout.

"Dr. Mazer," Gil said. "A heavily armed SWAT team is about to storm your house. Do you understand?"

Mazer was so drugged that his only reaction to what Gil had said was a slight wrinkling of his forehead, but he nodded, saying yes at the same time.

"You need to answer my questions in order for everyone to come out of it alive," Gil said. Mazer nodded again, and Gil continued, "Is Tyler Hoffman your son?" A nod from Mazer. "Is he alone in the house?"

Mazer shook his head and said in a hoarse voice, "Lupe is with him."

"Anyone else?"

He shook his head.

"What are the two other names on the list you gave to your son," Gil asked.

"Dr. Laura Goodwin and Chad Saunders."

"The security guard?" Joe asked. "Killing your boss I get—she is one cold fish—but what did you have against the security guard?"

Gil gave Joe a look and asked, "How many weapons are in the house?"

"I have a shotgun and two rifles," Mazer whispered.

"How much ammunition?" Gil asked.

"I don't know."

"Think," Joe said, closer to Mazer's ear.

"I don't—I have a box of shells for the shotgun and maybe a half of a box for the rifles."

"That's twenty-five rounds for the shotgun and ten for the rifles" Joe said to Gil. That was a lot of firepower.

"Dr. Mazer," Gil said, "I am taking you into custody for aiding and abetting a fugitive. While you are in the hospital, there will be an officer guarding you at all times. Once you are released, you will be brought directly to the county detention center, where you will be placed under official arrest pending formal charges. At that time, your rights will be read to you in full; however, you do have the right to speak to a lawyer immediately. Do you understand?"

"Don't . . . ." Mazer started to whisper, before stopping to cough.

"Don't what?" Joe asked.

"Don't hurt him," Mazer said, his voice fading as he reached the end of the sentence. "Tyler only came here to see me."

"Why would he do that?" Joe asked.

"He wanted me to meet my new granddaughter," Mazer said in a whisper. "Her name is Georgina Rose."

Kristen had kept watch over the Mazer's house until Gil and Joe arrived. The first thing Gil did was send her home. She tried to convince him to let her stay, hoping she could be there for the arrest, but Gil insisted she go. It was Christmas Eve after all, and her family would be waiting. Plus, she had her personal car, not an official vehicle, and was in street clothes, not her uniform. If things went badly, her fellow offers wouldn't automatically know she was one of them. And when it came down to it, not even Gil or Joe would be there to witness Hoffman getting handcuffed for the first time. That honor would be left to the Special Weapons and Tactics team, which, because of dangers inherent in their job, always operated alone. Gil and Joe would have to stay outside the perimeter and wait for the all-clear.

Kristen reluctantly drove away just as the SWAT team pulled up in their navy blue Chevy Suburban. As the men got out and started to gear up, Gil told the SWAT commander about the number of weapons and the amount of ammunition in the house. Then he got back into the Ford Explorer to wait, where Joe was supposed to be calling Chip Davis to tell him that Dr. Laura Goodwin and Chad Saunders were the next targets. Instead, he was saying to the person on the other end, "And this was during the outbound inspections on the Juárez–Lincoln International Bridge?"

"Who are you calling?" Gil asked.

"Yes, I can wait," Joe said into the phone, and then to Gil, "I'm on hold with Border Patrol."

"Why?"

"Wait a second," he said to Gil and then said back into the phone, "Huh . . . okay . . . what day was this? . . . Great. Okay, thanks."

Joe hung up, and Gil asked, "Did you call Chip Davis?"

"Yeah, of course," Joe said. "That's all taken care of. But listen to this. Just yesterday Blanca Escobar passed through customs on her way back into Mexico."

"With the baby?"

"Yep," Joe said. "Somehow Blanca had paperwork

showing she was the mother, so she got through no problem. Georgina Rose is safely in Mexico, where Tyler James Hoffman and Mazer can't get to her or fight for custody."

Gil saw a blur of movement out of the corner of his eye and looked up to watch as the SWAT team silently moved toward the house. A K-9 unit waited on the road, in case Hoffman decided to run. If the Santa Fe Police had been able to afford a helicopter, it would have been there. As it was, there were only the five SWAT members dressed all in black, moving like shadows against the white snow. Gil watched as they made their way up the driveway. Then they were out of sight. The plan was for SWAT to break up into two teams, Team A and Team B, when they were within twenty feet of the house. The three-man Team A would go to the front door, while the two-man Team B made their way to the back. Before getting into position to make entry, Team A had the job of covering Team B as they secured a sliding glass door on the side of the house by quietly laying a thick metal dowel into the door's running track. If anyone inside tried to slide the door open, it would jam in the track. Both teams would then get into position in the front and back of the house, but while Team A made entry, Team B would simply cover the back door and the perimeter. Once inside, a SWAT member would guard the front door from the inside while a now two-man Team A moved as a unit through each room of the house, looking for Hoffman as they went.

More than five minutes had passed since Gil had watched SWAT disappear down the driveway. He knew they had to be in position, ready to make entry, but the two teams were radio silent, which was protocol so the suspect wouldn't hear them approach. A minute later, Gil heard the SWAT team leader at the front door say, "Set." He heard the second-in-command with Team B say, "Set." Then the team leader said a single word, *Go*. There was a boom from the breaching round of a shotgun.

"Avon calling," Joe said with a smile. The breaching round, which was a twelve-gauge shell with a projectile made of powdered steel and covered in wax, fit into a regular combat-sized shotgun and would disintegrate a deadbolt lock or a door hinge with one shot. SWAT was inside the house with Hoffman, but there was no noise. Nothing on the radio. Silence. All Gil could see were the footprints SWAT had left in the snow.

To the left of the property, Gil heard scraping and crunching. Then he saw a dark Lexus SUV driving away from the back of the house, maneuvering its way through the underbrush and past piñon trees. The car came crashing onto the main road, pulling some downed bushes along with it, then went speeding off past Gil and Joe sitting in their SUV.

"What the . . ." Joe said, as Gil threw the car into reverse and made a quick U-turn. Joe picked up the radio and said, "All units. In pursuit of suspect going east on County Road Sixty-Two." Then he hit the light and sirens. Hoffman's SUV reached the end of the road and blew through a STOP sign.

"Crap, crap, crap," Joe said, looking both ways as Gil slammed through the intersection. "Clear right," Joe yelled, as he made sure no traffic was coming from the right side. Gil started to speed up as the residential road emptied out onto a county road. Both cars took a left. Joe picked up the radio, saying, "All units we are heading north on State Road Five-niner-one. SWAT, do you copy?"

"We copy," came the reply. "We're just a little ways behind you."

"Copy that," Joe said into the mike, and then to Gil, "Let me find a map to figure out where we are." Gil floored the gas as Hoffman sped up, the speedometer clicked up past seventy miles per hour, then eighty.

"Joe, I think there's someone in the passenger seat," Gil said. They both craned their necks to get a better look into Hoffman's car. As the Lexus took a wide turn in the road, a silhouette was visible sitting in the right seat. They watched as the passenger window slid down slowly. Then someone aimed a shotgun at them and pulled the trigger.

"Watch it," Joe yelled. The buckshot went too far to the right and missed their car. They were close enough to the Lexus to see the force of the blast throw the person holding the shotgun back and the butt of the gun hit her face.

"I guess we found Lupe Escobar," Joe said. "And lucky for us she doesn't know a damn thing about firing a shotgun. She probably got a bloody nose from that."

The highway started to twist slightly; Gil kept his eyes on Hoffman's wheels. When it came to sheer speed, their Ford SUV was outmatched by the Lexus, which had more horsepower and was about four hundred pounds lighter. According to the laws of physics, the Lexus would always be faster than the Explorer—as long as the asphalt was dry.

"Where does this guy think he's going?" Joe asked, looking at the map book. "There is nothing out here."

The police radio, which had been silent a second ago, was now difficult to follow, with every unit calling out where they were and what they were doing. Most were on their way to help in the chase. Gil was trying to listen for the SWAT team leader's voice, knowing it was likely that he and Joe would need their heavily armed backup. The state highway merged into another, this one heading even farther away from civilization and into the foothills of the Sangre de Cristo Mountains. Joe called out their position over the radio as they came to the top of a ridge. Hoffman took a quick left onto a dirt road. His wheels spun for a second, kicking up gravel and ice, and he swiveled as if he were about to go off the road. But he was able to correct himself and speed off. Gil was right behind him, with Joe calling out over the radio, "We're going east onto County Road Seven-six." They heard the SWAT commander start to say, "Copy that, we . . ." then he crackled out. Joe said, "Repeat, SWAT. Can you repeat?" But there was only static. Gil and Joe had hit a radio dead area.

"I think they got our last position," Joe said.

The wide, flat dirt road started to climb. It followed the top of a ridge, with almost vertical drop-offs on either side. They had left any houses far behind and were now in country marked with low piñon and juniper.

"God, I hope they get a flat tire or something soon," Joe said. "I really don't want to follow them if they go plunging off a cliff."

The road had gotten enough sun throughout the day to melt off the snow and turn the resulting mud into drying dirt. Below, in the valley, the setting sun was able to generously break its way through the building clouds, and sunlight glinted off houses on the horizon. Up in the much colder mountains ahead, Gil could see Mother Nature was being generous in another way: it had started to snow.

The radio, which had been silent with static, suddenly jumped alive with voices asking where they were and what roads to take. Joe tried to respond to the dispatcher, who was the only one he needed to be talking to at the moment, "Still heading on County Road Seven-six, heading"—Joe stopped to flip through the map book, jumping from page to page. After a moment, he closed it, threw it on the floor and said into the radio, "We are officially off the map." No response came back. They were in a dead area again. Joe took his cell phone out of his pocket, but there was no signal.

"Where the hell are we going?" Joe asked.

"I wish I knew," Gil said.

The road abruptly stopped climbing and topped out. The flat surface meant Gil could try to catch up to Hoffman. He hit the gas and inched the speedometer up, the sand and ice crunching fast under the tires. The barest falling of snow started swirling in front of the windshield.

"Wait," Joe said. "There's something up ahead."

"There's a sign," Gil said. "What does it say?"

"Hang on," Joe said. "It says, 'National Forest Road . . .' Damn, I couldn't see the number."

"Oh crap," Gil said as he started to hit the brakes.

"What's the matter?" Joe asked, as up ahead Hoffman's car skidded and started to buck like a bronco.

"In about one second, the road is about to get a whole lot worse," Gil said. Within three feet, the wide, level road became a narrow one cut with deep grooves and large rocks. The change in the road quality marked where the county ended its road repair responsibility and where the National Forest Service took over. And road maintenance was not a Forest Service priority. Gil and Joe watched as Hoffman hit the bad road ahead of them. His Lexus SUV went flying over rocks while his tires hit a hole and the windshield took out some overhanging branches, but he kept forcing his SUV down the road. Gil's braking meant they hit the ruts of the road at a much slower speed, but the impact still jarred them as they jumped over a large rock and took a swipe at some piñon too near the road.

"Welcome to the backcountry," Gil said, almost hitting the top of his head on the Explorer's roof as they bounced over a log.

* * *

Lucy sat in Nathan's car watching the snowy plains pass in the distance. The sun was setting, making the horizon look like someone had scraped the clouds with their fingernails and the sky had turned radioactive orange in protest.

After talking with Lucy last night, Tommy Martinez had tracked down Nathan, telling him that she had been arrested. Nathan had spent the night calling the county detention center and local lawyers, trying to find out where she was, what to do, and when he could post bail. He had given her a big bear hug the second he saw her, which made her burst into tears. She hadn't told him about her mother's hospitalization. She hadn't mentioned the cancelled trip to Florida. She hadn't called him when she'd been arrested. Yet he was still there, caring about her.

Now they were driving back toward town, listening to Christmas carols on the radio. They had stopped for food—a burger, which she ate gratefully. Now she was looking forward to her own bed. She noticed he didn't take the turn to her house and instead started down the bypass road.

"Where are we going?" she asked.

"You'll see," he said, smiling at her.

"Nate, I have been wearing these same clothes since yesterday," Lucy said. "Could we please just go back to my house?"

"You look fine."

"I just want to go home," she said, whining purposely.

"It's Christmas Eve," he said. "You're not going to spend it by yourself."

They took the bypass to downtown and searched for a place to park. He found a spot on a side street lined by galleries and low stone walls.

"What are we doing here?" she asked.

"You've never been in Santa Fe during Christmas before," Nate said. "I thought you'd like to do the Farolito Walk."

She pulled her coat around herself and sighed, then got out of the car and into the darkening night. They walked down the street, trying to avoid icy patches on the sidewalk. Then they turned onto Canyon Road and into a crowd. The street was shut down and people walked along paths lined in *farolitos*. These were not the electric kind. These were hundreds of brown paper bags, all with candles glowing inside, lining every possible surface—on roofs, chimneys, fences, trees, sculptures. It looked like fairies had been in charge of the Christmas decorations. Bonfires burned in the street, with people warming themselves near them.

"Okay," Lucy said. "This is beautiful." She wondered how something as simple as sand and a candle in a paper bag could be so picturesque.

"The whole neighborhood does this," Nathan said. "At the elementary school they make mazes of *farolitos* that you can walk through. A house down on Garcia Street sets up a bunch of toy railroad sets in the snow."

"What do we do now?"

"We walk," Nathan said, taking her hand.

The scattered piñon and juniper of the high desert had become a full-blown forest of aspen, spruce, and ponderosa pine. The road crashed up a steep hill and kept climbing, with cliffs down one side and up the other as it snaked its way through a narrow gorge. The elevation here was too high for the snow to melt much during the day; the road was covered in almost six inches, with more coming down. The snow cover meant Gil was no longer able to make out the grooves and holes in the road, so every bounce was a surprise.

But where the Lexus had the advantage on the dry road—this was where the Explorer took over. It had an extra inch of clearance compared to the Lexus, meaning it could plow through the snow much more easily. Plus, here, its size was a blessing. Gil could see by the tracks of the Lexus in the snow ahead that Hoffman had fishtailed several times as his back tires lost traction. As Gil followed along the same path, the Explorer kept its footing because its weight pushed the tires firmly down.

They hadn't actually seen Hoffman's SUV ahead for about a quarter mile, thanks to all the twists and turns. Joe kept trying the radio, calling out their position, "Heading into the mountains on some national forest road somewhere. Hello? Anyone?" He clipped the mike back into its holder and said to Gil, "I think it's you and me from here on out, buddy."

"Then maybe it's time to catch these guys," Gil said as he hit the accelerator. The road got steeper, skirting huge boulders half buried in snow, but they saw the Lexus just ahead. Another burst of speed got them within twenty feet of Hoffman's bumper. Joe snapped a rifle with a scope out of its holder on the dashboard, ready to jump out when it was time.

"Hang on," Gil said. "I'm going to bump him."

But Hoffman hit the gas hard, spitting out debris from under his tires. Gil sped up as well, turning the steering wheel to the right to nick the side of Hoffman's car. The two vehicles made contact, jarring Gil and Joe. Hoffman's front tires skidded off the road, getting close to the edge of an embankment. He hit the brakes, making the falling snow glow orange in the light of his taillights. But he was able to correct quickly, and plowed ahead down the barely discernible road.

"How in the world are they still going?" Joe asked. "They really should have hit a tree by now or something." Gil knew Hoffman and Escobar had few options. There were no turnoffs. There were no houses. There was only the forest. Their only real choice was to keep going until they either ran off the road or the drifts got too deep to maneuver through. And one of those things would happen sooner rather than later. It was getting dark, and the snow was coming down faster, bouncing through the beams of their headlights. Gil doubted Hoffman could still see the road. At best, he was looking for the largest open space between the trees, hoping he was still going the right way.

Gil had it easier. Hoffman's tire tracks meant Gil didn't have to cut his own trail through the snow, which let him concentrate more on his driving. They were going relatively slowly, given that this was a car chase. What had begun as an eighty-five-mile-per-hour pursuit was now fifteen miles per hour, but the combination of the snow, the darkening night, and the dense woods made this part of the chase much more dangerous.

"They're going to have to stop soon," Gil said. "We need to figure out how we want to handle it."

"Okay," Joe said. "With any luck they'll crash the car and hopefully be knocked unconscious. But more likely, they'll make a run for it on foot."

"Or turn to fight," Gil said.

They strolled past stores where people were handing out hot apple cider. Farther down the street, *farolitos* outlined even more houses, giving away the shapes of curved archways and long portals. It was clear from the architecture that the haciendas along Canyon Road were among the oldest in town. Many had been turned into galleries, but others still served as residences. But while the houses were old, the Farolito Walk wasn't. It had been started in the 1970s by the neighborhood association, which at the time was celebrating something as simple as winning a protected zoning ordinance. As for the *farolitos* themselves, no one was really sure where they came from. Some people thought they were a poor man's Christmas lights. Others thought they represented a light that would show Mary and Joseph the way to Bethlehem.

Lucy and Nathan turned down a side alley that was silent and only shoulder-width. There was no crowd here. It was cobblestone, with snow along the edges but even here there were *farolitos*. Lucy had to admit the romance of it all was starting to get to her. She walked a little way ahead, and the cobblestone alley opened into an enclosed courtyard with a huge cottonwood tree at the center, its branches lined with flickering *farolitos*. Nathan came up behind her and pulled her into a hug.

"Merry Christmas," she whispered into his ear. "And thank you."

CHAPTER TWENTY-ONE

December 24

When it finally happened, there was no warning. Hoffman didn't even hit the brakes. The SUV just swerved right and went twenty feet down a steep embankment. Gil lost sight of the vehicle but heard the crash—a twisting of metal and a splintering of wood.

Gil hit the brakes hard, which threw him and Joe forward into the dashboard.

"You okay?" Gil asked, looking over at Joe. He was worried he had bumped his head.

"Don't mind me and my whiplash," Joe said.

Gil jumped out into knee-deep snow and took his gun out of its holster. The Explorer's headlights showed that the path the Lexus had carved out as it went off the road and down the dark ravine. He made his way to the back of the Explorer, wading through the snow. Joe joined him at the back, holding the rifle. Gil opened the back of the vehicle and put a couple of extra magazines into his jacket pockets, then slung a shotgun over his shoulder. They already had on their body armor, as was department policy when assisting in any SWAT scene. Gil whispered, "Search-and-rescue protocol," as he handed Joe one of the handheld radios and held up six fingers. Joe nodded, knowing that, according to policy, Gil would contact him on channel six if they were separated for more than ten minutes. These radios might work in the terrain (even though the vehicle's radio did not) because they didn't need to bounce a signal off an antenna, only off the other radio. But the deeper they got into forest, the more trees there were to act as barriers, and the less likely it was that the radio signal would get through to the other person.

With a nod from Joe, Gil started down the embankment, following the tire marks left by the Lexus. After about ten feet, Gil crouched down in the snow to get his bearings. He unzipped his coat as quietly as possible and found the flashlight he had stowed in the outer pocket of his body armor. But he didn't turn it on, not wanting to ruin his night vision. Plus, the light would only bounce off the flakes, much like car high beams in a winter storm. They started down the steep hill, guns in hand, trying not to sink too deep into the drifts. The Lexus had made it to the bottom of the ravine, where it had crashed into a large boulder, but not before ripping down several aspen trees and leaving a trail of broken branches. Both front doors were open and the headlights were on, revealing a steep hill ahead much like the one they had just come down, leading up and away into the dark forest. Gil and Joe took cover behind the trunk of a ponderosa pine to catch their breaths and get a better look at the scene. Joe nodded to the right and headed in that direction, while Gil stayed still, surveying the area, ready to provide cover fire if needed.

Joe crouched low as he made his way forward, and stopped behind another pine tree. He nodded to Gil, who took a breath and headed left. He made his way toward the back bumper of the Lexus SUV and he knelt behind the vehicle, looking at the steep cliffs above and the cover of trees below for movement. He looked over to Joe's position, but couldn't make him out. Gil would just have to assume that Joe was covering him. Gil popped his head up to look in the back window of the vehicle, but the headlights of the Lexus bouncing back off the snow didn't provide enough light for him to see inside. Still crouched down, he moved forward, along the side of the car, toward the front driver's-side door. He stopped when he was flush with the back side door and popped his head up again to look at the inside of the SUV. He could see the interior more clearly now. One of the rifles was lying on the backseat. But there was still no movement inside. He kept low and made his way forward the last two feet to the open SUV door. From this angle, he could see that the driver's-side airbag had deployed, but there was no one in the driver's seat.

Movement on the other side of the car made Gil duck for cover again. He raised his Smith & Wesson, but he saw a flash of red hair and realized it was just Joe mimicking Gil's path along the passenger side of the car. Joe made it to the open passenger-side door, only his side of the car wasn't empty. The airbag there had deployed as well—not that it mattered to Lupe Escobar, who was slumped over in the seat, dead, a rifle wound to her head. They hadn't heard the shot, but the falling snow had probably muffled it. Her face had already been bloodied from the kick of the shotgun, when she shot at Gil and Joe; her weapon was still lying on the car floor. Hoffman really didn't like leaving an accomplice alive, Gil thought, even if she was the mother of his child. Joe rummaged quietly around her body, pulling out from her pocket a box of shotgun rounds, with one shell missing. He showed them to Gil, who nodded. Tyler only had a rifle, with at most ten rounds.

Gil and Joe were still crouched next to the open doors on either side of the car when the windshield shattered above their heads. A second shot hit the front part of the Lexus with a thud. Gil reached forward and fumbled around until he hit a switch, killing the Lexus headlights, which suddenly threw him and Joe into darkness. He closed his eyes, wanting them to adjust more quickly to the black. When he opened them again, Joe was using the space between the open door and the car frame as a rest for the rifle. He was peering through the attached night scope, scanning the dark forest ahead of them for movement. A third shot hit the door that Gil was crouched behind. A microsecond later, Joe fired a round from his rifle. He shot again. And again, giving Gil the time to get away from the vehicle, which Hoffman was probably using as his target. Unlike Joe, Hoffman probably didn't have a night scope on his rifle, meaning that, with the headlights off, he could no longer see Gil and Joe. At best, he could see the dark outline of the Lexus against the snow. By the time Gil made his way behind the trunk of another ponderosa pine and looked back toward the car, Joe was gone from his position. Gil scanned the edge of the tree line as best he could in the dark. He saw no sign of Joe. But he knew what Joe would do. Stay to the flank. Move up the hill. Shoot on sight.

Gil struggled through the deep snow and up the steep incline, toward the location where Hoffman's last shot was fired. Despite his thick combat boots, Gil slipped and tripped as much as he climbed. He tried to stick close to the tree trunks, where less snow had built up. Every few feet, he stopped to listen for movement, but all he could hear were thick clumps of snow falling off the branches above and into the drifts below. He looked at his watch. He'd been at this for five minutes. According to the department's search-and-rescue protocol, he had another five minutes to search before he would have to break radio silence and try to contact Joe. If that failed, he was to wait another ten minutes and try again. After that, if there was still no contact, he was required to head back to the Explorer, where they would rendezvous. There they would regroup and wait for backup. Gil had gone another thirty feet up the slope when he saw a flat shadow in the snow ahead. He crouched down and tried to make it out. It looked as if something or someone had trampled down a patch of snow. He waited for movement, then repositioned himself. It was hard to tell from this angle if a person or animal had made the large indentation. He took the flashlight out of his pocket and for one brief second turned on the light. The quick strobe showed a scattering of boot prints next to a bright red puddle on the white snow. Somehow, Joe had hit his target. They were now tracking a wounded suspect, which made their job both easier and harder—a wounded man cannot travel fast, but he will fight much harder.

Gil looked at his watch. Another five minutes had passed. Time to contact Joe. He took out the radio, made sure it was on channel six, switched the volume to low, and hit the mike key three times. If Joe heard the signal, he would hit his mike key three times as well. Gil waited. There was nothing. Gil hit the mike three times again. Still nothing. He looked at his watch again. It was now two minutes past contact time. Gil needed to keep moving if he wanted to catch up to Hoffman. He took a chance and keyed the mike, saying quietly, "Joe." There was no answer. He said it again. Still no response. Either Joe wasn't there or the radio signal was bouncing off too many trees to reach him. Gil put the radio back and started out again, picking up the pace as the hill started to flatten out. He followed the tracks and the drips of blood through the snow, but fresh flakes were quickly covering them. A few feet ahead, he heard a sound and crouched again as he tried to calm his breathing enough so he could listen. Something was moving through the snow. He could hear the crunching of feet. Gil stayed still—as still as possible. The sound was coming closer. Gil quietly slid the shotgun off his shoulder and leaned it against the tree next to him, within grabbing distance if need be. He leveled his Smith & Wesson in the direction of the sound, knowing it was just as likely to be Joe and not Hoffman—or even a bear. The sound stopped. Gil waited. His right calf was starting to cramp, but he didn't dare move, knowing that if the person was Hoffman, he would shoot at the smallest sound.

Then he heard someone whisper, "Olly olly oxen free."

"Joe?" Gil asked quietly, as he kept his gun pointed straight in the direction of the voice.

"Yo," came the reply. "Please don't shoot."

Gil lowered his gun while Joe covered the few feet between them in just a couple of steps. He offered his hand to Gil to help him up from his crouch. "It's good to see you," Joe said, as he gave Gil a quick hug. Without another word, they started to move forward. Gil knew Joe had probably been working his way toward the spot where Hoffman had been shot when he came across the same boot trail and blood drop trail that Gil was following. Otherwise, it was doubtful they would ever have met up, and both would have had to return to the rendezvous point to regroup.

It was getting too dark to see Hoffman's trail, so Gil took out his flashlight; Joe did the same. Every few feet, Gil would break a branch, which would act like a trail of bread crumbs when it was time to head back with Hoffman. Within a few feet, the blood trail was gone. Maybe Hoffman had bandaged up his wound. But his tracks through the knee-deep snow were still easily visible. They followed in his footsteps so they wouldn't have to cut their own trail. It meant they could go more quickly than Hoffman, who would have to expend extra energy fighting his way through the drifts. Plus, Gil doubted Hoffman had dressed for this kind of weather. Without gloves or a hat, he would already be losing heat in his extremities. All of that meant Hoffman would tire out well before they did. Both Gil and Joe were wearing parkas, hats, scarves, gloves, and waterproof combat boots, but even so the cold was still slowing them down. Their jeans had been soaked through and were starting to freeze. And they were breathing hard, as much due to the physical effort as the elevation, which Gil guessed was close to eleven thousand feet, given the change in vegetation and terrain.

Ahead, the dense forest started to thin out. As they got closer, Gil could see they were at the edge of a rockslide area, which was common at the higher elevations. Within a few more feet, they left the deep snow of the forest and were starting up a boulder-covered hill. With the cover of trees gone, the storm had nothing to hold it back. The blowing snow stung Gil's face, and he pulled his wool hat down over his ears, which were getting eaten raw by the wind. They walked on rocks peeking through a hard layer of snow that was swept smooth by the continual wind. They could move more quickly now, but every few feet, one of them would step onto the snow and break through the crust, sinking up to his knees into crevices between the boulders.

For the first ten feet or so, the ground was almost level, and they could follow the edges of Hoffman's footprints as he cut his way across the open area. Then the tracks were gone, wiped clean by the wind. Gil heard Joe yell something into the howling wind, likely a curse against the weather. Up to this point, Hoffman's trail had required no special skills to follow. Now Gil would have to actually put his tracking skills to the test. His father had taught him to track when he was seven. It had come in handy on the job, mostly when they were searching for lost kids or Alzheimer's patients who had wandered away from home.

Gil tried to yell over to Joe, "I need to cut for sign."

"What?" Joe yelled.

"I need to cut for sign."

"What does that even mean?"

"Just stand there and don't move."

Cutting for sign was a method of looking for a trail after tracks had been lost. Gil walked an *S* pattern as best he could in the terrain, away from where Joe was standing. Following a trail across a rock field meant looking for tiny details—a groove made by a boot hitting some ice, or dirt that wasn't the same shade as the surrounding surface, except Gil had to do all this during a blizzard. The wind and snow would quickly erode any signs Hoffman had left behind. The only good thing was the darkness. Tracking at night was much easier than during a sunny day. That's because tracking is a game of light and shadows. A tracker can use a flashlight to make shadows the noontime sun would blot out. A print not visible from above will be clear if a tracker crouches down, shines a light on it, and looks from the side.

It took a minute, but Gil found a rock displacement. A larger rock had been moved slightly, resulting in a half inch of disturbed soil above it. It was enough to tell Gil that Hoffman had pushed the rock backward with his foot as he walked toward the north. He whistled over to Joe, who came to join him.

They moved forward, with Gil crouched low to the ground with his flashlight, looking for the next groove that would tell them they were on the right path. The hill got steeper and the rocks got bigger, but the wind was unchanging. Gil found a toe dig in a small pocket of snow, which showed that Hoffman had dug in the tip of his boot as he pushed himself up to grab a rock above. Gil and Joe holstered their weapons, unable to keep a grip on their handguns while trying to climb up the boulders on the slope. Gil got small cuts on his wrist where his gloves did not quite meet his jacket. And he felt blood on his knee after he slipped and cut himself on a sharp edge. He heard Joe give a muffled "ouch" a few times as he tripped.

"We should head back," Joe said, close to Gil's ear so they could hear each other in the wind. "We can call in backup."

"Just a little while longer," Gil said. "We have to be gaining on him. He's wounded."

Joe shook his head, but kept going. They lost the trail two more times, forcing Gil to spend long minutes cutting for sign among the boulders. Gil was starting to have a hard time feeling his fingers. He tried to wiggle them slightly, knowing that if he had to pull the trigger, a stiff finger would make for a slow response time.

A minute later, Joe put his foot on a patch of snow and,

before he could react, the snow gave way. He slid into a coffin-sized crevice between the boulders, landing hard against the rocks a few feet below. Gil slid down to him, trying not to slam into him in the dark.

"Are you okay?" Gil asked, bending close to Joe, trying to help him up. Joe had a five-inch scrape on his left leg where a rock had sliced through his pants. They climbed up out of the crevice as best they could, both stiff from the cold. Their frozen jeans and parkas didn't allow them full range of motion. Even with Gil's help, Joe struggled to his feet as he got to the top and leaned against a boulder. His face was half covered in snow that he tried to wipe off but only managed to push down his neck.

"This is crazy." Joe had to yell through the wind just to be heard. "We have to turn back. No one even knows where we are."

"He can't be too far ahead," Gil yelled back. "He's losing blood."

"And so are we. These rocks are cutting the hell out of us."

"Just a few more minutes."

"He's got nowhere to go, Gil," Joe yelled, the wind taking most of the sound away with it. "There are no houses. There are no roads. There's nothing for hundreds of miles. He'll be dead in a few hours. And so will we unless we go back."

"He can't be that far ahead," Gil yelled. He got up and started to walk slowly forward again. But Joe didn't move.

"Look at you, you can barely walk," Joe yelled.

"I'm going to keep going," Gil said, moving again, the snow burning his raw face. This time Joe did move. He took a stride forward and grabbed Gil's arm, pulling him backward. This time they both slid into the crevice, and hit the bottom hard, a dusting of snow and small rocks falling on them. Gil felt his shoulder twist the wrong way under him and struggled to get up. But Joe held him in place, pushing on his chest and pinning his legs under him.

"We can't do this," Joe yelled in the wind. "We have to go back."

"Get the hell off me," Gil yelled, pushing back hard against Joe, who fell into the rocks behind them, hitting his head. They both sat up as best they could, Joe holding a hand to his head. They looked at each other as the wind quieted down for a moment.

"We have to go back," Joe said again, wiping the blood from his hands onto his jeans. Gil took the scarf from around his neck and handed it to Joe, who pressed it against his head to stop the bleeding.

"He'll get away," Gil said.

"We can't catch him if we're dead."

CHAPTER TWENTY-TWO

February 25

The fires had come early to the Southern Rocky Mountains. It was only the end of February and there was already a ten-thousand-acre one burning near Los Alamos. Mateo Garcia caught sight of the smoke plume stabbing into the bright blue sky across the valley floor as he and Baby turned a corner of the trail. There had been no real snowfall in almost two months, leaving the lower elevations of the Sangre de Cristo Mountains clear and dry.

Baby made her way up the path, going slowly because of rocks and branches that had fallen during the last big winter storm on Christmas Eve. Mateo could hear the wind clawing through the upper branches of the ponderosa pine, the wood groaning and creaking. They weren't making particularly good time, but that wasn't the point. Mateo preferred to be safe instead of fast. Today, his only job was to act as escort to the two riders ahead of him. He was their guide and baby-sitter. Riding Phantom was a tall Hispanic detective who, Mateo had found out, was one of the Montoyas from Gali-steo. He seemed to have a good seat on the horse and knew how to nudge her forward when she got lazy. The smaller detective, with red hair and a twitchy face, was less sure of himself. They had found an old mare for him to ride. He made a lot of kissing and clicking noises to his horse, which ignored his efforts to control her.

They were out here because of Willie. When the weather had turned at the beginning of January, it had gone from snowy and windy to warm and windy, and everyone be-came restless. In town, people started to work on their gar-dens. In the mountains, people started to roam again. That's when Willie came back into the shop.

Mateo had been busy doing the books when Willie walked into Garcia Hardware. His beard was still a squir-rel's nest and he looked as if he had lost ten pounds off his tall frame over the winter, but his walk was brisk as he came straight to the counter and said without prompting, "I found something."

"What did you find?" Mateo asked, noticing once again how greetings among the mountain men didn't seem to matter. He hadn't seen Willie in three months, yet they talked as if they were in the middle of a conversation.

"A man."

"What is this man doing?"

"He's dead."

"Is he in your camp?" Mateo was worried that maybe a squatter had wandered into Willie's spot and things had ended in violence.

"No. In the mountains."

"There's a dead man in the mountains?"

"Yes."

Matt had Willie point on a National Forest map to the approximate spot where he had found the body. Then Willie left, heading back into the mountains. It had taken three days to get a proper search party going. The posse members reasoned that if there was a dead body, moving quickly wouldn't make him any less dead. And those extra days would allow members to get their animals fed and get some time off work. They spent two days in the mountains doing a grid search as best they could in the rough terrain, often having to get off their horses and walk up the steep inclines. Willie's directions had been specific, but the area he'd circled on the map encompassed more than a square mile. He been able to describe in detail the way the body was propped up against a ponderosa pine, just north of a stand of Gambel oak and west of a double stump of a white fir, but those details weren't included on a topographical map. It would take a coordinated, long-term search effort to find the body, plus more than a little luck. As such, they weren't surprised when they didn't find the body during the first search. They came back a second time, spending twelve hours working their way through another search grid. The third time they came back, they used it as a training run for six new members who had signed up. Mateo had almost forgotten about the body, instead concentrating on measuring up the new members and their mounts. He was planting flags for the new trainees to find as part of an exercise when he stopped to look at the view. It was at that moment that he saw something lying against a tree, near a stand of Gambel oak and a double stump of a white fir. Right where Willie said it would be. Only then did Mateo call the police;

until that moment he'd been unsure if the body had been a figment of Willie's imagination.

It was two more full days before Mateo went back up the mountain with the detectives. In the interim, the posse members dealt with the necessary logistics of conducting a body recovery—setting up base camp, organizing transportation, arranging reliable communication, and finding extra horses, gear, and feed. They decided that one rider—in this case, Mateo—would bring the police up to the body first, so they could see the scene as undisturbed as possible. The body recovery team would follow with the field investigator from the Medical Examiner's Office, and together they would coordinate how to pack the body out.

Now Mateo had been on the trail for about four hours. Ahead, a Clark's Nutcracker landed on a sagebrush next to the trail. The gray-and-black bird bounced on the branch, which was almost too thin to hold him, then flew off as the horses approached. At the top of the next ridge, Mateo had the detectives get off their horses and walk the rest of the way on foot, so as not to fill the air with dust. As soon as the little detective got off his mare, he started complaining about soreness. But Mateo knew he would really be in pain tomorrow, after his muscles started to stiffen up. Mateo led the detectives the last ten feet to the body in a single file, like the posse members had been doing since they first found the man. They had been specially trained in forensic scene management, for when a search and rescue turned into a body retrieval, as happened all too often.

When Mateo was within a few feet of the body, he let the tall Hispanic detective take the lead. The dead man was lying up against a ponderosa pine. The body was in surprisingly good condition, but then, it would have been frozen and only just recently thawed. The animals and squirrels hadn't eaten much of him, and there wasn't a smell. The red-haired policeman stood a few feet away, not approaching the body, but casting nervous looks at his partner and the dead man. The Hispanic detective crouched down and stared intently at the body for a few moments before looking off at the trees as they swayed in the wind. He watched the forest for so long that Mateo began to wonder if he was waiting for something. Then the detective stood up suddenly and began to walk back to the horses. As he passed his partner, Mateo heard the detective say, "It's not him."

ACKNOWLEDGMENTS

I would like to thank Annice Barber, Angela Barber, John Barber, Kristen Davenport, Pat West-Barker, and Tasha Rath for their constant support, along with Deborah and Tania, who gave me great insight into their worlds.

I also wish to thank, as always, Anne Hillerman, Jean Schaumberg, the Tony Hillerman Mystery Writing Contest, Peter Joseph, Thomas Dunne Books, and everyone at St. Martin's Press for giving me my start in this business.

Finally, to the Santa Fe Police Department, the Santa Fe Fire Department, the Santa Fe County Sheriff's Department, the Santa Fe County Fire Department, and *The Santa Fe New Mexican* newspaper—thank you for being champions of the public, each in your own way.